# ALEX MCFARLANE

# Venturing North

*Islands of the Northern Sea Book 1*

*Second edition*

*ISBN: 978-1-0685038-1-8*

*Cover art by Etheric Designs*
*Editing by Brit Corley and Alyssa LaMedica*
*Proofreading by Gabby D'Aloia*

*This book was professionally typeset on Reedsy.*
*Find out more at reedsy.com*

*To Ed, the best writing companion.*

# Contents

# Preface

This is a spicy tale, so expect sexually explicit scenes between consenting adults (and the relevant language). There is also mention of death of parents and a complicated pregnancy (neither of these are main characters or on page). If these are something you'd rather avoid right now, put the book down and come back to it when you like.

*In Law & Order: SVU voice* Reader discretion is advised.

# 1

# Ursula

The carriage rattled along the road, and Ursula let her head sway along with the movement, too bored to fight the tedium and sit properly. She picked her cuticles and looked out the window. The landscape changed as they started their bumpy ascent up the hilly paths and wound up the spiked summits that jutted through the clouds in this part of the world. It felt much further than a few hundred miles from the windswept bluffs she was used to. The world was green and wet here. Dampness clung to her like the mist on the high mountain peaks. A shiver ran down Ursula's spine and her flesh pimpled. The north was more foreboding than even the ballads claimed.

"Stop doing that. You'll ruin your lovely fingers," her nurse said. She looked down at her own plump hands, speckled with freckles and age spots and sighed. "You've been brought up better than that, Ursi dear."

Ursula stopped her fidgeting and painted a serene expression on her face. Nurse Selwyn was right; it would do no good fussing and fretting, even if her stomach lurched at every jolt in the road while images of men in various states of decrepitude swirled in her brain.

She had tried very hard not to think about Elias Clearbould: not during her girlhood after her father proposed the marriage, not in that horrible expanse of time between when she was supposed to get married and the letter summoning her a few weeks ago, and not now. It had been harder to push those probing thoughts away in the lead up to her journey north. To not think what he looked like, how he smelled, if he drank too much or gambled or laughed with abandon. To disregard him as a vicious cad when he'd written to her father all those years ago declaring that he was going to fight the giants and would have to postpone their nuptials.

Did he even know the problems he left in his wake? It had been a fraught, tumultuous time in the Woodruff house then. Her father had been in a terrible mood, his pride so wounded he'd stormed around and snapped at every opportunity. Only letters from Anton Clearbould had smoothed things over, promising his son would return soon and things would go as planned.

It had been remarkably easy to forget Elias then, to cast him aside like a bad dream. To believe that if she just kept pushing thoughts of him away, he didn't exist. That had worked for a time. Long enough to fall for someone else, long enough to be discarded, long enough to realise her worth would always be tied to her father's coffers. There was still a part of her that wanted more, that wanted to *be* wanted. Not for what she could provide, but for who she was. It was a tiny ember of hope that burned in her. That maybe this marriage to a stranger would be the one place she could finally be loved for herself.

An ache settled between her lungs, stinging with each breath. Only that tiny flickering ember kept her going. It was much simpler to do something than think about these things. To occupy herself until she forgot how she felt. Ursula looked around the coach and wished her sisters were here to distract her. For her mind to be taken up with their chatter and petty squabbles.

She swallowed down the harsh dryness that invaded her throat and tried to ignore the prickling shivers down her spine. She wanted to shake them off, to run and never look back, but instead she sat transfixed on the wash of scenery through the window.

The coach trundled forward, its creaks and clacks adding to the unnerving atmosphere. The air was growing thicker as they climbed the mountain road and brimmed with life. Ursula shivered again and tucked her arms around herself. How could this wild, remote place ever become home?

"How long until we get to Allerbrock?" asked Ursula, an unconvincing chipper note in her voice. "I'm desperate to stretch my legs."

Maybe she could walk off the clammy tingling that felt like a second skin.

"We still have a few hours of travel ahead. We can have a quick comfort break, provided you don't decide to stretch your legs too far and scarper." Her nurse wheezed in a half-laugh.

Ursula rolled her eyes, unable to stop herself. Where in the heavens would she run to? She doubted she'd ever find a more inhospitable place, full of mountains and soggy air. Ursula tugged her arms closer, the press on her ribs giving her something else to think about other than Elias. No matter what she did, her mind returned to him.

"No need to look like that, dear. We'll stop," her nurse cooed, and Ursula felt like an ungrateful brat.

The last conversation she had with her father reared its ugly head. Cedric Woodruff's stoic countenance dropped when talking business. She recalled his animated display as he went on and on about tax levies, exclusivity contracts, and duty—yes, duty above all else. The word hung around Ursula like a shroud.

She didn't know much about the connections with the Clearboulds other than it was through his schoolroom acquaintance with Elias's father, Anton, that her own father had finally managed to infiltrate Currington society. Cedric Woodruff had his fingers in so many pies now, Ursula was surprised he still wanted her to go through with this. Even so, he was so proud to be sole importer of Allerbrock stone and had used that to levy his place in the world, she doubted he would ever forgo it, even for his daughter. Doors opened when you were the only one able to provide the southern elite access to the most sought-after mineral in Reul, even if you had been born a grocer's son. Her father had expanded his empire from importing to owning an ironworks and utilising the new stock exchange. In a way, she was proud of him for knowing what he needed to do and using all his might to achieve it.

Of course, her father never entertained the idea of one of his daughters taking on the business, no matter how competent they were. In his eyes, they could only marry to achieve his goals, and the Clearboulds offered the first step to this. They were a family with history and links to the aristocracy that only blood, no matter how diluted, could give.

Her nurse knocked on the carriage roof. "Stop here,

Driffan."

Ursula wiped her hands on her skirts. She couldn't stop the heat rushing to her cheeks; she'd always struggled with her nurse's easy manner and booming voice. Nurse Selwyn was the exact opposite to how she was told a southern lady should behave. It was no wonder the old woman got on so well with her untameable, continental mother. Ursula had never been so glad her father had forked out for the private coach. At least it was just the driver who had to deal with her full-voiced nurse and not a coachload of pinched-faced travellers.

"Nurse Selwyn, you know as well as I that I am not prone to running at the best of times. A quick turn around the carriage and seeing to my needs will suffice," Ursula said, mouth as tight as her stiff legs as she stepped down from the coach. "Anyway, when have I ever gone against my father's wishes?"

The last comment was tossed over her shoulder as she wobbled towards the overgrowth at the side of the road.

Her nurse was devouring an apple when she reappeared and motioned towards a basket of provisions the last inn supplied. Ursula rummaged and grabbed an apple and pork pie, eating them as she stared out at the view. The wind nipped at her ankles and swirled under the heavy cotton of her travelling dress. It felt like she added a layer of clothing for each mile they travelled, the countless petticoats she wore wrapped around her legs in the chill mountain breeze. Stray hairs blew across her forehead, sprung loose in the wind.

It would still be balmy at home, as summer held on in Currington for as long as possible. Warm days slowly gave way to cool autumn nights. Her family would still be able to eat on the patio with just a shawl for cover as the sun descended. She could see it now: her sisters lounging in the garden after their lessons, fingers stained with juice from the last of the summer berries.

Ursula scanned the landscape in front of her; there was a steep drop at the edge of the road that gave way to a blanket of trees. She'd never seen so many, like a sweeping green carpet. There must be more trees here in the valley than in the whole of Currington.

"It certainly is impressive here," she said to no one in particular.

"In a way," her nurse responded. "Bit too much of a chill in the air for my liking. Never been this far north before, and I'm not sure I would again."

Ursula looked down at her nurse's aged russet face. Deep lines were etched in her skin thanks to a lifetime in the sun. Neither of them had ever experienced a climate like this, and she fully expected her nurse to regale everyone back home about the arduous weather, no doubt exaggerating for comedic effect.

Ursula's gaze drifted back to the sweeping vistas. "I've never been this far north either."

"Is that right?" her nurse asked. "Thought you came up here with your father all those years ago."

"No, that was Theo. I was too young, and Elodie had just been born. I've never met any of the Clearboulds."

"Ach!" Her nurse swatted her away, face scrunching. "There were so many of you so quickly, I find it hard to keep track. Such a colicky baby was our Elodie. The Gods! I had to walk her around for hours to get her to sleep. Your poor mother was run ragged."

Ursula gave a faint smile. She had been too young then to

notice her father and brother's absence. Too young to realise that she was being bartered for stone. Stone so prized in the south, that a human life was worth it. It was such a hairbrained scheme; marriages like this were for the nobility to strengthen bloodlines and consolidate power, not for exclusivity on a product, no matter how rare. Only someone like her father could come up with it. Someone so fixated on bettering the position of his children—and himself with it—he might as well be a king in a court.

Old anger pricked at her. It was a war she had felt for years now, torn between what she should do and what she wanted to. She didn't want to feel the heavy, curdled weight in her gut anymore. She knew she should just accept things, but there was always a part of her that fought against it. A part that wanted to escape as Theo had.

Her nurse groaned as she clambered back into the carriage, snagging Ursula's attention.

"Let me help you!" Ursula dashed for the tottering old woman, levering her back into her seat.

The movement quickly turned to a wince, and her nurse grabbed her back as she plonked down in her seat. "These roads are too bumpy for my old bones. They're not even paved properly! I thought these people were civilised."

Ursula sat opposite the older woman and swung the door closed. She opened her mouth to respond but was cut short by her nurse gesticulating wildly like she was talking to a full assembly and not one person in a carriage.

"You'd think they'd be more like us, given the queen traces her lineage up this way, but you never know with northerners. Did you see the shrines lining the road? I haven't seen such a thing since I was a girl. Makes me feel all peculiar." She gave an exaggerated shiver, and Ursula would have found her words more foreboding if it wasn't so funny. She bit the inside of cheeks to stop a laugh from erupting, her nurse's blunt demeanour ever the source of entertainment in the Woodruff house.

"That's deep magic, nature magic. These northern types may follow our Gods now, but you better watch your back, my girl. You hear me?"

Ursula nodded in assent. There was no point interrupting her nurse when she was in full flow, even for agreement. Nurse Selwyn knocked on the carriage roof and the wheels groaned into motion. She looked out of the window, her eyes narrowed and lips pursed.

"Sneaky types, hiding away in their woods and mountains and hoarding like dragons. I wouldn't even be surprised to see one of those godless beasts fly across the sky."

Ursula smiled to herself and let the words wash over her. Her eyes drifted closed as she listened to her nurse, who would be going for some time now, talking about all and sundry. She gave herself over to the rocking motion again, falling asleep quickly.

She was woken by an avid tapping on her knee.

"Whaaa?" Ursula mumbled groggily, her mouth dry and skin tight across her cheeks.

"Look! Not long now, you can see the skyline over the ridge." Her nurse leaned out of the window, a bold move on a narrow mountain road with a steep drop at the side.

They had travelled quite a bit further up the mountainside since she fell asleep, and Ursula felt a million miles away from her fen hometown surrounded by bogs and flat lands. How would her legs cope with the steepness? She already felt bested by the carriage ride here, never mind traversing this terrain on foot.

Her nurse handed her the water flask and some herbs to chew on to freshen her breath while they rounded a bend in the road and started their descent towards the town. Ursula chewed and sipped on the water, feeling steered like a current in a stream as the carriage juddered along the path to her new home.

Finally, her nurse looked at her. "Gods, Ursula! You look like a frog! I've got some cream that should bring down that puffiness. We don't want the young lord to think he's marrying an amphibian!" Her nurse dove into her travel bag, clinking bottles and yanking out bits of knitting as she fumbled around, eventually pulling out a small jar of cream that she slathered unceremoniously on Ursula's face.

Her nurse sat back, inspecting her handiwork. "Maybe give your cheeks a little pinch to get some colour into them. Men like it when their women look flushed. I don't need to explain to you why…"

Heat spread on Ursula's cheeks, and she doubted they needed any pinching now.

2

# Elias

Elias paced around his study; the day felt interminable already. His work lay abandoned on the old desk, yellowing papers strewn across the entire surface completely covering the once shiny wood below.

His thoughts were consumed by Ursula Woodruff.

Would she hate him for leaving her dangling like a fish on the line? Would she be like all the other prim southern misses he'd met: tight-lipped and overly proper? He tried to remember what her brother looked like when they were at school together, but all he could picture was the vaguest outline of a gangly, dark-haired youth. He'd had a few classes with Theodore Woodruff, but the pair moved in vastly different circles. Elias had tried to care about his education, but he was not a natural scholar and the call of being outside often seduced him away from his books. Rugby, fencing, hiking, fishing, hunting—anything beyond the ivory towers of Stonebank Academy for Boys. Theo always gave off an air of contempt for the strictures of high school, bending—if not, breaking—any rule he could, and still managing to be at the top of the class. Elias wondered if his sister had the same spirit—defiant to the point of obstinacy.

He patched together Ursula Woodruff in his mind: dark-haired, petite and curvaceous, bright-eyed and elfin featured, as was the fashion.

He told himself it didn't matter, that he was doing this for reasons bigger and better than himself: to secure a future for the quarry and the town. Too many people depended on him now; he needed this to work.

Elias did another circuit of the room, knowing he was wearing the already thin carpet bare. He braced his hands on the mantelpiece and looked into the crackling flames in the hearth. Heat danced across his legs and chest, warming his chilled skin as Elias cursed his younger self. He'd been so foolish and foolhardy that he'd just run away. So afraid of missing out on adventure, of being stuck in a role handed down for generations, of being the one that failed, that he'd fled. The sword above the mantle glinted, and Elias traced his hand along the steel length. It was a museum piece now, a symbol of youthful make—believe and misadventure.

Above it sat his father's portrait. Eyes the same blue as his, but stern with determination. Anton Clearbould—confident in his position, proud of his heritage, devoted to tradition. Anton Clearbould who had been so sure of himself that he'd forged on, never changing in the face of modernity

Elias let out a long breath and walked back to his desk—and the document that changed his future. It stood out amongst the plain papers below. Florid colours and script wove across the page. His father's looping signature beside Cedric Woodruff's neat penmanship.

The betrothal contract had curled with age, the edges frayed and brittle. It had been in his father's wall, safe, neatly stacked with deeds and stock certificates. Most of those papers were now useless, unlike the colourful tract in front of him.

He sat down and ran a hand through his hair, tugging at the strands to ease the tension building along his scalp. Elias had always wondered why his father had entered into this bargain, why he hadn't just sold the stone himself. It was all there; how many tonnes of stone would be sent south and the percentage of the profits the Clearboulds would get. Things had become clear when Elias had sorted through his father's effects after his return to Cairden. Cedirc Woodruff sold the equivalent in one year that his father did in three, and this way Anton Clearbould could keep his hands clean and look his peers in the eye at the country club or the assemblies down in the capital. There were few things Anton Clearbould cared about more than dignity to the point of ego.

Elias picked up the contract. There were no clauses for violating the agreement, no need to pay back the signing fee or bride price, but he knew he could never break it. This one piece of paper had kept the quarry going and the sum that Ursula brought with her would help them survive for at least another year. It could even contribute to the modernisation the business desperately needed to make it a viable, livable thing again.

He looked down at his left hand and the space where his last two fingers used to be, where aches still bothered him from time to time. There used to be such power in his touch. And now? Nothing. Elias flexed his hand, the paper in the other rustling with the movement. Would he ever feel that again—be whole, be *enough*?

The contract fell from his grasp onto the desk. The paint

made the paper heavy, and it landed with a whispered thud. He turned his back on it again, tracing the same route around the room. His body was jangly, and he wanted to move, wanted to get the energy out. He wished he had the time for a run. It was the one form of exercise he could still do with some skill, and it was one of the few things that grounded him. Elias walked to the window and placed his hands on the wide windowsill. He rested his forehead against the cool glass, closed his eyes, and breathed.

In for three, out for three, just like he learned in the east. His breath fogged the glass, picking out the patterns on the wet pane. He watched a drip dance down until it vanished.

This is what he needed to do, what he should have done five years ago. A calmness washed over him as he kept his breath long and steady. Some deep part of him wished that this would work, that it would magically solve everything and become a proper, loving marriage like the ones he was surrounded by. It was the same part of him that looked beyond the quarry walls all those years ago, a part of him he never managed to grow out of.

There was a sharp knock at his door and Rodger, his valet, appeared. "Your guests have arrived, sir. They are in the parlour."

Elias straightened and tried to smooth the creases out of his shirt. "Thank you, Rodger. I'll be right down."

His valet pursed his lips, nodded, and left the room. Elias smoothed down the front of his shirt again and ran his fingers through his hair as he went for the door, one thought circling his mind.

He hoped he'd be better as a husband than he had been as a son.

# 3

# Ursula

Ursula's mouth dropped open as Allerbrock came into view. The town stretched down the mountainside, nestled amongst the trees that populated the landscape. It was built in the same pale sandstone the area was known for and had a golden glow when the sun managed to peek through the clouds. She could see why it was called the Pale City; the stone stood out in stark contrast to the greenery that surrounded it. It wasn't like she'd imagined. The few people who had visited always talked as if the north was quaint. Backwards, even. Not like the expansive edifice in view. The road evened out as they travelled under the city gate and passed the high walls that encircled the town.

The buildings were much taller here; long, thin structures that had slate on the roofs not like the squat timber-framed lodgings she was used to seeing back home. Ursula felt a wave of something like homesickness—not for the flat lands of her birth, but the uneasy feeling that she had left everything familiar behind. All she had now was Nurse Selwyn and her rough ways to remind her of life from before, even if that was just for a few short weeks before she, too, left.

The carriage slowly rolled to a stop and the driver hopped down, sprightlier than he had been the rest of the voyage. The prospect of the end of the journey and rest seemed to have buoyed him as much as it terrified Ursula. Her nurse leapt to attention at once and ordered the driver where to take their bags, even though she'd never set foot in the magnificent building in front of them. Their driver huffed and grumbled as he climbed onto the roof of the coach. Sweat shone on his furrowed brow as he hauled the heap of cases down and thumped them on the ground. No wonder the poor man was so happy to see the back of them.

Ursula made her way from the carriage, noting how the leaves on the trees were already mottled with yellow and had started to fall in piles on the ground. The large flagstones leading to the house were slick underfoot, like there had been recent rain. Her feet felt unsteady on the wet surface as she took in what was to be her new home. The building had a plain facade with large leaded windows and modest front garden with small ornamental hedges leading to a brown front door. Everything felt old here, like it had been around for generations.

Ursula's stomach knotted as she stretched her neck skyward, following the long lines of the house. She'd never been ashamed of her family, but everything about them felt gaudy next to Cairden Abbey's quiet grandeur. The Clearboulds didn't need to parade who they were, their roots or connections; it was all here in the stark stone house that dominated the landscape. Their distant ties to the aristocracy gave them a respectability her father had never been able to buy. She felt very small in the house's looming shadow.

Although the building was plain, the scale dwarfed the house she had grown up in, which was a rabbit warren of rooms added onto by the various inhabitants. Bowside House had always felt simultaneously too big and too small for her family; there was barely a room big enough to contain all her siblings, but you could get lost in the place without seeing anyone for hours. Cairden Abbey felt far more impressive, even if it didn't have Bowside's ornamentation or sprawl.

They made their way to the door as it swung open. The driver took the opportunity to grouse audibly about the audacity of southerners as he took their bags to the servants' entrance around the side of the building.

Three figures greeted them at the door: a young woman in a well-made but plain dress, a dour looking man, and the last was a green-skinned magical creature. Ursula assumed they were servants from their dress, but she couldn't be sure as they weren't in livery. She'd heard whispers that people dressed much simpler up north, that the weather was so cold and inhospitable they didn't care about how they looked. The green-skinned woman was short and stout, with long, pointed ears that stuck out from the sides of her lace cap. Thin, wispy white hair curled around the edges, which gave her the look of a kindly grandmother. She must be a hobgoblin, or a 'brownie', as they were known up here.

It took every bit of willpower in her body to not stare, but it was the closest she'd ever been to someone magic outside of a temple. Magic was rare back home, weakened by generations of migration to the cities. Real magic could only bloom in wild places, where connections to the elements hadn't been hemmed in by box hedges or eroded by smog from factories.

The servants paid obeisance as Ursula and her nurse arrived

at the door.

The small green woman tilted her head to the side, a warm smile on her face. She was at least half the height of Ursula but had an air of authority that told her who really ran this place. "Welcome to your new home, Miss Woodruff. I'm Mrs. Clough, the housekeeper."

She pointed to the man beside her, who was so still he could be a statue. "This is Rodger, Mr. Clearbould's valet."

The man gave a stiff nod as a way of welcome.

"We have been ever so excited for your arrival," said the young woman beside them. She had gleaming, wide eyes and a beaming smile. Ursula liked her instantly.

Mrs. Clough patted the girl on the arm. "And this is Maisie, the closest thing we have to a serving girl here."

"I'm a jack of all trades," Maisie added.

Ursula nodded down at the staff. She towered over them, even Rodger. "It's a pleasure to make your acquaintance."

She had imagined lines of new faces and names to memorise and was glad that there wasn't a litany of servants to manage. She looked past the group into the open doorway behind them to see if more people were lurking in the shadows. How could a house of this size manage with such a small team? Even Bowside had at least double the staff. Her thoughts were interrupted by Nurse Selwyn, who made a theatrical cough and looked down her nose at the people in front of her.

"I'm Nurse Selwyn. I've been with Miss Woodruff since she was in a swaddling cloth."

"I see. Loyalty is an often overlooked quality." Mrs. Clough ran her eyes up and down Nurse Selwyn with a gaze so formidable, Ursula would have withered under it. Nurse Selwyn held firm, eliciting a brief nod from the housekeeper.

"Your man has already delivered your luggage. Please follow me to the parlour for tea while you wait for Mr. Clearbould."

Cairden Abbey was more homely inside than the façade let on, and while the walls had the impressive height of the outside, they were covered in colourful wall hangings and pictures. There were impressive portraits of long-dead ancestors in wide ruffs and frilly pantaloons alongside bucolic landscapes and the odd pair of antlers. Ursula found herself smiling at a painting of a rather rotund, hairy dog sitting on its own velvet chaise. She followed Mrs. Clough down the corridor, her footsteps muffled by an expanse of red carpet that ran the length of the hall. Ursula felt her stomach unknot a fraction as she took in the room: it was rough around the edges and suggested an air of being lived-in, which was a far cry from the haughty institution she worried it would be.

Her knees felt unsteady as she turned left into a rather small, but well-proportioned parlour. All the worries and fears she had felt on the journey up coalesced into a strange sort of panicked static. It was like her insides were jumping around, as if her body had a mind of its own. Her lips felt dry, and she traced them with her tongue.

The parlour was comfortably appointed with brocade settees and an imposing leather armchair. Ursula arranged herself on one of the settees facing into the room, enjoying its soft sag after days of bumpy roads and hard tavern furniture.

Mrs. Clough came in with the tea and there was a flurry of movement as cups and plates with delicate fancies made of cream and candied fruit were passed around.

Ursula settled back into the chair, sipping her tea and awaiting the stranger who would be her husband. She fiddled with her skirt, flattening out non-existent creases and readjusting her cuffs. It was like being a prize sow at the summer fair. Even after all the pain, disappointment, and worry, she wanted to make a good impression for Elias to like her.

She also wanted to like him, too. Ursula gave a quick, sneaky prayer to Talia, the goddess of love and all things beautiful, that her husband-to-be would not be a complete wretch. Then she shoved the thought aside with as much force as she could muster and began fiddling with her hair, tucking an unruly strand that had been tickling at her chin behind her ear.

The chatter dulled, and hairs stood up on the back of her neck as the parlour door creaked behind her.

"Tea, sir?" Mrs. Clough asked, breaking the silence.

Elias gave a brief reply, his voice warm and lilting. It surprised Ursula that he didn't speak with the clipped tones she was used to; listening to Elias was like lying beside a stream on a summer's day.

Ursula now regretted her seating choice; she desperately wanted to sneak a look at Mr. Elias Clearbould, to see if he was the wretch she imagined when her anger overran the constraints she fastidiously tried to keep in place, or if he was just a normal man, buffeted along by fate like herself. Instead, she straightened her back and stood to face the man who would be her husband.

She watched as Elias moved through the room, unable to keep her eyes off him. He walked at an easy pace, his long legs devouring the short distance. Her heart was hammering in her chest, and she tried to commit as much to memory as possible. To file it away and think about it later. He had a rumpled appearance, his clothes lived-in and his face unshaven, yet he was unmistakably handsome.

Ursula lifted her hand in the air between them. "How do you do?"

Elias's eyes stared into her own. Ursula felt her shoulder drop an inch, as the worry she didn't even know she carried evaporated—she would not have to hunch for her husband. He was tall enough, her own height or maybe a fraction taller.

Elias bowed, clasped her hand, and brushed a chaste kiss on the back of it.

His lips skated across her skin, but Ursula felt every movement like a brand on her body. He tipped his gaze up, looking at her through impossibly long lashes. His blue eyes sparkled in the firelight, and Ursula felt unbearably hot.

"It is wonderful to finally meet you, Miss Woodruff." Elias straightened, properly fixing his eyes on Ursula's face for the first time. She looked away, feeling like a coquettish miss being wooed at a dance.

"And you, Mr. Clearbould," she said automatically, pleasantries that had been drilled into her tripping off her tongue. All she wanted to do was step away from him and get some fresh air; the room felt too small, the whole scene too intimate. She sat back down a little too quickly, her head swimming with the enormity of everything. It was actually happening.

Elias gave her a brief smile and walked over to the leather armchair.

The room was now empty besides them and Nurse Selwyn, who was ensconced in a chintz loveseat. The bulging cushions swallowed her short frame, and she caught Ursula's eye over the rim of her teacup and pumped her eyebrows a couple of times. She may have even mouthed something, but Ursula missed it on account of spending all her energy in staying upright instead of falling into a swoon.

She ran her clammy hands down the front of her dress, trying to get her breathing in check.

Elias sat on the chair, which gave a squeak as he reached for his tea on the coffee table. The noise gave the atmosphere a surreal air and Ursula had to repress a laugh. It was all too absurd.

"How was your journey?" he asked Ursula. The weight of his full attention scorched her, and she felt a blush creep up her neck. Ursula held his gaze for a beat, then lowered her eyes a fraction. His stare was overwhelming, and when Elias looked at her it was like she was the only person in the world.

She took a sip of tea and another, the action giving her a moment to breathe before raising her eyes to meet his.

He was striking, in his own sort of dishevelled way, with rich brown hair and blue eyes.

*Just my luck,* thought Ursula, *Elias has piercing blue eyes.* Ursula had always found the colour to be cold and untrustworthy, but maybe that was because men with blue eyes in Currington were cads chased by gaggles of adoring women. Blue eyes were an exotic rarity in a world of brown and hazel.

The more she looked at him, the more she liked. His hair had shades of red that glimmered under the lights. His eyes were warm, if not a bit guarded, with a hint of mischief. His jaw, though covered in stubble, was sharp, and his chin had a slight dimple—so small that it was easy to miss when you first looked at him.

Ursula tried to cling to the anger she had felt for him and was annoyed to find her resolve had melted away in his presence. For all his faults, Elias Clearbould looked like a decent, well brought up, sickeningly good-looking man. Perhaps he would make a good husband after all.

Once she admitted this to herself and didn't pass out, Ursula felt the clammy panic ebb. She was just about to reply when Nurse Selwyn cut in.

"Oh, it was very slow, Mr. Clearbould! You ought to get those roads smartened up. Makes travelling through the mountains an ordeal. We were flying along the road through the fens, but that all stopped when we crossed the border and the hills started."

Ursula was glad for the reprieve from her own thoughts, but not her nurse's overfamiliar manners. She plastered a smile on her face and added, "The scenery is beautiful here, so taking extra time was no real hardship."

"Yes, mountain roads are tough going but it stops people sneaking in and pilfering our goods. We don't want anyone with a chisel and a cart getting our sandstone. I see the mountains as nature's gate keeps, Nurse…" He looked at her expectantly and Ursula kicked herself for not introducing them. Had all her manners fled? The whole situation had her upside down. She had made an assumption about Elias Clearbould, and he was proving to be the very opposite. He was welcoming and erudite, handsome and curious.

"Selwyn," her nurse replied, preening herself under Elias's gaze. It seemed that no one was immune to his sapphire stare.

"Ah, a good southern name if ever there was one," Elias said, and Ursula was sure she saw her old nurse redden and flutter her eyelashes.

"You've had a long journey. I'm sure you will want to rest before dinner, but would you like a tour of the house first?" Elias placed his cup on the occasional table beside his chair and slapped his hands against his thighs. His eyes darted between the pair expectantly.

It was then that Ursula noticed his ring and pinkie finger were missing on his left hand. For all his obvious charm, she realised she still knew so little about Elias.

Nurse Selwyn had a wicked gleam in her eye and went to speak, but Ursula cut in.

"Thank you for the offer, Elias, but I think we'd better rest now."

She could have sworn he looked crestfallen, and she hoped she hadn't overstepped. Though she was itching to see more of the house, Ursula felt a heaviness in her limbs that no amount of nosiness could overtake. She wanted to be bright-eyed and able to take everything in.

"I'll ring for Mrs. Clough, she'll show you to your rooms." He stood and tugged on the long brocade pull cord by the door, and Mrs. Clough appeared moments later.

Ursula helped Nurse Selwyn out of her chair as she made exaggerated moans and complaints about her back.

"If you'll follow me this way," Mrs. Clough said as she came to Nurse Selwyn's side.

Ursula gave Elias a brief nod and followed the two older women out into the hall, drawing her first deep breath since the sight of Elias had stolen it away.

# 4

# Ursula

A woodpecker thundered against the carriage door. Ursula waved her hand in an attempt to get the infernal beast to fly away, waking with a start as it flopped back onto her face.

Unfamiliar walls came into view as she rubbed the sleep away from her eyes. A clock clanged on the mantle, and Ursula stared at it in disbelief. The last of the day's light painted the sky a watercolour of pinks and blues. She had slept the afternoon away.

It all came flooding back then—she had decided to lie down for a quick nap when she arrived in her temporary lodgings. Panic bloomed in her gut. Had she slept through dinner?

Someone rapped an insistent knock at the door, and Ursula fumbled over to it on sleep-leaden limbs.

Maisie stood before her, her cheeks bright like a springtime apple as a huge smile spread across her face.

"Ah, miss, I'm so glad you are up! I've been knocking on for ages." The young woman bustled into the room. "Mrs. Clough said I was to act as your lady's maid, seeing as you don't have one."

"There's no need, Maisie. I don't have my own lady's maid at home. My sisters and I help each other when necessary—"

"See! You need me." Maisie grinned, rubbed her hands together, and eyed Ursula from head to toe. "Now, where shall we start? A bath? I'll draw you one and we can unpack your valise while it fills."

"That would be wonderful." Ursula beamed at Maisie; her cheerful candour was infectious and rubbed away the last of her tiredness. Before she knew it, Maisie whizzed out of the room and Ursula was left to her own devices again.

She stretched, easing the last of sleep from her body, and looked around her accommodation, noticing details she had been too tired to see before. The room was well proportioned with sage green walls and pictures of flowers dotted around them. The furniture was mahogany or stained oak, dark and sturdily built. It was a peaceful place, with a calm atmosphere and restrained grace. Her shoulders eased, the sore bunches in her muscles she didn't even know were there, loosening. She liked this room immensely.

Ursula wandered over to the window and peered out. It had gotten dark while she slept, but she could make out the silhouette of trees and buildings against a star-filled sky. You couldn't see the stars in Currington; there were too many factories downstream, and their fumes clouded the sky at night to conceal even the brightest constellations, including her namesake. The world suddenly felt very big as she looked out into the inky dark, and she felt a shiver go down her spine.

The chill sent her to the hearth, and she noticed the fire was getting low. Ursula pulled her dress closer around her to keep the cold out. If only she could remember where her robe was packed…

She picked up a poker and took to the embers, stirring up the flames before adding a new log. Maisie reappeared just as she was finishing the job.

"Oh, Miss Woodruff, you must leave that. We don't want you getting ashes all over your nice dress." The maid waved her away from the fireplace and Ursula jumped like a startled cat. Maisie busied about, bringing a wooden rail in front of the fire and draping linens over it.

Ursula looked down at her, feeling like an out-of-place giant. "I was just trying to help."

"That's alright, miss! We're here for that now. It takes a wee while for the water to heat up, but it'll be done in a jiff."

Maisie seemed to be in perpetual motion, bouncing around the room like a determined rubber ball. She stopped and smiled with glee as she opened Ursula's luggage.

"Now then, let's get you in a nice frock for tonight."

Before she knew it, the room was a riot of colour: dresses, petticoats, ribbons, and shoes scattered everywhere.

"Aha! This will do!" Maisie exclaimed as she held up a burgundy taffeta dress. Ursula gave a taut smile; the evening ahead did not inspire the same enthusiasm in her. She'd met Elias for all of five minutes and found him distracted and unkempt. Heavens knows how he would turn up for dinner.

After a few minutes, Maisie went to check on the bath in the adjoining bathroom, picking up some scented oil that had been sitting on the dressing table as she went. There was some splashing, and Maisie poked her head around the door with an expectant look on her face.

"Are you going to get in, miss?"

Ursula paused. It would be good to have help scrubbing

off the grime from the road, but it felt strange to accept help from anyone besides one of her sisters.

"Thank you for all your help, but I think I'd like a bit of privacy now, Maisie."

"It's nothing I haven't seen before, miss, but I understand. We all need moments of calm in our day, don't we?" Maisie smiled softly.

Ursula smiled again at the warmth of this stranger. "Thank you, Maisie. I'll ring when I'm done."

She lowered herself into the bath, grateful for the way the warm water eased her stiff muscles. She hadn't the faintest clue what to expect from tonight's dinner, but she couldn't deny her eagerness to see Elias again.

Heat that had nothing to do with the water's temperature flooded her cheeks, her thoughts drifting to a pair of clear blue eyes as she sank beneath the surface.

# 5

# Elias

He'd picked up the whisky to busy his hands, but the peaty burn was the perfect antidote to his overactive mind.

He was more consumed by Ursula than ever.

Silly musing had solidified when he met her. She wasn't how he had pictured; her striking beauty completely different from northern women with their pale skin, elfin features, and demure build. She was tall—nearly his height—with a long, regal nose and a face that tapered to a soft oval. Her hair was a literal crowning glory, very long and very dark. Just a shade off black, it caught the light like a raven's wing.

He swigged his whisky and propped his arm on the mantle, determined to stay in that spot and stop his fidgeting.

It was her eyes that intrigued him the most: amber and mottled with flecks of green. He'd never seen eyes like that before.

Elias was lost in his thoughts when the door finally opened, and Ursula walked in. Her steps were hesitant and slow at first, but once they locked eyes, she gave him a beaming smile that made Elias feel like he'd been punched in the gut.

The light bounced off the striking planes of her face, all jewel tones and shadow. Her dark hair had been swept up and pinned in intricate whorls. Unbidden images of pulling out those pins one by one swept through his mind, and he imagined his hands raking through the dark tresses as they fell over her bare shoulders and back. He tried to mentally douse them in cold water. Now was not the time to think such things; he could contain himself until later.

"Good evening, Miss Woodruff. Do come and sit down." He motioned to the settee she had sat in earlier.

Ursula made her way to the chair, the wide hem of her gown rustling as she moved through the tight space. Her back was as straight as an arrow, hands clasped in front of her.

"Would you like an aperitif?"

She sat silently for a moment, her bottom lip worried between her teeth. Elias found himself so lost in the sight of her that he almost missed what she said.

"Yes. A sherry would be lovely, thank you."

"Oh yes, of course."

He went to the drinks cabinet, the image of her full lip pillowing against her teeth in his mind, and poured a healthy measure into a small, etched glass before handing it to Ursula. She gave a quick nod of thanks, and he sat down in the same armchair as before.

She lifted her glass and looked him in the eye. "Sallot."

"Ah, I forgot your mother was from Esmarna." Elias raised his glass in response. "Sallot, indeed."

He took the moment to study her, to watch the way the firelight danced in her amber eyes. They were remarkably appealing, like they held the fire within them.

"How did your mother end up on our fair island?  Most people are clamouring to leave Reul for the continent."

She relaxed back into the chair as she sipped her drink, the stiffness of her arrival ebbing as she held his gaze.

"It's a rather boring story," Ursula said as she tipped her head to the side, and Elias's eyes felt glued to the long column of her neck. "My mother moved to be a companion to a widowed marchioness, but then she met my father and absconded to a hotch-potch house by the marshland, much to the lady's chagrin." Ursula gave a small chuckle. "Although she can't be that annoyed, as she sends chocolates every Yule."

Elias smiled back. Ursula spoke in the same abrupt cadence he had come to expect from all southerners, but her laugh was gentle and melodious. It floated around the room and crept down his spine, leaving goosebumps in its wake. He promised himself to make her laugh again tonight.

"How do you find your lodgings?"

"Lovely, thank you. The room is very peaceful."

"It was my sister's room," he replied. "You will have to give her credit for the decor. But it does have the best view in the house, right down the hillside to the river."

"I did have a look out this evening but couldn't see much. Although the stars are extraordinary here." Ursula shifted in her seat, smoothing out the fabric on her lap. She looked around the small room. "Don't we have a chaperone?"

"We're not as concerned with these things up here, but I could ask Mrs. Clough or your dear Nurse Selwyn. She seems like the type to come after me with a fire poker, should I try to tarnish your reputation before the wedding." He shot her his most roguish grin and raised an eyebrow.

A laugh bubbled out of Ursula. "Oh no, it's quite alright. I know your customs are different here. I just expected that we'd be accompanied before the wedding."

Elias sat taller, pleased that he had made her laugh again, and heartily. He sipped his drink with a small, satisfied smile on his face.

Ursula traced her eyes around the room, and he followed her gaze.

"This is one of my favourite rooms in the house."

"Oh?"

He liked it when he had her full attention on him. The way her face was a placid mask, but her eyes held a cunning spark like she wanted to devour all the information in front of her.

"It's a bit more…"

"Intimate?"

Lightning charged down his spine, settling in his groin and tingling across his skin.

"I was going to say friendly, but intimate fits as well." Her cheeks had reddened, and Elias hoped it was from their conversation and not the blazing fire. "It's a bit of a mishmash. This armchair was my grandfather's, and the sideboard was part of his mother's bride price."

"That's nice," Ursula replied, her eyes scanning the walls again. "I like the pictures."

Her spine had straightened at the mention of a bride price, and Elias wanted to run out and employ a chronomancer to turn back time and say anything else.

"I'm no art maven, but I do know about some of them. I could show you, if you like?"

He hoped his voice wasn't too eager, but he wanted to get closer to her now that they were alone. To see the rigidity drop from her shoulders and watch her eyes sparkle again.

"Alright."

Elias was at her side in a flash, his hand proffered to help her up. Her skin was soft against his own and her long fingers wrapped around his palm. He wondered how they would feel against other parts of him.

"Excuse me, but dinner is served," Mrs. Clough said from behind them. Elias silently cursed his housekeeper's impeccable timing. Of course, dinner wouldn't be late.

The housekeeper tried to hide a smile. "Now, if you'd like to follow me."

"Another time." Ursula patted the top of his hand, and they filed out of the room.

Mrs. Clough showed them into the dining room; there were candles burning in sconces on the wall casting a golden glow over everything. A fire roared in the hearth, the room's diminutive dimensions making it easier to talk here rather than shout across a vast expanse of wood in the main dining hall.

Elias pulled out her chair, and Ursula lowered herself into it with all the grace of someone raised to sit on a throne. His stomach twisted into an uncomfortable knot. Ursula deserved to be on the arm of some master of business or an old money duke, lighting up a ballroom and not sent off to the wilds to wed a stranger with watered down blue blood and a failing industry.

"On tonight's menus," Mrs. Clough announced, interrupting his miserable thoughts, "we have parsnip, carrot, and mutton soup to start, followed by venison in a blackberry sauce with roast vegetables."

She poured a healthy glass of red wine from the carafe on the table for the pair before leaving the room and returning a moment later with a huge silver tray with two steaming bowls of soup on it.

A silver basket full of perfectly round bread rolls sat between them and Elias ripped into one, slathering butter all over it. Dipping it into his soup with one hand and lapping it up with his spoon in the other.

He caught Ursula's eyes widen at the ferocious speed with which he was devouring his soup and paused. She was demurely supping at her broth, her arms delicately placed on the edge of the table. He felt like an oaf hunched over his dinner and uncurled his back.

"I can't help but eat like a soldier now. When you're in the army, you never know if someone is going to pinch your pudding or bestow a second helping. Better to eat fast for all eventualities."

She smiled in response. "I have six siblings. I know what it's like to have to fight to keep what you want to eat on your plate and what you don't want off. This is a nice change of pace."

Elias nearly choked on his food. "Seven children!"

He would never imagine this refined creature in front of him in such a melee. She held herself with such poise; her back was so straight, like there was an invisible thread tethering her from above. Elias bet Ursula Woodruff could run an obstacle course with a book on her head and it wouldn't move an inch.

"This place must feel empty to you."

Ursula gave another small, almost conspiratorial smile. "I wasn't joking when I said the room was peaceful. I've never had one on my own before."

Before the war, he could never have pictured living so closely with another. It had always just been him, Susannah, and their parents. They could rattle around Cairden for hours without any interruption—something he and Susannah had taken full advantage of when growing up—disappearing into nooks and crannies during their games. It was the same with the woods that butted up against the grounds; they felt like an extension of the house, their very own plaything. School had been the same. The tight leash the teachers kept on them effectively stopped their shenanigans…well, most of the time.

The army had been a rude awakening: too many men shoved into tents, the inescapable desert sand that got into everything, the constant jostling for a bit more room, an extra blanket to fight off the cold desert nights, or a razor that had somehow gone walkabout.

Elias felt an ache in his chest. It was so easy to focus on the bad that had come from his service, but he missed the noise, the business, the camaraderie. If he felt this now, all this time later, how must Ursula feel having left such a full household behind?

"You mentioned a sister. Does she live nearby?" asked Ursula. She looked at him intently across the table.

Elias sat back in his chair, his bowl now empty, and fiddled with the stem of his wine glass. He wished he'd taken more time to eat, if only to give his hands something to do. "Susannah is a year younger than me and lives in the next county. She's been off and married for a while now, has two boys and a doting husband."

The ache returned, and he couldn't fight the sad smile that crept on his face as he talked of his only family. "They were a love match and met as teenagers. You know, the whole star-crossed lovers' story—except they've been madly in love for over a decade. It's positively sickening." He chased away the lump in his throat with a long pull of wine. "She was born under a lucky sign. As the saying goes, she could fall in muck and come out smelling of roses."

"I think I know the type."

The conversation lulled as she finished her food, and Elias reached for another roll to occupy his mouth.

"She'll be here the week before the wedding to help with any arrangements and whatnot. I'm sure the family will be in tow. Hopefully, you'll get to meet the boys. The young ones, I mean. My nephews, not Cal—but maybe he can be lumped in, too," Elias babbled. He was grasping for something to say, and words kept pouring out. Anything to keep her talking, to find out more about her. Maybe to even coax one of those sweet smiles or her bubbling laugh.

"Oh, that's nice," Ursula replied.

Her hands now neatly folded in her lap as she conspicuously looked anywhere other than him. He kicked himself and hoped he'd done the right thing inviting Susannah. He wasn't sure what it was like for a woman in the lead up to nuptials, but he assumed she'd like a sisterly presence. Given Ursula's response, he was thinking otherwise.

"Since we are on the subject of siblings, how is your brother? Theo, isn't it? I must admit I have few memories of him from school, apart from making mischief and scaring the local wildlife. Settled down?"

Ursula's mouth twisted as she fidgeted with the napkin in her lap.

"Oh no. Theo is over in the continent. He first went after university to connect with our Esmarnan history and ended up staying."

She looked like she was about to say more but thought better of it.

He was about to try and guide the conversation onto easier topics when Mrs. Clough re-emerged to clear their dishes and replace them with the main course.

The venison was juicy and pink, and a delicious sweetness was radiating from the blackberry sauce. Elias vowed to take his time with this dish.

"This looks wonderful," Ursula said as she stared at her plate, eyes wide in adoration.

"Trust me, it'll taste even better knowing Mrs. Dyce's talents." Elias pulled at his napkin and fanned it over his lap.

"I can only imagine."

"No need to imagine, dig in and live it." Elias speared a piece of venison on his fork and ate it with a flourish as if to underline his point.

She gave him a quick smile and followed suit, diving into the meal with gusto.

"I thought your parents were accompanying you. It would be nice to see your father after all this time."

Ursula paused, the tightness returning to her face. Elias felt like a fool all over again. It was like one step forward, two steps back.

"Well, you see the thing is…my mother is indisposed, and my father didn't want to leave her alone."

Elias squinted as Ursula fidgeted around. He was about to make a platitude about good health and a speedy recovery, but Ursula cut in.

"She thought it was the change of life but it's…well, the healer has said that she must have bed rest until…it…arrives."

Nervous laughter bubbled up in him. Of all the things he

thought she was going to say, it wasn't that.

"Oh my. Well that is a justifiable reason, indeed." He lifted his glass in a toast. "To their health."

Ursula copied the motion, taking a sheepish sip.

She looked down at her plate again and Elias noticed the sprouts were left untouched.

"Excuse my ignorance, but what are the green vegetables? I've never had them before."

The tension in the room lessened as the company focused on vegetables rather than parental procreation.

"They are called Bulin's sprouts. They are a bit like a tiny cabbage." Elias stabbed one on his fork and bit in.

Ursula cut one in half and took a tentative bite. He could see the exact moment the sprout touched her tongue. Her face screwed up, and though she tried to cover it with a calm facade, her strained, purposeful chews gave away what she thought of it. He watched the charming crinkle of her nose with rapt attention as she determinedly swallowed the vegetable and washed it down with a healthy gulp of wine.

Elias caught her eye and smiled, admiring her candour.

"They are an acquired taste. No one would judge you for leaving them on your plate." He shrugged and speared another with his fork, eating it whole. "I, personally, love them."

Ursula grimaced as she pushed the green spheres away from the rest of her food. "Well, you can have mine, too."

"Gladly! Tip them over here." Elias brandished his plate and was pleased to see Ursula give a little chuckle as she rolled the offending vegetables onto it.

The conversation quietened again, but the silence didn't have the same frantic edge to it as it had in the parlour. Perhaps it was the cosier dimensions of the room, or the noise from the fire, or the fact they were eating, but time passed quickly, and soon enough Mrs. Clough was back again to clear the dishes.

"Now, my dears, we have carrot and walnut cake, or some apple crumble and custard. Or both?" the housekeeper asked with a devilish smile.

"Oh goodness, Mrs. Clough. I don't think I could eat another bite…although the crumble does smell divine."

"I'll give you a small portion. My mother always used to say, *A little of what you fancy does you well.*" Mrs. Clough filled a bowl with the dessert, pouring on lashings of custard. She then turned her attention to Elias, who gave her a beaming smile in response.

"You know me, Mrs. C. I can't turn down a sweet."

The housekeeper gave a little chuckle as she served Elias. A flush crept up his throat as the tiny housekeeper wobbled over with his plate. He could have sworn it quivered under the mountainous portions and he felt like a pig about to bury its head in a trough. This was further compounded by Ursula's delicate nibbling of her plate. It looked like she'd hardly touched the pudding.

Elias gave his mouth a self-conscious dab. "Would you like a tour after?"

Ursula laid her cutlery down, her hands coming to rest in her lap again. "After dinner? Won't it be too dark?"

Elias could feel his shoulders slump. She was avoiding him, that had to be it. This had happened twice now, and he didn't think his ego could handle another rejection. Of course she would be distant; she'd met him and decided to keep him at arm's length. Isn't that what all respectable southern ladies do? Isn't that what he'd do in her position?

He just wanted to spend some time alone with her without the pressure of other people or the need to keep conversation going. He wanted to show her where he grew up and see how she reacted. It felt important, like he would glean some vital piece of information or that it would be a bellwether for their relationship.

"How about tomorrow? After breakfast?" Ursula asked.

His chest puffed on its own accord. *She* had asked *him.* Maybe it wasn't all lost. "Perfect."

# 6

# Elias

Sweat prickled the back of his neck as he stalked behind the commander.

Rows and rows of casters stood in formation, ready to strike.

The giants were miles away from them, but their huge forms stood like mountains against the candy-coloured sky.

Dawn was here, and the battle would soon follow.

"Positions!" the commander bellowed, and the soldiers hunched into a phalanx. Shields of magic materialised, glistening in the early rays of sunlight.

Elias kept his eyes trained on the back of the commander's head. He would see these men soon enough, bloody and battle worn with injuries he couldn't imagine. He couldn't face seeing them now, faces full of determination, only to find them destroyed later.

A commotion broke the line to the right of him and Elias abandoned his vow to keep his distance, instinctively chasing after the caster running across the golden sand.

His feet sunk into the shifting ground, dancing in the last of the chill night air.

*He reached for the young infantry man and grabbed his arm.*

*"This is not the way to do it." Elias's hand held fast, but his voice was soft.*

*The boy looked at him with pleading eyes. His face was clammy and flushed, eyes wide like a trapped animal.*

*"I can't. I can't," the boy said over and over.*

*"Come, let me help—"*

*His words were cut short by a blast of blistering light. Elias threw his hands up in front of his face and the world went black.*

Elias gasped awake, soaked with sweat, his arms flung out above him.

No, he had survived.

He had defied the odds and survived.

He looked at his left hand. Yes, he had survived—but barely.

Elias lowered his hand to his torso, feeling the web of scars down his side. They had faded over time, the raised skin still pink and puckered. He kept them covered now, and no one had seen them since his return.

The bedclothes were bunched around him, and Elias untangled the knot of covers as he shifted towards the edge of the bed. His chest heaved as he braced his hands on his thighs, staring into the dark. Finally, he rubbed his face and stood.

He trudged to the window, weariness clawing at him, and looked out. It was still dark, but he knew that he would not sleep for the rest of the night and decided to go for a run. Physical exercise was the only way to dispel the nervous energy his nightmares brought on.

The rhythmic pounding of his feet on the path steadied his mind. Each step slowed his whirring brain, bringing him back to the present.

He fought against an onslaught of memories. The metallic

tang of blood, the groan of other soldiers around him, and the sickeningly sweet stench of death. More prominent than any of them was the searing pain of the caster's spell as it struck him, liquid fire melting away his clothes and pooling on his skin. He lost his footing, almost tumbling back into those dark days after his accident.

He pushed harder, spurring his legs to run faster. The wind whipped around him as he ran up a steep incline through the trees. The scenery was so familiar, and it washed over him as he strode past. He always took the same route—through the side gate, down the hill, and a wide loop round the western woods.

He could hear the forest shift and move as he wove through it. Groaning trees creaked and rattled as they crept along the forest floor. Tales of disappearing travellers, meandering cabins, and fell voices on the wind luring people to their demise didn't worry him. The woods were as much a part of him as the bones in his body, the hair on his head, the beat of his heart.

The forest was like a second home, and it always welcomed him.

He paused on a rocky overhang, breathing deeply, and looked down at the blanket of green below. A harsh wind blew in his face, and Elias closed his eyes to savour the sting. The smell of pine needles crushed underfoot as he traversed the rough terrain that caught out many a weary traveller, the dank air sharp enough to cut through the best cloth.

He could feel his body relax, the nervous energy draining away.

This place was his refuge, and it replenished him.

Elias took off back towards the house.

He was halfway down the hall when he saw a shadow move. He froze; no one was usually awake when he went for his nighttime runs.

He prowled up the corridor, his ears trained for any sound.

A floorboard creaked up ahead and Elias leaped forward.

Ursula shrieked, slamming her back against the wall. She was as white as a sheet, her chest heaving.

"It's just me, it's just me." Elias held up his hands in surrender and slowly moved towards her. "I'm sorry to have scared you."

A thin shaft of light peeked through the leaded window at the end and cast her in a sliver glow.

She released her hands clasped over her mouth, easing the shawl that had slipped back onto her shoulders. Her hair was undone, framing her face like a dark halo. She looked beautiful and otherworldly in the dim light, like a spectre made to haunt only him. Shadows highlighted the curve of her cheeks, the arch of her brow.

He wanted to run his fingers over them. To feel the strong line of her nose, the jut of her jaw.

He let out a rattly breath. "Are you alright?"

Ursula nodded, wide-eyed, as she licked her lips. His gaze followed the peek of pink.

He wanted to feel that, too.

Those plump lips against his throat, her clipped voice low and husky.

His heart hammered against his chest, blood singing in his ears.

He wanted her.

"I was going to heat up some milk, but I…I think I'll just go back to bed." She brushed past him and went down the hall to her room, closing the door and locking it without a second glance.

He placed a hand on the wall and dropped his head, letting out a long breath.  It was their first night together, and he already scared her witless. Elias shook his head and made his way downstairs.

Warmth drifted from the cup as he set it on the floor by her door. The scent of honey filled the hall as he lightly rapt the wood, racing back to his room before it was opened.

He hoped that this would help; that she would understand.

7

# Elias

He scooped another spoonful of scrambled eggs onto his plate as he eyed the older woman across the room. Ursula hadn't appeared for breakfast yet, and Nurse Selwyn hummed a jaunty tune as she buttered a wedge of Mrs. Dyce's rye bread, an open newspaper spread out on the table in front of her. She had tiny half-moon glasses perched on her nose.

Elias surreptitiously added another spoonful of eggs, a few slices of bacon, and a couple of sausages to his breakfast.

Nurse Selwyn looked up with a wicked gleam in her eyes as he sat down. "I've always liked a man with a good appetite."

Elias blushed like a pre-teen as he picked up his fork, but it hung in the air just above his plate. Ursula may not be here, but he wanted to make the best impression with her companion.

Nurse Selwyn licked her fingertip and turned the page of the newspaper. "Don't stop on my account. Strapping lad like you has got to keep his strength up."

His cheeks burned like he was standing next to a fire, but it

45

jolted him out of his thoughts as he dug into his food.

"How did you sleep?" he asked after a few bites.

"Oh, wonderfully," Nurse Selwyn replied. "It's very peaceful here. It's not like in Bowside, where there's always someone coming and going. I feel like I could walk around Cairden for hours and not bump into anyone. Lots of little nooks and crannies to hide away in, away from prying eyes."

Elias nearly choked on his breakfast. Nurse Selwyn just stared at him with wide-eyed innocence.

"I suppose so. I've never thought about it."

"Oh, I doubt that."

He could have sworn the older woman flashed him a wicked grin and fluttered her eyelashes.

"You have me there, Nurse Selwyn," he conceded.

Nurse Selwyn had a mischievous streak that belied her age. He bet she was a hellraiser in her youth—in fact, she probably still was—but could now hide behind those little brass glasses of hers and plead innocence.

"Age isn't just a number, young man. Remember that." She swept over another page of the newspaper. "Very kind of you to get the Currington Gazette sent up. It's a few days out of date, but it's always nice to hear news from home. Our Ursula has never been one for current affairs, but she does love to read."

Ursula burst in then, looking rather flushed and harried. "I'm sorry I'm late, I slept in by accident. I'm only here at all because Maisie woke me." She rushed over and sat next to her nurse, poured a cup of tea and drank it, then poured another.

Elias was struck by how different she was compared to dinner last night; morning had completely worn away her composure. He didn't realise he'd disturbed her sleep so badly last night.

"Ursi, dear, you'd sleep through the end of time, if you could," her nurse teased with a smile. "Now, go and get yourself a plate before you waste away."

Ursula took another swig from her tea, nodded, and went over to the sideboard laden with breakfast food. She judiciously picked at the food, selecting each piece with care and attention. Her brow was furrowed in concentration, something Elias had come to notice she did often. It was like the world was a puzzle that she had to figure out. He wondered what else her analytical brain could do.

Elias sat back in his chair, uncurling his hunched shoulders and gave them a quick roll to work out any knots. He also placed his cutlery down and gave his chin a furtive dab with his napkin.

Nurse Selwyn let out a tiny huff across from him, but her eyes never strayed from the newspaper in front of her.

Ursula glided over to the chair beside her nurse, only a tiny shred of the gangly tiredness from her arrival left in her limbs.

"Morning," she announced to the table in a sort of sing-songy voice.

Elias replied, but he missed the unvarnished manner he witnessed moments ago.

"How did you sleep?" he asked, feeling like a parrot, but not sure what else to say.

"Quite well," Ursula replied. "Although there is a lot more wildlife here than I thought. More things prowling around after dark."

She looked directly at him then, and Elias felt the tawny stare on every inch of his skin like lightning crackling over water. She'd seemed panicky last night when he'd seen her in the hall, and he'd assumed he'd scared her. Yet, the intense look she gave him now made him think otherwise. He didn't have a chance to think more as Nurse Selwyn chimed in.

"What are you two youngsters doing today?" she said, eyes peering over the top of her tiny metal spectacles.

"Elias is taking us on a tour of the house," Ursula said.

Elias wilted, his confidence dented again. He'd been buoyed up by Ursula's suggestion of the tour today, of getting to spend time with her alone. His hopefulness had only been heightened by her searing look, but he'd read it all wrong. She wanted her nurse to come along, and the stare was more likely a reprimand and strong suggestion he keep his mouth shut in front of the old woman.

"Oh, I couldn't possibly go on a tour!" Nurse Selwyn shrieked. Her tiny glasses fell from her face and dangled on a chain around her neck as she grabbed at her side. "My poor back has not recovered from the journey. A long soak in a bath and a day in front of a fire is what I need."

"But I heard movement is best for a sore back." Ursula had turned and was looking directly at her nurse. Her eyes were narrowed, and she enunciated each word.

"Now, now, my girl," Nurse Selwyn swooped in, wincing theatrically. "We'll call a healer if need be. Isn't that right, Mr. Clearbould?"

He nodded, trying not to draw attention to himself. This morning had the beginnings of being a disaster.

Nurse Selwyn gave Ursula's hand a squeeze. "You go on with Mr. Clearbould, and don't worry about me."

Ursula looked from her nurse to Elias. "Only if you're sure."

"I insist," her nurse said at the same time Elias replied, "Absolutely."

"Alright then." She looked firmly at Elias. "It's a date."

His stomach did a tiny flip, and he could have sworn he saw Nurse Selwyn give him a sly wink across the table.

"The parlour is just across there," he said. "But you know that already."

The tour wasn't going to plan. Elias had wanted to dazzle Ursula with Cairden Abbey, to talk about it as his father did, with reverence and an air of authority. Instead, he'd tripped over his words like uneven flagstones and kept coming up blank.

Ursula looked around the hall. Her face was as serene as a swan gliding on a pond.

"It's a very nice room."

"Yes, very cosy."

She tilted her head and gave him a closed-mouth smile. Elias wanted the ground to swallow him up.

"If you follow me through here, I can show you the ballroom."

The hinges squeaked with disuse as he pushed at the huge, ornate oak door that held Cairden's most impressive room.

The ballroom was practically empty now, save for the huge antique table and chairs that had been pushed up against the far wall beside the fireplace. Old scorch marks from centuries of use fanned around the sandstone surround. The Allerbrock stone glimmered in the midmorning sun.

Elias held the door open for Ursula and nodded for her to go in ahead of him.

"We don't use this as much now that my parents aren't here. I'm not one for elaborate parties." His voice echoed through the empty space. Elias felt a cold, hard pain of longing for his family, for Ursula to meet them and see this place full of people and cheer.

"It's so charming," Ursula replied, her voice tinged with awe.

The south side of the room was filled with huge, leaded windows that let the light in all day and long into the night. Magnificent swags of fabric were pinned to each side, framing the woodlands beyond. Burnished wooden carvings covered every wall, making the vacant space feel alive.

Ursula walked over to the wall nearest the door and ran her hands along the sculpted surface.

"This is fascinating."

Her fingers followed the undulating scene of a satyr playing a flute in the woods, a flock of birds nestled in the tree above him.

Elias walked up beside her, and the oak door screeched closed behind them.

"It's an old tradition up here. To carve stories into your house." He pointed to the panel above. "Clearbould history is in these walls."

Her eyes followed his outstretched hand to the carving of a long figure walking through the woodland.

"That's my ancestor, David Clearbould. He was a great northern lord, the first to find the quarry. Story says that he bought a divining rod from a travelling witch, and it led him here. It was his grandson, also called David, who built Cairden Abbey."

Ursula's eyes went wide, her beautiful mouth agape as her eyes roamed over the image. She turned to look at him, and her fingers fidgeted with the end of her braid.

"My father bought Bowside House from a local gentleman

who fell on hard times. I can't imagine living somewhere my family has been for generations."

"It's a double-edged sword. Hard to make a place your own when it's belonged to so many. But I'm sure there are secret passages lost to time that even Susannah and I couldn't root out." Elias took a step closer and pointed to the next carving. "This one here shows what the quarry originally looked like."

Ursula turned back to the wall, sending an alluring, spicy scent into the air. He closed his eyes and let it wash over him for a second.

"Have a look at the border. Do you see anything unexpected there?"

Ursula's eyes squinted in concentration and then she burst into a fit of giggles. "Is that what I think it is?"

Elias chuckled. "Apparently, David—the grandson—was an awful man and a notorious tyrant. He fell out with one of the carvers he hired to make the piece, and the man did this in retribution. I'm not sure if he ever noticed or if he was just too pig headed to say anything, but it's been a favourite of mine since childhood."

They both shifted closer, looking at the woodwork as they laughed at the image of a tiny man mooning from the hedges of an elaborate floral scene.

Ursula's eye caught on the next panel as they moved around the room, Elias explaining each one. Her neck craned to look at the panels, eyes drifting up to the ornate ceiling emblazoned with the Clearbould crest in the centre. She looked just like a dancer, moving with easy poise. Elias suddenly felt the urge to spin her around like they were at a grand ball.

"It's wonderful, Elias." She stopped and looked at him, her amber eyes glassy with emotion and walked towards him.

"Thank you."

He almost jumped when she moved in to embrace him. The spicy scent from earlier nearly brought him to his knees. Her statuesque form moulded against his body, and he lifted his shaking hand around her. She fit so perfectly against him, and his heart squeezed in a strange new way as he realised he never wanted to let go.

He dropped his hands quickly, worried he'd held on too long. "Now, I have it on good authority you like to read."

Ursula narrowed her eyes. "Who told you that?"

"A little bird," Elias said with a smile. "Would you like to see our dusty old library?"

The beaming grin he got in response told him he'd said the right thing. Gods bless this old house.

8

# Ursula

Maisie stood behind her, lacing up her stays. Ursula hoped she'd leave some room to breathe. Corseting wasn't worn as much in the north, and Maisie was prone to getting a bit too enthusiastic with the strings.

The wind buffeted the trees outside, branches tapping out a secret code. The click-clack of Nurse Selwyn's knitting joined in the gentle melody.

Ursula stifled a yawn. She was sure she had heard someone cry out last night, only to find Elias panting and sweat-soaked when she finally got up the nerve to investigate.

She could see him now, his hair framing his forehead in damp curls. How his shirt strained over lithe muscles. It was strange to see him like that at night, the musk of exercise clinging to him.

A shiver ran down her spine. Surely it was fear that had made her pulse race?

"Miss?" Maisie looked at her quizzically. "I was just saying that I think you'll need something warmer than this if you

53

are going to survive a northern winter. These cotton dresses won't do, although they are rather pretty." She picked up a light blue one with a wide neckline trimmed with lace that showed off her decolletage. At home, it didn't look as frivolous or impractical. "It's good we got you booked into the atelier so quickly. You'll beat the Yule rush this way."

Maisie held up the dress, face furrowed in concentration as she looked between the blue confection of fabric and Ursula.

"I prefer you in jewel tones, miss, but I think this will do."

"Thank you, Maisie." Ursula couldn't help but smile at the young woman's blunt affection.

"I'm ever so excited! I walk past there on my way to work. They've always got the dreamiest fabrics and dresses to die for in the window," sighed Maisie. "My mam makes all our dresses. I'm lucky if it's not my sister's hand-me-down."

She reached into the wardrobe and pulled out the wedding dress, still wrapped in its box. "Better not forget this," Maisie said, tapping a brief, jaunty beat before placing the box on the bed.

Ursula's stomach fluttered; excitement and anxiety were such close cousins that she couldn't tell which one rippled through her. Maybe it was both? This would make it real. She would finally be married, finally fulfill the contract. No longer be a Woodruff, but a Clearbould. Someone's *wife*.

Her heart joined in with a pitter-patter of its own, and Ursula had to admit to herself that excitement had won.

It was the first time she'd be exploring Allerbrock. Part of her wished it was Elias that was showing her around; she had enjoyed the small amount of time they had spent together and wanted to see the town through his eyes, but even that couldn't dim the excitement that bubbled up. She gave Maisie a quick squeeze on the shoulder.

"Let's get our cloaks. I think we might be able to fit in a quick trip to that tea house you mentioned if we hurry. Although, you'll have to show me the way."

Maisie smiled broadly, plucking Ursula's cape from the wardrobe and fitting it on her shoulders. "Mine's downstairs, miss. I'll meet you at the front door." She promptly left the room, grappling with the dress box as she moved through the doorway.

Ursula looked around her room, fetching her coin purse and shawl. The former went into her pocket and the latter was wrapped around her neck to keep out the chill. It was the height of autumn, and already she couldn't shake the constant damp. She had taken to wearing a shawl and woollen stockings since her arrival to try and beat the climate.

They set a good pace into the town, stopping at various points as Maisie talked to one person or another. Ursula was happy to sit back and take in the scenery.

The buildings were tall and thin, gleaming in the late autumn sun. This part of town felt like a labyrinth of stairs, and Ursula was surprised at how everyone nimbly moved around. She felt herself grip onto the edge of buildings as she descended, navigating doorways cut into the hillside and steep roads of packed earth.

"The tea house is this way, miss," Maisie called out over her shoulder, gesturing for Ursula to follow her down a thin, winding paved path. Her knees knocked together as they wandered down the steep lane.

"You'll love Elaria's. It's got every tea imaginable. It comes upriver from the coast," Maisie chattered as she shifted the dress box in her hands. Watching the girl navigate the tight bends and drops of Allerbrock with such ease, Ursula wondered if she would ever get used to the hilly landscape.

"That shop's been in her family for generations. Word has it her great-grandmother was a witch from the Western Archipelago. Brought over moss and herbs and bits with her, and some of that well water they have. Nonsense fairy stuff. Anyway, it makes the best cup of tea this side of, well… anywhere."

The girl stopped and turned to Ursula, her young face etched with concern. "You alright, miss? You've gone a bit green around the gills."

Ursula nodded, ignoring the churning in her stomach. Maisie was a dose of sunshine keeping her occupied as she struggled with the topography.

Maisie nodded, her eyes wary as she continued down the serpentine slope. She resumed her remarks on this thing and that, but it went over Ursula's head as she followed mutely behind.

"Here's the teashop, miss!"

They were greeted by a building bursting at the seams with people. A wide set of windows were flung open into the street, chatter, laughter and delicious smells pouring out. There were a few round wooden tables scattered on the thin patio that ran the length of the building. A puny awning fluttered above it, and people sat swaddled in thick cloaks against the cold, their drinks sending plumes of steam into the afternoon air.

Maisie led Ursula through a stained-glass door covered in loops and whorls of colour. Outlined in thick black lines read *Blankenship's Tea Emporium* in the middle.

There was no jingle of the bell as they entered. Instead, a plump, lime-green parrot squawked at their arrival.

Maisie looked up at Ursula. "That's Waller. He's mostly harmless."

The air was moist and fragrant. Bold, malty notes melded with refreshing citrus and tart berries. The scents swam all around her, propelled by the breeze from the window, and Ursula sighed. It was like the air itself was relaxing, warming her from the inside out.

They walked through the space, shuffling past tightly packed tables towards an empty seat at the window. Maisie placed the dress box gently down on the wide window ledge beside them. The decor was endearingly hotch-potch with mismatched chairs and china. Richly decorated plates lined the room, and it reminded her of those first moments in Cairden when she followed Mrs. Clough down the corridor and read the history of the house—of the Clearboulds—on the walls.

A server walked over and placed a jug of water, two glasses, and menus on their table.

"Nice to see you again, Maisie," they said with a quick nod, then retreated behind the wooden counter at the opposite side of the room.

There was a small selection of pastries, buns, and scones, alongside pages and pages of tea. Each section was broken down into type, taste, and the properties. Blends for stamina, balance, and sleep, as well as curative infusions for coughs, colds, and stomach upsets.

Ursula scanned her eyes over the selection greedily. She felt like her father and could imagine him poring over the menu, seeing where each ingredient came from, how it was transported and stored.

"What'll it be, ladies?" the server asked, returning as silently as they had before. This time they were holding a small self-writing pad. Ursula gawked; she wasn't used to seeing such everyday uses of magic since it was usually the preserve of clerics and priestesses back home.

Maisie smiled at her. "Oh, you must try the sticky buns."

Ursula was glad Maisie had taken over the order, as her mind had gone completely blank. All she could do was stare at the menu, trying not to watch the pen as it propelled itself across the paper out of the corner of her eye.

"I will defer to you in this instance." She smiled at Maisie, who put in their order for buns and ginger blend, with liquorice root and sea kelp.

"Do they not have magic where you're from, miss?" Maisie asked once the waitress had withdrawn with their order. Her head was tilted to the side as if she was appraising a curio in a shop window.

"No, not ordinary people," Ursula said, a bit ruffled.

"We all hold a bit of magic on us up here." Maisie flicked her fingers, and Ursula swore the air swirled around them. She wondered if they used magic in Cairden. Ursula hadn't seen any, but then again, she hadn't been looking. There were so few staff, so few people in the house, Ursula had just assumed it was maintained through Mrs. Clough's sheer force of will.

"Do *you* use magic like that?" She stumbled over her words.

"When I need to." Maisie shrugged. "It's a big help when clearing the chimneys."

Ursula stared back in disbelief, imagining a cloud of soot rising on phantom wind and scattering across the grounds.

Maisie gave a small chuckle. "There's no need to worry, miss. See?"

Wind twisted around, ruffling their hair and wafting the pungent air of the cafe out the window.

Ursula wanted to ask more but wasn't sure what to say or how to say it.

Maisie looked at her with kind eyes, and she felt the words disappear back into her. It was like being at school again, better to save face and pretend to understand than ask and look stupid. Ursula had always covered her own deficiencies by working extra hard, whether it was picking up a book or practising the piano until her fingers cramped. It was easier if she relied on herself.

Maisie reached across the table and placed her hand on Ursula's arm. "The house is the house. There's no trouble there. It's out and about you've got to keep your wits about you—especially in the woods. They are a tricksy place, miss. If you treat them with respect, they'll do the same to you. But don't go in there thinking you're loftier than the forest, for it'll teach you."

The hairs on Ursula's arms stood up and a shiver went down her spine. It was like every cautionary tale she was told as a child came true. The forest was so beautiful from the house, she could sit at her window and watch it for hours, but the trees now took on a sinister edge. What had been strange and enchanting suddenly felt ominous, the trees full of foreboding.

Soon enough, twisted sticky buns with cinnamon sugar, tea in an enormous pot, and a jar of honey arrived before them, and Ursula lost the moment to ask any more.

She took a bite of her bun, the sugar coating her lips. "This is delicious!" she said between bites, trying to not talk with her mouth full. "We have something similar at home, but never as good."

"Elaria is a miracle worker. I'd think they were a sorcerer, if I didn't know better," Maisie said, plopping a bit of bun in her mouth. "You should get them to make the cake for the wedding," she added excitedly.

Ursula thought for a second, her eyes unfocused as the busy ambience of the tearoom washed over her. The happy chatter that filled the room was like a melodic lullaby. The warm atmosphere settled into her bones and muscles that had tightened from the walk down. "I think you might be right," she said as she smiled at Maisie. "Will you point them out to me once we've finished?"

Maisie grinned. "Oh, certainly, miss."

The women chomped quietly on the sticky buns, the dessert too messy for any real discussion.

"Now, what is Sinjorro Zavaran like?" Ursula asked. "Fore-warned is forearmed, as my nurse would say." She dusted stray sugar from her fingertips and took a sip of tea. This was the closest she'd felt to normal since her journey north.

"Oh, he's eccentric. Big bushy moustache." Maisie held her hands either side of her face to show the size of it. "He looks like a walrus most of the time, but a fancy one with a monocle. He's from the continent, Istany or Esmarna. I can't remember which one."

Ursula's ears pricked up when she heard her mother's homeland mentioned. "My mother is Esmarnan."

Maisie's eyes scanned Ursula from head to toe. "Interesting. Very, very interesting."

"Why?" Ursula couldn't tell if she felt more flushed from the busy room or Maisie's enquiring gaze.

"I reckon you might be able to swing a cheeky discount if you throw that in with Zavaran. He loves talking about the continent." She rolled her eyes and took a slug of tea. "You wouldn't think he'd chosen to live here the way he goes on.

*One simply has not lived until they have seen the great tower at Taria."*

Ursula had never met the man, but Maisie's perfect impression of Esmarnan accented common tongue had her chuckling. They both burst into peals of laughter when Maisie twirled and tugged at her now humongous imaginary moustache.

One of the cuckoo clocks on the walls squawked into life, adding to the cacophony.

Ursula wiped her eyes and looked up at the clock, laughter fading when she read its face.

"Oh no! Look at the time, it's half past. How long will it take us to walk to the dressmaker?"

"With me, five minutes. I know a shortcut," Maisie said with a wink.

Ursula felt her stomach bottom out again. She wasn't sure she could handle another winding march down Allerbrock's steep streets.

They shuffled over to the till and stood behind a couple of fauns, their hooves clip-clopping on the floor as they moved. Ursula studiously looked at the painted plates on the wall, worried she'd stare again.

Eventually they made it to the counter and a person with grey-streaked black hair pulled back into a sleek ponytail and sparkling eyes stood in front of them.

"Miss Ursula Woodruff, may I present the aforementioned baker-slash-sorcerer, Elaria Blankenship."

Elaria gave a small nod, a warm smile on their face. "The one and only." They pulled their order down from a row of paper clipped to the back of a glass display case lined with so many cakes, pastries, and buns Ursula thought she'd be here until dinner just reading them all.

"See anything you like?" Elaria asked.

"Oh, it all looks so good." Ursula managed to tear her eyes away. "I had one of your buns and it was delicious."

"That was your suggestion, I'm assuming?" Elaria asked Maisie, a hint of teasing in their voice.

"They're the best, though."

"So says you." Elaria bent over and cut five small slivers of cake from the case. "Try these and let me know what you think then."

Ursula glanced up at the cuckoo clock that had signalled their leave. Her eyes darted back and forth from the clock to the cake a handful of times before she picked up her fork. Surely, they had a few minutes to spare. Maisie did say she could get them there in five minutes, and the cakes would make the hilly descent worth it.

"Where you off to?"

"Sinjorro Zavaran's," Maisie replied, her mouth full of cake.

"Oh, that old windbag won't mind if you're a few minutes late. No doubt his previous client will still be in when you get there. I swear he likes to overrun on purpose just to tell the rest of us down the Shop Owners Guild how hard he works."

Elaria huffed out a laugh as Ursula speared what was left of a white layered cake. It was marbled with rich slashes of icing and fluffy buttercream on top. It tasted divine, like sunshine and summer and something tart underneath.

"That's apple, elderflower, and gin." Elaria smiled and gestured to the plate. "This one's peach and brown butter, then orange and raspberry, honey and lemon drizzle."

Ursula groaned out loud as she finished off the pieces. The cakes were light and flavourful, and she wished she could eat them all over again.

"Do you make larger cakes?" The words were out of her mouth before she knew where they had come from.

"Like events? I suppose I could." Elaria shrugged. "What for?"

"My wedding." Ursula swallowed, her mouth dry. "I'd like to order a cake and some buns."

Elaria reached for one of the pads on the counter, and the pen on it snapped upright the minute their hand touched the paper.

"What were you thinking?"

"I'd like three cakes please—elderflower, peach and raspberry—and twenty buns."

The pen skittered along the pad.

"You can add it to our bill now, if you like." Ursula smiled and fished out her coin purse.

"Alright. You've got a deal." Elaria stretched out their hand and Ursula shook it.

This was the first time she had engaged in any wedding planning and felt that it was a good sign. It was happening, she might as well try to put her stamp on the proceedings.

They made it to the dressmaker's with time to spare, and Ursula only had a thin sheen of sweat on her top lip to show for their swiftness. She hoped the bracing northern wind would cool her sticky skin enough before they entered.

The shop was in a spindly building covered in yellow render. Two rectangular windows stood on either side of a narrow door, each displaying dresses made of undulating fabric covered in intricate embroidery. The dresses here were different from the bows, lace, and nipped-in waists of home.

A bell above the door tinkled as they entered, and a man

with an outlandish moustache that swept out from his face like the tusks of a walrus waved them over.

"Ah, *virina*. Please take a seat while I finish pinning the hem for Mrs. Howe. So sorry for this to run over but I cannot accept anything less than perfection." He plucked some pins from a pincushion at his wrist with an exuberant flourish.

Ursula and Maisie sat on the velvet loveseat on the opposite wall, the dress box resting on their laps. They tried to avoid looking directly at the woman ahead of them, but the curve of mirrors made it unavoidable. Mrs. Howe stood on a circular podium with three weighty gilt mirrors surrounding it. Ursula hadn't anticipated being quite so on display, and she understood at once why Maisie had suggested she wear such a lavish dress to run errands.

Mrs. Howe had her nose so high in the air, Ursula was surprised she could see anything in the mirror. She pointedly avoided catching their eyes—a feat, given her surroundings.

Sinjorro Zavaran moved her round and round on the podium, stepping back to scrutinise his work with a furrowed brow.

"You may now leave, Mrs. Howe. Mrs. Clearbould, you will be up next, yes?" Sinjorro Zavaran said through a mouthful of pins. Ursula nodded, keeping her eyes trained on the atelier.

She could see Mrs. Howe's ears prick up at the mention of her soon-to-be name. She didn't know all that much about the Clearboulds's standing in Allerbrock, but the name carried enough clout down south thanks to the queen being a distant relation. Given the haughty woman's response, it looked like it was the same up here. Ursula felt a pang of joy in ignoring her. People like her were always happy to shower attention on people that were advantageous to them and disregard those that were not. She had seen it with her father who had made a small fortune in her lifetime, people shifting from treating her family like a social burden to falling over themselves to send invites and calling round to see her mother.

"Now, *virina*, you have the dress, yes?" Sinjorro Zavaran asked, the pins now safely back in the pincushion.

Maisie brought the box over to him and returned to her seat.

Sinjorro Zavaran opened the box, peeling back the tissue paper inside with a reverence Ursula had never shown any of her clothes. In fact, it had often been the opposite: clawing dresses from her sister's tight-fisted grasps. A small smile crept onto her lips at the thought. She was surprised there hadn't been more casualties in the Woodruff wardrobes.

"Ah, your Ladyship, this dress is very…continental." Sinjorro Zavaran leaned forward and inspected the dress, tracing his fingers along the garment in slow strokes that bordered on reverence. He looked up at Ursula and tipped his head to the side as if seeing her for the first time. "It will need a lot of altering to make it more fitting for this environment."

"Sinjorro Zavaran, I do trust your opinions, but I'd like to keep the style of the dress the same. My heritage is southern and Esmarnish."

The dress personified the Woodruff children, a melding of two worlds. Her mother's people were loud, emotive, and colourful, and the dress reflected this. It was gold, with a shimmer like a sunset on water. It was cut close to the body and the silken fabric moved with the wearer. It was a dress to dance in—to *live* in—not like the stiffer silhouettes often seen in Currington. As much as Ursula enjoyed southern fashion, the whole purpose of the dress was to showcase whoever wore it, without the frills and adornment of the usual southern wedding dresses. It still had a similar demure cut, though, with boning in the bodice and a modest neckline that skimmed across the top of the bust. "Perhaps we could do minimal alterations on it, just enough that it fits?"

"Yes, *virina*. I think you are correct with this one. Although you will freeze in such flimsy attire." He held up the hem of her gown for emphasis. Sure enough, the delicate material was practically translucent under the bright shop lights.

"That's the other reason we're here, Sinjorro, to get her kitted out," Maisie piped in from behind them. She was sipping on a cup of tea supplied by the atelier's assistant, and Ursula wondered when it had materialised. She couldn't help but smile at the girl, catching her eye in the mirror. In the short time she'd know her, Ursula came to realise that Maisie could charm the birds from the trees.

"Oh yes, you must, *virina*. A northern winter will wreak havoc on your thin blood," Sinjorro Zavaran said with the gravitas of a general. "Now, what would you like?"

"Well, everything, I suppose." Ursula shrugged.

"Odette, cancel the rest of my appointments today!" he shouted, lifting a hand so Ursula could manoeuvre off the podium. "Now, we will choose some fabrics. We have just had a delivery of the most enchanting velvets this side of the Strait."

# 9

# Ursula

The wedding was in a week, and Ursula felt pulled in two different directions. The little ember of hope inside her was burning brighter: the hope that this marriage would work and that she could find a purpose. The hope that someone would see her—the real her. But every time that hope shone, a voice in the back of her head reminded her that she was merely a pawn in someone else's plan. That this would all fail, and the hopes that burned in her chest would be extinguished for good.

A bang on the front door made Ursula jump, the sound reverberating around the old stone walls of the house. She squared her shoulders and went to investigate, glad for a reprieve from her swirling mind.

A clatter and chorus of voices echoed up the staircase as Ursula padded down the steps. She was hit by a bundle at her legs once she reached the bottom. Looking down, she saw a mass of red hair.

The bundle looked up at her with twinkling eyes as she heard, "Goodness, Nicolas, what are you like?"

"I was just greeting my beautiful new auntie," Nicolas said with a mischievous grin.

Ursula's gaze caught on a woman looking back at her from across the foyer, a broad man standing beside her. She was dressed in a dark green gown that complimented her deep red hair. The dress fell in straight lines to the floor, pinched in lightly at the waist by rows and rows of smocking. There were none of the accentuated curves of southern fashion, and Ursula felt overdressed in her floral ruffles.

"Nico, you are such a flirt," the man said and smiled at the toddler in his arms.

"I don't know where he gets it from., the redheaded woman said with a sigh.

"You." The man laughed, and the toddler leaned into his father's embrace before echoing the sound.

The woman across from her smiled, the skin around her eyes crinkling. They were the same piercing blue eyes as Elias's and every bit as warm. She was compact and lean, more angular than Elias's lithe frame, but held herself with the same effortless grace. There was no mistaking it; Susannah and family were here.

"You must be Ursula," the woman said as she rushed across the hallway.

"Pleased to meet you." Ursula extended a hand, but instead of shaking it, Susannah pulled her into a fierce hug.

She only let go when Nicolas shouted, "Mummy, you're squashing me!"

The women broke away from each other and looked down at the boy who was standing with his hands on his hips, a posture he surely picked up from the adults around him. Nicolas's cheeks shone like apples, and he looked like a cherub from a temple despite the serious look on his face. A wooden train dangled from his hand that whipped around as he moved. Ursula pinched her lips together to stop from laughing.

Susannah looked down at her son, a stern expression in her eyes. "Serves you right. You don't go grabbing at ladies."

"But you did," Nicolas pouted.

"It's different when I do it." She ruffled his hair and ushered the boy away, turning her attention back to Ursula. "It's so wonderful to meet you! I've heard so much about you."

Ursula began to answer, but Nicolas interrupted.

"Where's Uncle El?" His voice was dripping with excitement as he looked around for his uncle, the annoyance from moments before completely forgotten.

"He was off for a run the last time I saw him," Ursula said.

Obviously bored by the adults, Nicolas then turned and ran down the corridor in search of Elias.

"Stay out of cook's way. You know she likes to make pies out of naughty boys!" Susannah shouted at his retreating figure. She gave Ursula a knowing look. "Boys, eh? Until you came along, I was completely outnumbered."

Ursula smiled. "It does make me feel some sympathy for my father and brother. They were two to seven."

"Blimey! The poor man!" Susannah laughed and turned her attention to the gentleman behind her. "Ursula, let me introduce the other agents of chaos in my life—my husband, Calvin, and this is Felix." She reached out and touched the plump cheek of the toddler her husband held.

Calvin hitched the young child higher on his hip and held out a hand. "Pleasure to meet you, Ursula."

Felix gave her an adorably suspicious stare, breaking any awkwardness.

"I see I have someone to win over," Ursula said.

Mrs. Clough appeared from the kitchen corridor, and Susannah sprinted over and bent down to envelope her in a hug. "It's so wonderful to see you, Mrs. C.!"

The housekeeper gave her a forceful, brief squeeze in return. "We were expecting you at lunch time, Lady Lockston. Cook even made young Nicolas's favourite sandwiches."

"Cucumber with the crusts cut off," the adults all said in unison, leaving Felix and Ursula to look at each other with bewildered expressions.

"Oh, he's probably made his way to the kitchen and scoffed down half by now," Susannah said, rolling her eyes as she wore the same honeyed smile as before on her lips.

Ursula instantly liked her soon-to-be sister-in-law. The world appeared to glow brighter when Susannah smiled; it was as if she was the sun, and they were all in her orbit. Her husband looked at her as if she were a dream made flesh, and Ursula was reminded of Elias's comments from their first dinner together. It seemed that two children and years together had not dimmed those flames.

They made their way into the drawing room at the front of the house. The fire was high in the hearth, and it crackled a welcome at them. Light filtered through the delicate curtains, throwing patterns onto the floral wallpaper. The furniture was more ornate than the parlour, and the spacious room lacked the restful ambience of other parts of the house.

Ursula sat on one of the settees, smoothing her skirt over and again. They were expecting the Lockstons earlier that day, and she'd been so caught up in her own thoughts that time had slipped past her this afternoon.

"Is it tea tonight? Or would you like something stronger?"

Mrs. Clough asked the group, the mischievous glint in her eye the same as when she offered seconds to Ursula or snuck her a scone straight from the oven. She could see why Mrs. Clough was so beloved by all the Clearboulds.

"I can never say no to your brandy, Mrs. Clough," Calvin said, casually leaning back on the settee he was sharing with Susannah, baby Felix propped on his lap.

Susannah thought for a second. "Make that two. The journey over was chilly, and I need some fire in my bones."

"And you, Miss Woodruff?"

All eyes turned to her. The power of speech abandoned her, and she swallowed as she fought to regain some control over her body. This would never have happened at home; even her boisterous mother rarely drank. Theo was the only one in the family who she had seen drunk. She'd caught him countless times trying to sneak back during his breaks from school or university, getting more brazen as he got older. Ursula would have to wrestle him into bed after she found him bent over and heaving into the rosebush by the front door.

Mrs. Clough looked at her with stern concentration. "It's good for the blood."

It was like she was sitting for a test she hadn't studied for, but somehow she knew the answer. Part of her wanted to stay in the safe confines she was used to, to be the prim southerner everyone expected her to be. But not anymore. She was forging her own path, one tiny, rebellious step at a time.

"Please, can you make that three, Mrs. Clough?"

"Good choice," Susannah said. She gave Ursula a wink so fast, she almost missed it.

"I feel I've caught a chill, too. Too much reading by my window," Ursula added, a bit too quickly. Her cheeks were burning now, and it was not from the roaring fire. This small act of defiance felt good, even if no one else in the room knew or cared. Northern life might suit her better than expected.

"I found him!" Nicolas shouted from the doorway.

They all turned to see Elias hand-in-hand with his nephew as they walked through the door.

"Let me guess, he was in his study?" Susannah asked, and Nicolas nodded empathically before dropping his uncle's hand and making a beeline for some wooden blocks that had been laid out for the children by the fire.

"Not my fault. You said you'd be here at lunchtime, and we were all ready for you then," Elias said to his sister. His tone was lovingly mocking, and though Susannah glared at him, everyone could see the smile she was holding in.

"I'd like to see you try and get this lot ready for a deadline," she huffed back at him.

Elias continued into the room, earning a giggle from Felix as he tickled under his chin before planting a kiss on his sister's cheek.

"It's nice to see you, Sus."

"You too, you big lummox."

Susannah smiled up at him and settled back, and Calvin plopped the toddler on the carpet and draped his arm behind his wife on the sofa.

Elias nodded down at his brother-in-law, who gave a swift salute back.

"I see you've met Ursula," Elias said in an unsteady voice. "I would have made introductions, but you were late, and we waited but Bruce had to talk to me about the horses—"

Nicolas shouted his uncle over, interrupting his deluge of words. Elias was flushed and his hands fluttered around as he spoke. Nicolas called over to him again, flapping his hand insistently until Elias kneeled stiffly beside him. He gave Ursula a quick, pleading smile and the temperature in the room rocketed. Her mouth went dry, and she wished she had asked for a glass of water along with her brandy. It had been fleeting, but the moment Elias glanced at her and gave that small, genuine smile, the world melted away until it was just them.

Ursula couldn't tear her eyes away from him. His hair was still damp from what she could only assume was a post-run wash, and there was a disarming curl right in the centre of his forehead that bobbed every time moved.

She wanted to pull it taut and watch it spring back, to wrap it around her finger and see if it felt as soft as it looked.

To see if Elias liked the sting of a light tug on his scalp.

He laid out a solid foundation of blocks, encouraging the young boys to stack some on top. Ursula could almost feel her heart melt. There's no way someone who played with children this patiently would ever be a cad. Felix plonked himself onto his uncle's knee while Elias helped him put the trickier blocks on the structure, but he soon got bored of tower building and bashed two blocks together in his hands instead.

Elias kissed his fluffy head and popped him back on the carpet. "I'm going to sit by Ursula now."

Nicolas looked up, his face contorted in petulant confusion. "But why?"

"Nicolas!" Susannah gasped from across the room.

Elias just smiled down at the boy. "Because I want to."

Nicolas huffed a bit and returned to his playing. "Fine, she is pretty. I'd sit next to her, too."

Elias rolled his lips like he was trying to keep a laugh in. "I know."

Ursula felt her stomach do a somersault.

Nicolas nodded, more interested in swatting his brother's hand away from stealing blocks.

Elias leaned heavily on his right side as he pushed himself off the floor. Ursula watched as he walked over to her. It was almost like a prowl, slow and deliberate. Her stomach did another somersault as her pulse ratcheted to a thundering pace. Seeing this side of Elias made her body lose control.

"How are the wedding preparations faring?" Susannah asked, halting the spiral of her thoughts.

"Oh, swimmingly," Ursula replied, only telling half of the truth. Bar the cakes she ordered, most of the preparations had been arranged ahead of time, her own mother taking the reins from afar before she had been ordered on bedrest. They had arrived with so many packages for the wedding, Ursula couldn't even remember the contents of half of them. It had all felt so remote then, like planning a fundraiser or a luncheon.

Elias settled into the chair to Ursula's right, and she tried to ignore the blush that crept up her neck and flooded her cheeks. Heat radiated from him, and she was acutely aware of every breath, every tiny movement he made. Her gaze kept drifting back to him, like she was a compass, and he was due north.

"And your dress? Do you need me to strong arm Sinjorro Zavaran?" Susannah asked, leaning her head against her husband's arm.

"No, that's all in hand. I'll be wearing my mother's dress. She gave it to me before I travelled to Cairden. My sister wore it at her wedding, and I suppose it's become a bit of a tradition." Ursula felt her face flush at the unknowable look in Elias's eye.

"How delightful! I wish I had a girl to pass my dress onto," Susannah said with a sigh and looked up at her husband, who gave her an intense stare in response. Elias coughed lightly, and he rolled his eyes briefly at her. Ursula felt warmth spread through as they shared a conspiratorial smirk.

Susannah blanched, easing herself away from Calvin's body. "I thought your parents were attending?"

Ursula reddened and went to speak, but Elias jumped in instead. "They were held back with some family matters. Nothing to worry about."

Ursula looked at him, sharing a grateful smile. She did not want to have to discuss the reason her parents were not here. It was a cause for scandal back home, and while northerns may be more understanding, she couldn't face telling people quite yet. Although, judging by the empathetic looks that were passing between Susannah and Calvin, they would understand.

"More's the pity," Susannah sighed.

Mrs. Clough came in bearing a tray of drinks for the group, glasses tinkling as she deposited them in front of everyone. "I took the liberty of pouring you a whisky, sir."

Elias thanked her and grabbed his drink from the tray.

Susannah started to regale the group with a story about the local baker, and Ursula watched from the corner of her eye as Elias sat back a fraction in the chair, nodding along to the story.

He looked as rumpled as ever: his shirt open at the neck, exposing the milky white column of his neck. The firelight cast him in a wash of gold, sparking the red undertone of his hair that stood out at odd angles, like he had been running his fingers through it. Ursula's gaze snagged on his Adam's apple as he sipped his drink. She wondered what his skin would feel like under her fingers, against her tongue. She gulped down the last of her brandy to quench her thirst.

There was no artifice with Elias, and Ursula had to admit that she found his straightforward bearing enchanting.

Susannah started talking wistfully of her wedding day, but the words washed over. Ursula's mind kept drifting back to the man who sat next to her, the man who would be her husband in a week's time.

Elias had grown on her, and the more time she spent in the Allerbrock, the more she noticed about him. His easy smile, the way he doted on his nephews, how he treated the staff and people around him with care.

Ursula went to put her empty glass down on the occasional table in front of her, her hand brushing against Elias's as he did the same. Her skin burned at the brief touch, the heat she felt roiling off him almost scalding her in that moment. She wanted to touch him again, to burn away all trace of herself and exist only in his touch.

Ursula knew that if she looked up at him, his gaze would be as blistering. Instead, she kept her eyes trained on his hand. His fingers were long and lean, clean, clipped nails showing as his hand still cupped the etched glass tumbler. Ink splatters dusted his wide hand, that gave way to strong arms peeking out from the undone cuffs of his shirt. He was more robust than she initially thought, his frame made of neat, corded muscle.

They both paused momentarily, slightly startled at the closeness, until the moment was broken by Felix toddling over with a block in his hand. A cry soon erupted from Nicolas, and Susannah hurried over. She scooped up her eldest son as the little boy sobbed into the crook on his mother's shoulder.

"I think it's time for these young gents to get some rest," Susannah said. Her hand skirted up and down Nicolas's back, the little boy's heaving gasps slowing with each pass.

He was soon asleep in her arms, and Felix started to grizzle. Ursula hopped off the settee and pretended to steal his nose. Felix exploded into a fit of giggles, and Susannah mouthed a thank you.

"Why don't I help you with the boys before dinner?" she asked and held out her arms to Felix. The toddler gave Ursula one final once-over and tottered into her embrace, settling quite happily on her hip as she followed Susannah out the door.

The cold whoosh of air in the hall crackled against her skin as she padded up the stairs, unable to rid the images of Elias from her mind.

"You do have a way with children," Susannah said in hushed tones over Nicolas's sleeping head on her shoulder.

"It comes with being the eldest daughter," Ursula replied with a small laugh. It was true she had been tending children as long as she could remember. She looked down at Felix nestled against her and couldn't stop her mind picturing a child with unruly dark curls and sapphire eyes.

"If you say so," Susannah said ruefully.

Ursula snapped back to the present, to the family she was about to join and halls that didn't feel like her own yet. She was a week away from the wedding; better to focus on that, she chided herself and continued up the stairs in silence.

# 10

# Elias

With the ladies gone, Elias crossed the room and sat down next to Cal with a huff. The man was like a brother to him, and most of the time he revelled in having someone who knew him so well, who never judged. Only now, he hated the way Cal eyed him with a knowing look.

"What?" Elias asked, as surly as a teenager.

Cal just laughed in reply and brought the brandy to his lips.

"What? You can't keep smirking at me like that."

"Oh yes I can," Cal said, the smirk deepening to a chuckle.

"Fine, smirk away."

Elias took a gulp of whisky, and he focused on the burning in his throat instead of the look on Cal's face.

"You are a goner, my good friend," Cal said as he sat back in his chair, his long legs crossed at the ankle.

Elias said nothing as he twirled the whisky glass in his hand.

It all felt too good to be true. Their fathers had made this madcap decision for them decades ago, but he had landed on his feet. Is this how Susannah felt? He could have ended up with an uptight, prissy southern lady. Instead, fate pushed him and Ursula together.

Ursula, with her umber eyes that took in everything around her, even when she didn't realise it. Her wit that lurked just under the surface, ready to be coaxed out with a daft joke or silly glance. That ridiculous hair that seemed befitting of an underworld goddess, so dark he could bet ravens would be jealous.

Elias felt like he'd played a hand of cards with the universe and won. He had never been religious—only going to the temple when school or his parents dragged him—but tomorrow he vowed to go into town and leave an offering for Alvis, the trickster god.

The silence between them stretched on in the way it only can with those that you care about most. He turned to look at Cal, feeling guileless and out of his depth.

"Tell me what you think, Cal. Be honest."

His friend puffed out his cheeks, blowing the air out slowly. "I saw the way you noticed her, El. I've never seen two people so inherently aware of another's presence without acknowledging it. The pair of you practically jumped out of your skin when you touched. A blind man could see you've got a thing for her." Cal took another swig of his drink. "Honestly, there were so many sparks tonight, I'm surprised you didn't catch fire."

Elias sunk further into the sofa, the words tumbling through his mind.

There *were* sparks. He could almost feel them under his skin, prickling and pressing at him. It was like there was energy flowing through him, a stirring of something dormant.

"It's just so strange. We're thrown together without ever

having met, and somehow it feels like I've known her all along." He scrubbed at his face. "I should show you the betrothal contract, it's flimsy at best."

"Why not have the Elders dissolve it? It should be easy enough."

Elias closed his eyes, worried he wouldn't be able to continue if he looked at Cal. "Because it's what he wanted, and I didn't follow that very often when he was alive, but I can do that now. Because her bride price will pay to keep the quarry afloat for a few more years."

"You know you can always come to me for that," Cal cut in, and Elias turned his head to give his friend a warning stare. Cal held his hands up in supplication.

Elias gave a taut smile. "Because I feel this pull towards her. It's not just because she's beautiful, and by Gods, she is, but because I don't think I've ever met anyone like her in my life."

"Like what?" Cal asked. His brow was raised to the most irritating angle possible.

"I don't know, alright. She just makes me feel like more than some decrepit lump. When I talk, she listens. *Really* listens, Cal. And she remembers things, silly little things that I've said."

"And likes to eye you like a piece of meat when you're not looking."

"Oi, that's my future wife you're talking about!" Elias snapped, earning another of Cal's smirks. "Oh, yeah, you've gotten a rise out of me. Laugh away!"

His friend reached over and gripped him on the arm, suddenly serious. "You may not have chosen this, but you can choose to make the best of it."

"I know, I know. It's just hard, I feel like I'm floundering.

She's not what I expected. None of this is what I expected."

"Good unexpected or bad unexpected?"

Elias looked up to the ceiling. "So much better."

Calvin moved and sat on the settee beside him. "I know what it's like to fall for someone, how scary it can be. But you don't need to keep avoiding happiness. You deserve it. We all do."

Elias nodded slowly, hoping his friend was right.

# 11

# Ursula

She was on her second helping of crumpets when Elias and Calvin shambled into the breakfast room.

Nicolas was playing with some tin soldiers and a hugely out of proportion wooden horse. He held both aloft when he caught sight of his father and uncle. "Goooooooood morning!"

Elias and Cal visibly winced at the boy's screeching welcome.

Susannah burst out laughing, which brought on another bout of wincing as they piled their plates high from the breakfast dishes on the sideboard.

"You two look a bit worse for wear," Ursula said to Elias as he flopped down into the chair next to her. The table felt smaller than their first dinner together with all these people around it. Ursula imagined this is what it was like when Elias and Susannah were growing up. Cairden Abbey suddenly felt like a bustling family home, and it reminded her so much of her own upbringing. Mornings at Bowside House were always boisterous affairs. Her youngest sisters ran ragged to get their things ready for school. Someone usually misplaced an important piece of homework or their uniform. Miranda was always at her most surly first thing, snipping and sniping at anyone who dared talk to her before she could get her hands on some caffeine. It twisted in Ursula like a knife; she missed them all so much now. She vowed to write to them tomorrow, once she had a bit more time to herself.

"Awful," Elias said with a grimace.

"Serves you right." Susannah pointed at them with her fork. "I don't know what you did to him last night, but he came to bed singing a tavern ditty that is not meant for polite ears. Luckily, we brought our nurse along to help with the young ones, as I had to play nursemaid to this big galoot."

"You're a terrible nurse, though," Elias chuckled as he scooped a mound of eggs into his mouth.

"I didn't say I played the part well," Susannah replied, smiling.

Calvin stayed conspicuously silent, pushing eggs around his plate and necking a cup of tea.

"I hope he didn't go serenading you with ballads about busty maidens and sea captains?" Susannah asked Ursula. She had an innocent smile on her face but mischief in her eyes. Ursula blushed; she'd never heard such a song, but the promise of such lewd words spilling out of Elias's lips sent her pulse fluttering.

"Of course not," Elias snapped. He rubbed his temples as he speared a whole sausage on his fork and took a gigantic bite off one end. "Sorry, Sus, my head feels like there's a troupe of dancing mice in it."

"As I said before—serves you right. And don't talk with your mouth full. You'll give the young ones ideas." Susannah nodded to her sons, Nicolas to the right of her and Felix happily picking food off her plate in her lap. "You're no spring chick now, El. The pair of you can't go gallivanting around like you used to."

"This sounds like an interesting story." Ursula caught her soon-to-be sister in law's eye from across the table, and Susannah gave her a conspiratorial wink.

"Oh, Ursula. You have no idea," Susannah said. "They used to sneak out to go drinking down at this old run-down pub at the edge of town. What was it called again?"

She looked at the two men who avoided her gaze.

Susannah looked thoughtfully into the air. "Was it the Shaking Swan? The Agitated Chicken? The Trembling Goose?"

"Quivering Duck," Calvin finally conceded.

"That's it! The Quivering Duck." Susannah beamed. "It was always full of young lads from the town." She covered Nicolas's ears and leaned across the table. "The barmaid had huge knockers."

Elias rolled his eyes and audibly groaned. "Sus, can you not?"

"But it's true!" She looked aghast at her brother with mock censure.

"It was also the only place that would serve us. We had about three chin hairs between us."

Ursula chuckled as Elias looked to Calvin for support, who nodded silently, then groaned and grabbed at his head.

She tried to imagine him, young with a face full of peach fuzz, mooning over a busty barmaid, but all she could think about was the man in front of her. His taut muscles bunched under his rolled-up shirtsleeves and his oceanic eyes hooded with tiredness. How Elias Clearbould could look so handsome with a hangover was anyone's guess.

Felix squirmed in Susannah's lap, reaching for his father. Calvin scooped the toddler up and the young boy snuck a piece of bacon from his plate, chomping on it with contented mumbles.

"Oi, you cheeky toe-rag." Calvin laughed and kissed his son on top of his fluffy red hair, and the boy's face scrunched up in response.

"Daddy smells."

Ursula caught Susannah's eyes, and the pair burst into laughter as Felix swatted the air at Calvin's breath.

"What're your plans for today, Ursula? I have half a mind to leave these two on childcare duties."

"I'm picking up my dress from Sinjorro Zavaran with Maisie, you're welcome to join."

"Only if you're sure." Susannah's voice was steady but Ursula was sure she could see a twinkle of mischief in her blue eyes.

"I insist," Ursula said. Once the words were out of her mouth, she realised they were true. She missed her sisters terribly, but even spending a small amount of time with Susannah had lifted some of the heaviness from her heart.

Susannah leaned down to her older son. "How do you feel about a whole day with Daddy and Uncle El, Nico?"

Nicolas's eyes went wide with excitement. "Uncle El, let's play pirates!"

Elias let out a muffled groan. "Maybe tomorrow, Nico. How about we play sleeping lions today?"

Nicolas's smiled widened even more, and he growled at his uncle.

"Penny for them, miss?"

"Oh, it's nothing, Maisie," Ursula replied. "Just thinking about the next few days. There's a lot to do."

"I'll say!" Maisie replied, catching Ursula's eye in the huge gilt mirror. "But you and Mr. Clearbould are having a rather relaxed affair, so that should help. Plus, I've seen all those packages you brought from down south. You're in good hands, even if some are afar."

Maisie scuffed her foot across the floor. She was sat in the same loveseat as before, only this time squashed in next to Susannah. The women were drinking tea and nibbling on some round shortbread, and Ursula's stomach gave a jealous grumble.

It had been hours since breakfast, and Sinjorro Zavaran was silently walking around her, stroking his chin in concentration.

Maisie washed down the last bite of her biscuit with a gulp of tea. "When my sister, Judith, got married half the town was invited. Whew, it was something else. Old farmer Dean got in a fight with the butcher's son, Jed, and Mrs. Sudberry had to be carried off to bed after she'd had too much ale. It was fun, though."

She brushed the crumbs from her fingers and smiled at Ursula in the mirror. "I'm sure yours will be beautiful. Just a bit less…rowdy."

Maisie turned to Susannah. "What was your day like, Lady Lockston?"

"It was just magical," Susannah sighed, a faraway look on her face. "The ceremony was held in the woods near Lockston Hall, and Cal just looked so handsome in his jacket. The embroidery was done specially for it, and it glinted in the sun as it set."

She sat up a bit straighter under Ursula and Maisie's attention. "It was a summer wedding, and I had flowers braided through my hair. I still can't walk past a sweet pea without thinking of that day. Once we got back to Lockston Hall, we danced all night with everyone we love until the stars came out."

Maisie sighed. "It does sound magical."

Sinjorro Zavaran snapped his fingers in the air with a flourish, like he had just finished a particularly taxing dance routine. "It is done."

Ursula looked at her reflection in the mirror; the deep brown jacquard dress was exquisite. It was pulled in at the waist tighter than anything she'd seen Susannah or Maisie in, but it still smoothly followed the lines of her body unlike the narrow nip she was used to wearing. The floral pattern also felt like an ode to her southern roots while the umber tone suited her current surroundings, and the high neck and voluminous sleeves that tapered to her wrists were a guard against the weather. She smiled at herself in the mirror; she finally looked like a proper northerner. Ursula shook her head. No, she didn't look like a northerner, not fully. She looked better than that—this time, she looked like *herself*.

"You like?" Sinjorro Zavaran asked, a distinct hint of worry in his voice.

"I love it."

Sinjorro Zavaran stood a little taller at the praise. "The items that are ready will be sent up to the house today and the rest will be delivered the same time next week. Now, it is time to try on the most important one."

Ursula nodded and took his proffered hand as she stepped off the dais. Her wedding dress was hanging behind the screen next to the mirrors, and Sinjorro Zavaran's assistant stood to attention to help her into it. It was strange to wear the dress without her sisters. The ache that had been soothed by being with Maisie and Susannah came flooding back, and Ursula rubbed at her chest in slow circles. She had forgotten that sadness hurt so much, or maybe it was just worse now. That the pain of missing her sisters was bone deep.

The atelier's assistant undid her new dress and carefully laid it aside, then lifted the wedding dress over her head. It was just like helping Elodie into her dress on her wedding day; holding her trailing mane of hair out of the way as Miranda had fastened the back, the pair of them bickering while Elodie stood there, serene as ever, in her pre-marital bubble.

Tears pricked at her eyes as the assistant pulled the bodice tightly around her and arranged the sleeves to hang on the edge of her shoulder. "There, that's you ready."

Ursula's hands were shaking so much she smoothed non-existent creases down the front of her dress for something to do with them. She took a deep breath and walked out from behind the screen.

The room went quiet. Maisie and Susannah were still sitting on the loveseat while Sinjorro Zavaran showed them fabric samples from a huge flip book.

"You look wonderful, miss," Maisie said eventually.

"You have rendered me speechless," Susannah joined in. "And that is no mean feat."

Ursula felt the tears sting again and smiled broadly at the people around her. The people who barely knew her, but whose faces were full of warmth and affection. She wanted to say something, but it didn't feel like enough.

"I think this calls for a celebration," Susannah said, breaking the moment. "And I know just the place."

"It's the middle of the day," Ursula said, unable to keep the incredulous tone out of her voice. She eyed the white-washed front of the tavern, its wooden sign outside swinging in the wind so violently she couldn't read the name.

"Precisely! What better way to celebrate than with a spot of fizz," Susannah said as she pushed the heavy-studded door.

"Is this allowed? I've only been to a pub when travelling," Ursula stammered. She looked around wide-eyed at the panelled walls. Dappled light filtered across the room through the wavy glass window panes. It was nowhere near as busy as the tearoom had been, but there were enough patrons to give the place atmosphere. People were talking and laughing as they took their time over steaming bowls of stew that had Ursula's stomach rumbling.

Susannah smiled. "Of course, you're in the barbarian north now."

"I go to the pub all the time, miss. The Alder and Badger has the best food in town," Maisie added.

They wound around stout dark wood tables until they found one big enough to accommodate them. Ursula shuffled at the edge of her seat and tugged at her sleeves. She tried to settle into the cheerful atmosphere of the place, but her body wouldn't relax. It was as if it wasn't ready to leave all her southern decorum behind quite yet, no matter how much she willed it.

There was a wide chalkboard above the bar with today's menu on it, and a few dishes had already been scored out.

The barmaid sauntered over after they'd been browsing for a few minutes, a bottle of sparkling wine and three glasses clinking in her hands.

"It's my usual.  I used to be a regular here," Susannah whispered across the table.

Ursula ordered sausage casserole with mustard mash, Susannah opting for rabbit stew while Maisie chose the fish pie.

"To new beginnings," Susannah toasted. They all lifted their glass to meet hers, and Ursula felt her shoulders soften a smidge. As the glasses clinked in the air, Ursula realised she had never done this before. She'd never spent time with other women like this that weren't her sisters. Currington society was so wrapped in propriety, the only events people attended were teas, luncheons, and the occasional dance. It was nice to sit and genuinely relax with other people.

Susannah took a healthy swig of her wine and plonked it on the table. "Now, let's chat. Ursula, you're spoken for. Maisie, do you have someone special?"

Maisie made a squeaking noise and shrugged her shoulders. "Oh, not really, miss. I don't have the time."

Susannah turned to Ursula without missing a beat. "You are working the girl too hard. Maisie, there must be someone."

Maisie arched her brow. "There's always a kiss to be had at Beltane, but I haven't found anyone I'd like to go in for seconds with."

Susannah raised her glass.  "Wise words.  Don't get tied down when you don't need to."

Ursula looked at her askance, sipping from her own wine. "Weren't you and Calvin childhood sweethearts?"

"Oh, Elias has been talking, I see." Susannah gave Ursula a knowing look. Ursula tried not to squirm in her chair, even though Susannah was smiling. "I believe we are the exception not the rule.  I think it's best to know yourself before you decide on forever. I'm just lucky I already happened to know who my forever would be with."

They all toasted again.

"My sister was the same," Maisie said quietly. "She met her husband in first class at the school. Think they held hands at lunch, and that's been them since. I'm going to wait a bit, though."

"And right you should!" Susannah clinked her glass with Maisie and took another gulp of wine.

Ursula felt at sea. She had never had a conversation like this with anyone, and it poked at her old sores. This was supposed to be a new beginning, but she felt the old hurt eat away at her. She was only here to fulfil a bargain, a duty. Would she ever be able to talk about Elias in this way? Good-natured gossiping, sharing stories, comfortable in her place, knowing she's cared for. She felt a chill creeping through her.

Susannah noted her change in mood and reached across the table to squeeze Ursula's hand. Maisie hicccughed lightly beside her. "Thank you for being such a good sport. I worried I would scare you off with my savage northern ways."

Ursula shook her head, squared her shoulders, and lifted her glass. "I must admit, I'm starting to like some of these unconventional customs."

The barmaid came over then with a huge tray covered with their food and another bottle of wine. Ursula knew her head would be swimming by the time they got back to Cairden.

Susannah held up her glass again. "To new beginnings."

"You've already said that," Maisie giggled. Her face was rosy now, and her eyes had taken on a faraway sheen.

"I know that, but I like to think we can always start our story at any point."

They all clinked their glasses again. "New beginnings!"

Her nurse gave her a worldly stare. "Had a good afternoon, eh?"

Ursula braced herself on the banister to keep from swaying. "Lovely, actually." Her words had a perceptible slur. "I picked up my dress from the atle…atel…from the dressmaker."

"Oh yes, and where is said dress?"

Panic suddenly gripped her; the clothes were supposed to be sent ahead. "They should have already been delivered."

Nurse Selwyn gave her a nod, and Ursula could have sworn she was fighting against a smile but couldn't be sure on account of her wobbling vision. She held onto the banister for dear life.

"True enough, they were delivered a few hours ago. At least you've still got your wits about you. I suggest a quick shuteye before dinner. And rinse your mouth out. You smell like a brewery, Ursi dear."

"Yes, Nurse." She felt about eight years old, being told off for eating too many berries in the garden, and tottered up the stairs.

# 12

# Elias

"You promised me, Uncle El."

Elias looked down at his nephew's serious face, and any tiny bit of resistance he had was demolished by the boy's cherubic charm.

He looked so like Susannah at that age, completely innocent until you caught the look in his eye that told you trouble was brewing.

"I didn't say I wouldn't play. I just have to finish this tiny bit of work first."

He hated the words that came out of his mouth, the same that had been echoed to him years ago. It had felt like being dismissed when he was growing up, cast aside for something more important. Still, he knew if he didn't finish his thought now, it would be gone forever.

Nicolas gave him a concise nod, and Elias felt momentarily stupefied by the adult gesture. Is this what he'd been like while trying to grab his father's attention in his youth?

"Nico, I promise I will be finished in a hundred seconds. Can you count to one hundred?"

His nephew looked at him with a cocked brow. "Obviously."

"Alright. I bet you I can finish my work by the time you finish counting, and I'll buy you and Felix ice cream for a week."

"One!" Nicolas screeched loudly in response.

Elias's pen scratched at the paper as he flipped through each timesheet at record speed. It was imperative that he finish them today, otherwise the workers wouldn't be paid on time. Nicolas seemed to be faltering over some numbers, as he had only gotten to twelve by the time Elias was halfway through his work. He was fairly certain he'd heard eight and eleven a couple of times, and Elias smiled to himself as he continued signing. When he had finally reached the last sheet, he kept his pen moving by drawing circles on the blotter on his desk.

"One hundred!" Nicolas announced, proud that he'd made it all the way there despite all the tangents.

Elias finished his last doodle with a flourish. "You beat me to it, Nico. Looks like it'll be ice cream after all."

His nephew smiled with his whole body, every inch of the boy shaking with glee. Elias gave the boy an answering grin, and he was glad he'd taken the time to put his pen down and include the young boy in his life.

"Right. Where to?"

Nicolas looked up at him with sparkling eyes. "The library."

"Die! Die, you beast!"

Elias felt his back twinge as he rolled to avoid Nicolas's imaginary sword. The wooden slats of the library were far less forgiving than he remembered. Nicolas was standing over him, a lethal look on his face as he plunged the make-believe weapon at him again and again.

He convulsed on the floor, making his best attempt at

extravagant gurgles as a death throe. Finally, he slumped in submission, conscious not to move a muscle lest the young boy dare descend on him. Elias cracked one of his eyes open to find Nicolas looking at him with a very disapproving air.

"C'mon, Uncle El, let's go on an adventure. I'm the Pirate King after all!"

Elias groaned from the floor. "But I'm dead. I can't move."

Nicolas kept staring.

Elias sat up, his joints groaning as he moved against the worn wood floor. "Also, when did you become a king?"

"When I killed the kraken," Nicolas said matter-of-factly. "I'm going to sail and conquer new lands."

He jumped into position, shielding his eyes as if he were looking into the sun from the prow of a ship as he scanned the horizon for pastures new. Elias levered himself from the ground, ignoring the click in his hip as he stood. Nicolas suddenly took off running, narrowly dodging shelves and tables leaden with books as Elias looked on with his heart in his mouth. He doubted he could survive Nicolas getting a knock on the head, no matter how many he'd sustained in childhood.

Nicolas came to an abrupt stop in front of a range of books at the far side of the library.

"Oh, hello. What are you doing here?"

Elias trotted up behind him, intrigued by who else would be in the often-overlooked room.

Ursula shuffled out of the shadows. Her dress was creased, and she gave Nicolas a wide-eyed smile as she smoothed down the fabric.

"I was writing a letter…" She stumbled over her words, the blush he'd come to recognise flooding her bronzed cheeks.

There were abandoned sheaves of paper in the nook behind her. She looked so guilty, so adorably abashed, Elias wanted to run his thumb over her reddened cheeks and feel the heat from them. To feel the pitter patter of her pulse at the base of her throat as she swallowed.

"It's alright we were—" He was going to say some platitude, to explain she needn't join in their games, when Ursula raised her hands and crouched in front of Nicolas.

"…I was writing to the witches' council asking how to catch a Pirate King! I've been trapped on this island for millennia, and I need his crown for my freedom."

Nicolas burst into peals of laughter and ran in the opposite direction, ducking behind an enormous stack of books.

Ursula made chase, making elaborate shapes with her hands and cackling maniacally.

Nicolas popped his head up from his book shield, a look of mischievous delight on his face. He raised his pretend sword. "Oh, no you won't, Island Witch!"

He sprinted back to Elias, landing against his legs with a dull thud. "Kraken, come back. You're on my side now!"

Elias wobbled his arms around as he made the same grating shout he had earlier, but his eyes kept drifting back to Ursula. She had snapped into this game as if it were nothing, and he could never imagine any of the sniffy southern girls he'd met at school or the well-to-do ladies of Allerbrock doing the same. Her dress was creased, and she gave Nicolas a wide-eyed smile as she smoothed down the fabric.

Nicolas's voice broke through his thoughts. "Stop staring, Uncle El, you've got to help me. She's trying to get my crown!"

He could have sworn Ursula snorted with laughter, and his heart squeezed at the sound.

Nicolas ran back behind him. His little hands gripped the back of Elias's legs, and he felt the boy press against him. His head rested against Elias's thigh as he reached behind him, ruffling the resplendent curls on his head.

Nicolas panted out a breath like it was his last and ran past Elias, imaginary sword held high. "Charge!"

They chased Ursula around the library as she ducked and dove behind bookshelves, pretending to fire lightning from her fingers and making zapping noises with each movement. Ultimately, she was skewered by Nicolas's sword and fell to the floor in a heap, gasping for breath and loudly ruing the day she dared to fight the might of Pirate King Nicolas.

Ursula's breathing was laboured by the time they finished playing, but she unfolded herself from the ground like a swan about to take flight. Each of her movements were so deliberate and graceful, Elias was awestruck by how naturally her body moved. She unsuccessfully tried to wipe the creases from her dress, and Elias found his eyes glued to her. It was as if she were a flower slowly blooming in front of him.

The more he saw of Ursula, the more he liked.

She finally looked at him, a small smile on her face. He would have marched across the space and kissed those lips were it not for the young boy beside them. Instead, he held out his hand to Nicolas.

"I think it's time for some tea and a rest. What do you say, Nicky? Shall we find your mama?"

Ursula moved to leave, and Elias caught her stare. "Will you be joining?"

She nodded, her face so radiant and lovely it took his breath away. "Sounds perfect. My throat is dry from all the cackling."

# 13

# Ursula

"Goodness! What are you doing?!" Mrs. Clough exclaimed behind Ursula.

Ursula straightened, tucking the broom close to her body. "It's a southern tradition," she said, hooking a stray piece of hair behind her ear. "We sweep every entrance to a house to welcome in good luck for the marriage."

"I can do that, Miss Woodruff," Mrs. Clough said, reaching for the broom. "You needn't spend the morning of your wedding doing chores."

"Oh no, it wouldn't be right if you were to do it." Ursula smiled, holding the broom firm. "This is important to me, Mrs. Clough. It's like a new beginning."

The housekeeper gave her a sceptical look and raised her bushy green brow.

"If you insist," Mrs. Clough sighed.

Ursula felt she was laying it on a bit thick, but she needed a few moments to herself. Butterflies had taken root in her stomach, and she had been fighting fluttery jitters all morning. Her mind kept dancing over all the worst things that could happen: she would be left at the altar, a storm would flood the forest and they'd be stranded there, all the food would suddenly spoil and there would be nothing for the guests to eat.

The increasingly nervous tumble of her thoughts perturbed Ursula as much as the dreadful daydreams themselves. It was only the rhythmic action of sweeping that grounded her in the hubbub of the day.

"I'll be finished shortly, in any case," Ursula said, returning to her work.

She meticulously went to each entryway in Cairden Abbey, sweeping until they were pristine.

The ceremony wouldn't be until late afternoon, once the world was draped in twilight.

The days were much shorter this far north and Ursula found it jarring, missing the sun in a way she never would have anticipated.

She returned to her rooms to find them a flurry of activity, with Nurse Selwyn at the helm. Ursula smiled meekly at her nurse as she thundered, "Where on the Gods green earth have you been, my girl?!"

"I was sweeping," she said in return, and a look of pride coasted across her nurse's face at the confession.

"Oh, you darling girl, keeping our traditions alive." Her nurse swept her into an embrace. She smelled like buttery baking, cut through with the floral, green scent of the neroli oil that she always wore. Ursula clung to her, her head resting against the much shorter woman's shoulder, fondness for her companion swelling. She would miss these moments of unguarded affection once she was gone.

"Ursi, dear, your mother wanted me to give you this." Nurse

Selwyn straightened and threw her thick pewter braid over her shoulder. She walked over to Ursula's bed and retrieved a cream box tied with a golden silk bow.

Ursula held it in shaking hands and manoeuvred to one of the chairs by the fire. Her sneaky, wonderful mother.

She rested the box on her lap and tried to open it as carefully as possible, wanting to savour the contents.

A letter written on thick paper sat on top of layers of tissue paper, her name written on the envelope in her mother's sure slanted hand.

*My wonderful Ursi,*

*I hope this letter finds you well and you are not overwhelmed by thoughts of the wedding. I know how you fret.*

*I'm writing from my childbed, and though I love this little one very much, I am ready to get up and stretch my legs. It is so boring only having books for company—especially as Nurse is with you and cannot give me any local gossip. Your sisters try to tell me about the goings-on in town but they are not as good as Nurse Selwyn. She must hurry back soon, the Mastersons' garden cottage is up for lease again!*

*The box we assembled for you should bring you thoughts from home and carry all our well-wishes across the miles. I am sad to miss your special day but know we will have many more to come.*

*I instructed your sisters to pick flowers from the garden to make a crown, and they outdid themselves. (I saw your father out walking the grounds last night and think he may have added his own. Don't tell him I saw; you know how he is!) Please wear it on your wedding day so a part of all of us can be with you.*

*All my love,*

*Mama xxx*

A hush fell around the room as Ursula peeled back the tissue layers and lifted out the headpiece. It was a riot of flowers, the colours muted as they had dried, but still full of life.

She sat there, the crown in her hands and a shaky smile on her face.

Ursula ran her hands over the delicate petals. The blooms were dried and had no fragrance, but when she shut her eyes, she could imagine walking through the garden at Bowside with them, tracing the scent as they went.

Their absence was like a tinny, rawness in her throat. It flared when she thought of them, all the women who she had spent her life with, argued with, and missed so much.

Irises from Miranda, a small token of respect from her hard-headed sibling. Pink heather for good luck from Alexis, practical and old beyond her years. Baby's breath from Elodie, proper, orderly and traditional, and the only one of the Woodruff children who was married. Red camellias from Margot, a hopeless romantic, even as a young child. Purple aster from Gwen, the baby of the family and the only artist. It was probably Gwen who made the crown, and Ursula pictured her youngest sister with a fierce frown of concentration on her young brow as she assembled the blooms.

Finally, she saw the small springs of forget-me-not, which she knew were from her mother, and a single white gardenia at the centre from her father.

Tears pricked at her eyes then, and she marvelled at how, with this one gift, her family was here with her.

"Oh, that's so lovely!" Maisie sobbed as a cool breeze whipped around the room, ruffling paper and flapping the curtains violently.

"Sorry," she mumbled. "My powers get a bit out of whack when I'm excited."

A furious blush overtook Maisie from head to toe and Mrs. Clough comforted her with a pat on the arm.

"Enough of this!" Nurse Selwyn proclaimed loudly as she swatted away tears from her eyes, the volume doing little to mask the wobble in her voice.

Ursula was then ushered into a bath, the water filled with sweet-smelling oils. She could feel her muscles relax as the warm water enveloped her and scrubbed off the dirt and grime she'd accumulated in her morning activities.

Her hair was washed by Nurse Selwyn's capable hands, who deftly tamed her tresses.

Ursula couldn't help the sigh that escaped her lips; it would be the last time she was waited on in this way by someone who knew her so well.

The next few hours passed in a blur, Ursula willingly going along with the flow of activity. Soon, she was ready. The final piece was the crown of flowers from home.

"Lovely, just lovely." Nurse Selwyn beamed, and her voice was full of emotion.

Ursula looked at herself in the mirror, her reflection startling her. The last time she had seen this dress worn it had been on her sister, Elodie. It followed every dip and curve of her body. She had tried it on at the dressmakers, but standing now in the low light of her room, with her hair dressed and finished with the crown, it looked so different— like it was made for her.

Ursula took a slow, unsteady breath. The tangle of nerves in her chest unwound as she exhaled.

"Ready?" Maisie asked, her voice calm as she smiled broadly. She had worked her magic on Ursula's hair; an elaborate plait ran down her back, woven with tiny crystals.

Ursula turned to look at them, glimpsing the darkening sky in the window.

"Yes," she said with a tentative smile on her face. Hope flared in her chest, melding with the butterflies in her stomach and sending her mind spinning. It was like being on a carousel at a fair—dizzying and intoxicating. She was about to do it, she was about to solidify her future.

She squared her shoulders and took her first shaky step into the unknown.

Ursula walked down the aisle of torches that led to the altar, enjoying the feel of the soft woodland ground beneath her bare feet.

The forest felt alive around them, like it was the true witness to their union. A soft breeze blew through the wood, rustling the straggling leaves still on the branches. The pine trees swayed along too, sending their sweet, sharp scent into the air.

She finally understood why northerners were wed in this way; it felt so natural, so intimate. There was none of this in the pomp and ceremony back home. The weddings she had previously attended were held in the central temple, an imposing building that sat at the core of Currington. Its bright stone turrets twisted into the clouds, the hard stone floors polished to perfection. Everything about the place was cold and unyielding, the complete opposite to the world around her now.

Her feet sunk into the loamy earth. Soil peaked between her toes, and she knew she left her imprint behind, that she was a part of the forest now. The earth gripped her, held her in place. Ursula felt anchored in the moment, it was as if these were the first real steps she had ever taken.

Creatures scuttled and snuffled in the overgrowth as they began their night's work. Life teemed around them, so different from the noisy gossip and oppressive silence of a temple.

A smile curled at the edge of her lips as she reached Elias, who looked at her with such a serious expression it nearly rooted her to the spot. His blue eyes were stark against the backdrop of green and shadows. Excitement, fear, impatience, and hope bubbled as she focused on his face.

The world fell away in those long moments as she stood in front of him. The intensity of his stare was like looking into the sun, and it burned away the rest of the world.

He was resplendent in a deep navy dress coat to match his dark stare. Gold embroidery circled the collar and ran down the front, twisting and turning around the buttonholes like vines on a tree.

Light from the two low braziers beside them picked at the golden threads, glinting and dancing in the darkness. The finery of his clothes only accentuated his dishevelled charm; his hair was still its usual mop, with tendrils brushing against the creamy skin of his brow. There was no denying he was handsome, and it warmed her that he made an effort for the wedding. For *her*.

There were no attendants for a bride in the north, no need for anyone other than the couple and the celebrant. Ursula thought she would miss her family, but she was so captivated by the man in front of her that she was glad she did not have to share this moment—share him—with anyone else.

Heat poured from the braziers and from Elias himself. He was so close she could see every fleck in his gemstone irises, read every freckle on his face. His eyes creased as he smiled, and after a pause the priestess started a quiet chant to begin the ceremony.

"We call upon you, Brannen, Goddess of Marriage, Fidelity and trust.

We call upon you, Brannen, commander of the owl, of knowledge and devotion.

We swear fealty to you, Vanquisher of Perfidy, to see these souls brought before you at this time of change. As one year fades, and another is born."

Elias smiled at her. A ground-shaking, wonky grin that made Ursula's heart flutter. The forest responded with a wave of chittering; it was like they were all one.

"We look to you, all-seeing Brannen, to cast your eye on the mortal plain on this night when the veil between our worlds is thinnest," The priestess continued. "May you grant us your presence on this Samhain Eve. A day that marks a new year, a new beginning, and judge those before you and see them worthy."

The priestess's monotone voice rang through the clearing.

She gestured to the couple and then at the stone altar before her. There were two basins carved into the rock—one with fire, the other, water.

She lifted an owl feather to her brow then lowered it into the fire. The fire rose, consuming the feather until there was only ash.

The priestess walked around the altar and reached into the ash-filled hollow, coating her fingertips in ash before running them over Ursula's and Elias's brows.

"We ask for balance in this union, for equity.

We ask for your care and your protection, as you give your consort, Lireth.

Lireth, who commands the waves and brings life to our world.

These souls before you swear to uphold your laws, to nourish and guard one another.

To tend the bonds they have formed tonight.

They swear to honour you both, so you may honour their union."

The priestess turned, picking up a wide, double-handled pewter bowl from the altar and dipping it in the water until it filled.

"Please say your commitments," the priestess said.

She held the bowl between the couple. Elias reached for it and held it to Ursula's lips.

"I promise to do all this and more," he said gently, tipping the vessel. Ursula swallowed the cool liquid, her eyes never leaving Elias's.

She took the cup from him, repeating the gesture, saying in return, "I promise to do all this and more." A shiver passed down her spine as Elias drank the water, his eyes burning into hers.

The priestess took the cup from her hold, laying it back on the altar before looking to the couple. "Please bring your hands together and seal this union with a kiss."

Ursula placed her right hand on Elias's upturned palm and leaned forward. Time slowed as his lips touched hers. They were firm and warm in the cold forest air.

His kiss was light at first, almost timid, but Ursula felt him ease against her as he wrapped his left hand around her waist, pulling her close.

Her left hand splayed against his chest, the lustrous embroidery on his jacket tickled her palm.

His mouth was hot and giving, and she sighed against him as he lightly teased her with his tongue.

She wasn't sure who broke the kiss first, but they stood there for long moments afterwards, their faces close as they shared the same air.

It was like they were one. She could feel the beat of his heart underneath her palm, the steady rhythm in time with her own.

All she could think about was Elias. The way he held her, kissed her, looked at her. She was at sea and happy to be pulled along by his current. He smelled musky and so, *so* masculine, like soap and cedar and the tiniest hint of whisky. Ursula wanted to bury her face in the crook of his neck and drown in him.

"May it be so." The priestess's voice was a distant whisper, and all Ursula wanted to do was lean in to feel his yielding lips on hers again.

"May it be so," the pair replied, and a bright light flashed in between their palms. A searing heat flared—hot, but not painful—and skirted over her flesh.

A feeling of wholeness swept through her, and she hoped Elias felt the same.

Ursula turned her hand around, seeing a thin thread of gold along the heart line on her palm. A corresponding line glimmered on Elias's.

There may be disparities in how people lived in the north and south, but their faith—and, by extension, their marriage— was one of the links.

"Then it is done. Your union is anointed by Brannen, and her consort, Lireth.

May it be fruitful, fulfilling, and may it remain until the seas swallow the sky."

The priestess announced the union to the world around them, and the forest responded with its own natural harmony of rustles and chittering.

That was it.

They were finally wed.

# 14

# Elias

The evening had been a blur with well-wishes pouring from the guests like fine wine.

Elias couldn't take his eye off Ursula as she flitted around the ballroom; she looked every inch the lady of the house as she laughed and danced with the guests. They had been like ships passing in the night, barely able to utter more than a few words to each other before being pulled away. The party may have been small but the music, dancing, and good cheer filling the ballroom made it feel as though there were a hundred people in attendance.

They had decided against a formal sit-down meal, instead laying food out for guests to have at their leisure. Elias plucked a fig from a platter of fruit, relishing how the jammy sweetness complimented the smoky whisky in his other hand. Juice ran down his hand, and he caught the trickle with his tongue. Hairs lifted on his arms and a tingle ran down the length of his spine as he suddenly felt someone's eyes boring into him. Elias looked up to find his wife's piercing amber gaze. She stood next to her nurse across the room, and the vast expanse of space vanished in that second as he was transported back to their kiss in the woods—the give of her pillowy lips, the soft noise she made when her tongue breached them. Like her laugh, it was another thing he wanted to coax from her again and again.

Ursula nibbled on her bottom lip, and Elias wished he could magic everyone away with the click of his fingers and rush over to take her mouth again. To forgo the restraint he had wrestled with in front of the priestess. She looked ravishing and ravished. The light gold of her dress shimmered every time she moved, the soft fabric skirted along every curve, hinting at what was underneath. Elias couldn't tear his eyes away; the square neckline framed her face and highlighted her brown skin. Stray hairs fanned around her face, the apples of her cheeks flushed and glowing in the candlelight. He could picture her like this below him in the heat of the night.

Elias downed the dregs of his whisky and strode over to his new bride.

Her eyes tracked every step, drifting from his toes to his head. He smirked when they snagged on his thighs, the thin fabric of his dress trousers straining as he stalked across the room.

The band had just started back up after a short break for their repast, and a jaunty northern reel filled the room that had everyone, including Nurse Selwyn, up dancing.

He held out his hand. "Shall we, *wife?*"

She slid her hand into his. "Naturally, *husband.*"

He pulled her close towards them. His hand splayed on her lower back like earlier, and he heard her gasp. Another smirk played on his lips. He was willing to bet all his money she was thinking of the kiss, too.

They spun around, the world melting away until all he could focus on was the way Ursula met his stare, her amber eyes daring him. He got so caught up in her he stumbled and snagged the hem of her dress, the thin fabric ripping easily under his foot.

"I'm sorry," he whispered. They wove around each other, their hands clasped in the middle.

"It's alright. Not the first time a husband has ripped at a wife's wedding dress." Ursula blushed. "Ignore me, I've had too much wine."

"Perhaps another dance will help."

Elias felt his blood heat as he fought the urge to whisk her away right now, but instead he held her close. The music slowed to a waltz, and Elias couldn't—*wouldn't*—let his new bride go. Ursula's back straightened as they glided across the floor, and he was determined not to lose his footing as he guided them around the room. She fit against him perfectly, her body moulding to his as they moved to the music.

Eventually, it was time for the married couple to depart.

Susannah rushed over and pulled Ursula into a tearful embrace. "Welcome to the family, Ursula. I am so happy to finally have a sister."

Elias felt his eyes smart as he watched his new bride give his sister an equally forceful squeeze. The women whispered to each other, chuckling in low tones, their arms still wrapped around each other.

Elias felt a tug on his trouser leg.

"I was supposed to give you this before, but I forgot." Nicolas held up a horseshoe tied with a ribbon. "Mama says it's good luck."

He bent down to eye level with his nephew. His shirt was askew, and he was barefoot. Elias ruffled the boy's hair, then picked him up under the arms and whirled him around in a circle. Nicolas burst into a fit of gleeful giggles as he spun. His arms spread wide like a bird, the horseshoe clamped in his tiny fist.

Elias slowed and settled the boy on his hip, taking the horseshoe and putting it in his pocket.

"Thank you, Nicolas. I'll cherish it always."

He walked over to Ursula and Susannah, who picked up Nicolas from his hip.

Elias brushed his hand down Ursula's arm. "I think it's time we go."

Her eyes swept around the room, her smile beaming. "I think you're right."

Part of him wanted to stay.

They exited the ballroom through the front door, their guests waving and cheering like a crowd of thousands behind them.

There was a carriage decorated with ribbons and bells waiting for them outside. They jumped into the coach, leaving their guests to continue the revelry without them. Progress was slow on the rain-soaked roads, the decorations tinkling with the movement.

"This is where my parents went on their wedding night," Elias said, his body pressed up against Ursula on the coach's narrow bench. Her dress seemed to fill the rest of the space.

"Oh, that's nice," Ursula replied with a wan smile, then returned to staring out of the window. Her back was rigid again, and her gaze had been fixed on the view for the entire journey. Elias felt the smart of unease in his gut; the wild abandon he'd seen during the dancing earlier had vanished.

"It won't take long to get there," he continued, nervously filling the silence. "The manor is further down the hill, just on the outskirts of town."

"I don't mind. The scenery is fascinating," Ursula sighed, almost to herself.

Sure enough, the outline of a house came into view as they swung down a steep slope. The pale stone stood out against the charcoal sky.

The carriage bobbed along the gravel drive, and Ursula put her hand on Elias's thigh to steady herself. He just about jumped out of his skin at the touch but settled his own hand on top of hers. Her eyes darted to his, but she left her hand there as Elias inched his head forward. It was a test for him, to see if he could kiss her. They were married now, but this somehow felt momentous. Ursula wet her lips and edged forward. It was a minute movement, but it knocked him dizzy. She had told him so much in that tiny tilting of her head.

She wanted this as much as he did.

He leaned closer to her, and his nose brushed against her cheek. He could feel her breath on his lips, just like he had in the forest. He had planned a chaste kiss for their vows, but all proprietary fled him once his lips touched hers. Only a tiny shred of decency had held him back from devouring her like he wanted. There was no starchy priestess standing over them now. They were alone, they were married, and they could do what they liked.

Elias edged closer, his hand skimming along her jaw and cupping the back of her head. His eyes nearly rolled back in his head when he touched the sleek strands of hair at the nape of her neck. Ursula made a tiny gasp as he inched closer, his mouth a whisper from hers.

A footman appeared and swung the carriage door open, scattering them like school children caught up to no good round the back of a barn.

The manor stood before them, resplendent in the autumn moonlight with torches lining the drive and up a stone staircase to the entrance.

"It is a beautiful place," Ursula said. Her voice tinged with awe as she stood down from the carriage.

Elias had always admired the manor in the many times he had visited with his parents, but it looked even more dazzling now that he was experiencing it with Ursula.

"It belonged to a favourite of a long-dead King. They would rendezvous here, and it is rumoured to give any couple who stay in good luck," Elias whispered over her shoulder, letting his hand linger on her waist before he held it out his arm. He could have sworn she quivered as she looped her arm through his.

They walked the rest of the way towards the house in silence, a palpable tension in the air. It took all his might not to haul her into the shadows of the garden and finish what they started in the carriage.

"...and here's your key." The jovial receptionist handed over an ornate gold key with love hearts and vines all over it.

Elias thanked them and guided Ursula down the hallway, his hand on the base of her spine. They moved through the building and up a sweeping staircase until they stopped at an expansive white door, the fixtures matching the key that Elias clicked into the lock.

"In the south, it's good luck for the groom to carry a bride over the threshold after their wedding," said Ursula, her tone verging on playful.

"Then we shall!" Elias declared as he scooped Ursula up, earning a theatrical gasp in response. She stiffened at first, her arms looping around his neck, but a giggle escaped her as Elias dipped to open the door handle and wobbled back and forth like a ship in a storm. The absurdity of the situation left them both shaking with hysterical laughter, which did not stop when Elias deposited her on her feet in the room.

"I'm sorry…" she said, trying to suppress her laughter. "I didn't think it would be quite so…wobbly. What a silly custom, it's positively vertiginous."

"I must admit, I could have used some guidance on how to do that smoothly. Southern men must be more suave than us parochial northerners."

"You handled it well. I'm just a bit dizzy," Ursula replied, her breathing returning to normal.

They took in the room. It was decorated in various shades of pink with the odd gold accent. Magenta was layered on top of rose, rouge, fuchsia, and blush. Elias blinked a few times as his eyes adjusted, but it didn't help. It was like being inside a giant striped sweet from the confectioner rather than a wedding suite.

Their luggage was already waiting for them, as was a roaring fire and some sparkling wine resting in an ice bucket in the shape of a rather grotesque fish.

"It's certainly not dull here," she noted.

"Yes, I'm starting to doubt my parent's taste, in all honesty," Elias said, looking around.

Ursula skirted around to the other side of the ostentatious four-post bed, untying her cloak as she went.

Elias wasn't sure where to put himself and decided that one of the chairs in front of the fireplace was best. He shrugged off his jacket and propped his foot over his knee.

Ursula was looking at him intently, her brow in the faintest of furrows. "There's something I should say, or at least I think I should, so I will."

She squared her shoulders, and Elias sat up a bit straighter, his foot falling back to the floor as he listened. He knew instinctively that now wasn't a time for him to talk—he'd grown up around enough women to know when to be quiet.

"I'm not a maiden. I don't want to imply that you were expecting anything physical, but I know that we have to…to consummate the marriage for it to be legal." Ursula picked at her nails and took another deep breath. "I want to—I'd *like* to, but I had to tell you. I just did."

Elias took him a minute to gather his thoughts. He cleared his throat. "I must admit, I hadn't really thought about it."

It was true he hadn't thought about it, but he had assumed and assumed wrong. The same had been true of Ursula. He had assumed he would get a prissy southern lady as a wife, but he had her. He just needed to square this circle and find his footing. It was just like being on the rugby field and being unexpectedly tackled.

Elias opened his mouth to speak, then closed it again. The oppressive decoration and stifling heat in the room bore down on him, and he needed out. "I think I'll go down to the bar for a nightcap. Alone."

He rushed out of the room before Ursula could protest.

Elias wandered down to the bar at the back of the manor. It was completely empty and tucked away from the rest of the building, both of which suited him just fine.

The barkeep came over and asked for his order.

"Make me something warm, something comforting," he replied dolefully.

The barkeep returned promptly with a tall, steaming glass mug. He could smell brandy, and there was a cinnamon stick bobbing around in it.

"Old family recipe," the bartender said. He slipped away to the other side of the bar before Elias could say anything else.

He took a long inhale before taking a sip. When he said warm, he hadn't meant literally, but he was all at once grateful for the barkeep's perception. It was exactly the comfort he needed, and he gave the man an appreciative nod.

He'd assumed she would be a maiden, that she would wait, even though he never had. The conventions around marriage in the south were so strict, he'd never given it any thought. Women there were married young, and he had been surprised her parents had waited until she was twenty-two. He was starting to realise the Woodruffs were different from the other southern families he'd met. Elias assumed that it came from Ursula's mother; he didn't know much about her, but had gleaned enough through conversation to know she had successfully stemmed some of the southern stiffness in her children with her iron will and continental wit.

Elias took another sip, and the liquid gave a soothing burn as he swallowed. He motioned to the barkeep for another, enjoying the enveloping warmth. The drink went down easily, and soon it was drained.

The barkeep came over to replace his empty glass with a third, and Elias shook him away, the night's revelry sitting heavily on him.

Why had he left their room? He knew he was being close-minded and petty, but he couldn't shake the feeling that he should have been her first.

This was the norm, wasn't it? Virgin brides that a groom coaxed with sensual touches and encouraging words. Grooms were supposed to arrive at the marriage bed with a base arsenal of sex acts to corrupt a pure bride.

*Why was that?* Elias sat back; he had never considered this.

He felt the world tilt as he nodded to the barkeep for a brandy. The swirling amber liquor made him think of Ursula's eyes, and he groaned internally.

The night had not gone as he had intended.

He wasn't sure what he wanted beyond getting to know her, and her disclosure scared him.

She had a life beyond him, and he worried now that he may never live up to it.

He sat there silently, staring in his glass like it would give him all the answers he needed, but there was only one person he should be speaking to now.

The clouds in his mind started to clear, and he felt a pang of guilt over his reaction. He was being churlish. Ursula had once found solace in someone else's arms; was that so bad? Hadn't he done the exact same thing during his campaign with exotic beauties in far-flung cities? His betrothal had never entered his head during those times, and certainly never before them. He had never thought twice about her in his numerous dalliances. A small grimace fixed on Elias's face. The double-standard for women had never felt more apparent.

He took a final, long swig. The rules of the game were so stacked against women. One blight, one indiscretion, one liaison and they could be ruined. Men could act with impunity, and now, after years of ignorance, it rankled him.

Elias understood that he was now at an impasse; he could censure his new wife for living her life in his absence, or he could accept—appreciate, even—who she was now. He drained his glass, decision made.

# 15

# Ursula

Ursula had read the same page five times, the words spinning around as her thoughts kept drifting back to Elias's face before he stormed out. She had hoped it was different here, that women were held in greater regard. What was the point of all those stories about the wild north if they treated women in the same antiquated way as home? He had left her for a war and was now upset when she told him the consequences. Ursula flung her book away in frustration, and it skidded along the bed before landing on the floor with a thump.

If only she had just kept her mouth shut. She could have just lied, pretended that she didn't have a past, that the last five years had never happened. It would have almost been easier to hand-wave it away and make some excuse as to why she didn't bleed. Naively, Ursula didn't want to enter into her marriage with lies. She didn't want to pretend it didn't happen, that she had cared about someone before. She may have ended up with a battered and bruised heart, but she would always be proud of herself for going for what she wanted.

Ursula had always been aware of the world she had grown up in. The expectations of what a woman could achieve was of a wife and mother. She was sure she could do those things, and do them well, but a tiny part of her had wanted more—to be successful in her own right, to do something lasting beyond the traditional roles set out for her. But that dream felt too unsteady, like a rickety ladder that took too much courage to stand on.

The door swung open and she braced, unsure of what would come next.

Anger burned like fire in her belly. She was ready for a fight, ready to spew forth everything she had kept down all those years.

Elias walked into the room, his hands up in supplication like the night in the hallway. A blush spread across her cheeks.

"Before you say anything, let me say my piece," he said warily. "I am not going to probe you for details but know this: I am glad you have lived your life, as I have done mine. I see no shame in how you behaved, because I am no hypocrite, but I am glad you shared this with me. Above all, I wish for us to be equals."

Ursula gave a half-smile. "Thank you, Elias, I would like that very much, as well. I will say it was nothing more than a case of two people finding comfort in each other, and I'm glad you understand this."

Elias's gaze swept around the room until they landed on their cases on the wooden luggage stand. He bustled over and frowned when he found the case empty.

"I packed your things away. I felt it was something a wife would do. Your night clothes are in the chest of drawers, and I put your toilet bag on top." Ursula smiled up at him and inclined her head to the huge baroque monstrosity on the opposite wall.

"Thank you. I'll change in the water closet," he said. He rustled through the wash bag and pulled out a small glass vial, dropping some liquid under his tongue before grabbing a pile of night clothes from the drawers and dashing into the adjoining room.

Ursula watched him as he left for the bathing chamber, glad that they had come to an understanding but not really knowing what that meant.

Elias returned before she could get her thoughts in order, and the sight of him had them scattering again. His skin was fresh and gleaming, the apples of his cheeks pink like he'd come in from a winter walk. He wore a loose tunic and bottoms of brushed cotton or flannel. The high-necked design was left open, and Ursula found her eyes glued to his throat. His Adam's apple bobbed as he swallowed, and she felt her insides turn molten.

There was a hint of worry on his face, his brows creased to a neat vee and blue eyes narrowed like he was working a maths problem out in his head as his gaze flicked between the bed and the settee. Her resolve melted some more; he looked so charming and fresh-faced, like some country cottier and not a worldly soldier.

"If we are to be equals, then we can share the bed. I'll try not to steal the covers," Ursula said, giving him an understanding smile before retrieving another book from the nightstand.

Elias moved to the bed and slid in between the covers, his long legs getting tangled in the sheets as he rolled onto his back. He fussed with the knot before giving up and lying down, eyes trained on the ceiling. Ursula watched him from the corner of her vision, turning the pages of her book but not reading. His eyes were closed now, long lashes fanning out on his cheeks. They were thick and dark, and Ursula wanted to run her hands over them and continue down the slope of his nose, his pinkened cheeks, all the way down to that dimple in his chin. To trace her tongue over it and taste the salt of his skin.

The anger from earlier moved lower, warmth trickling through her veins and pooling deep in her core. She shifted uncomfortably, and the bed linen bristled against her heated skin. If she were alone, she would let her hand inch below the covers and work herself to oblivion. Ursula took a few deep, steadying breaths, leaned over, placed her book on the nightstand, and snuffed out the light.

There was a clock ticking on the mantelpiece, the mechanism sounded like a gong in the silent room.

"Are you asleep?" she whispered into the dark.

The clock ticked on, marking their silence.

"No."

Ursula lay there a moment longer, feeling flushed and frustrated. Elias was just a handspan away.

She rolled onto her side, facing her new husband. Her eyes tracked the topography of his silhouette in the darkness. His nose was straight, but not as prominent as her own. The way the end curved made it almost delicate. His jawline jut out like the bluffs at home. There was a tension in him, something even the night couldn't hide. She followed the sweep of his eyelashes as he blinked into the night, and Ursula imagined him lying there, staring at the ceiling as she had been.

Her hand slid across the bed. Cold sheets gave way to warm flesh as she laid her palm across his stomach. His breathing hitched, muscles tensing below the soft cotton of his tunic.

"I meant what I said earlier. I want to do this. I want you."

Silent moments passed, and the only thing that stopped Ursula's mind from completely spiralling was the heat that seeped into her outstretched hand.

Should she pull away? Let him take the lead? Did he think her wanton? Would this be the end of marriage before it had truly begun?

Ursula's hand tensed, the doubt in her mind slithering through her body. Elias silenced her racing mind when he lay his palm over her own.

Time slowed again. The seconds lazily slipped into each other as they lay there, bound by just their hands.

He didn't move or trace tiny circles on her skin, and Ursula fought every urge to pull away. Had she misjudged his ration just moments before? Was he stopping her? Making a boundary of who could touch who?

The heat in her soured at the edges, curdling with panic. She wanted to run and lock herself in the bathroom, to douse herself in water and scrub all of this from her memory.

He turned then, closing the space between them.

"I do, too."

She felt his lips on hers now, soft and seeking in the gloom. His hand clutched at her waist, the fabric of her nightdress bunched in Elias's desperate fingers as he pulled Ursula even closer.

It was like an eclipse, the light giving way to something magical. Sight was replaced by touch, taste, and scent.

Ursula wrapped her arms around his shoulders, her fingers delving into his untamed mane.

"You want this?" he asked, his breath hot against her neck.

"I do. I really do."

Ursula sighed as he pulled her flush against him.  The cool night air caressed her legs, leaving goosebumps as her nightdress bunched even more under his incessant touch.

His mouth trailed down her neck, kisses fluttering against her pulse. He moved lower and nipped her collarbone, teeth swift and feather-light.

Ursula gasped, and the sound was reciprocated as Elias groaned against her.  She swept her hands down his back, feeling the jut of bone and knots of lithe muscle under the soft fabric of his clothes. She tugged at the hem of his tunic, letting her hands dance along the waistband of his bottoms.

A strangled half-moan escaped Elias then, and he ground against her.

Ursula let her hands dally over the sensitive strip of skin, enjoying the feel of his hardness through the cotton bottoms before her hands shifted to the hem of his shirt and pushed it upwards over his torso.

Elias caught her chin in his hand. Though she couldn't see his eyes in the dark, Ursula could feel the way they burned into her skin.

"My turn." His voice was playful, devilish as he let go of her chin. His fingertips brushed down the centre of her throat, fanning out slightly over her decolletage.

Her throat caught as one finger trailed between her breasts, making them swell to aching points. Ursula willed her eyes to stay open, to watch Elias in the dark and feel his scorching gaze on her. But that one finger sent so many shivers across her whole body, all she could do was let herself go and bend into his touch.

"Take this off." His voice was rough when he reached the

fabric circling her waist. Ursula's hand met his, and she tugged the nightdress over her head. The fabric fluttered through the air and hit the floor.

Elias's hand splayed on her stomach, his thumb lightly caressed the bottom of her breast in tiny, maddening circles. Ursula willed his hand to reach higher and grasp her, the pain like a balm to the torment building inside. Instead, his hand slid down her body in a sure, slow stroke. She sucked in a breath as his palm moved down her abdomen, through the faint line of downy hair from her navel to the dark thatch below.

To where she ached for him the most.

He gasped then, and Ursula forced her eyes open again. Elias was just a shadow above her, but she fixed her gaze on him where she knew those dark, gem-like eyes would be.

"I meant what I said." Her voice was a firm whisper. Direct.

Ursula couldn't wait anymore. She had planned to eke things out, to taste and tease until he was as shaken up as she felt. Now, she just wanted him.

Words failed her, and Ursula pulled him to her in a clattering kiss.

Elias moved then, swiftly kicking off his pyjama bottoms as he settled between her legs. His lips never left hers, and his tongue plundered her mouth as he nudged her thighs open with his own. She could feel the length of him, hot and hard against her skin, and she wished she could see this. See him enter her, *claim* her.

Ursula instinctively curled into him, enjoying the way Elias's lithe frame felt nestled between her thighs. She could feel his forearm beside her face on the bed, his hand tangled in her hair.

Elias hooked his right hand under her bent knee and slid into her.

She gasped at the intrusion, welcoming and filling in equal measure.

Had it always felt like this? Elais was strong and caring and wicked, nothing like she had experienced in her life.

Elias stilled, his face so close to hers she could feel his breath against her lips. "Is this…?"

The question was the only thing that hovered between them.

"Yes," Ursula breathed, her hips rocking against his, coaxing a grunt from Elias.

"Yes," she said more forcefully as she pulled him down for another kiss, her heel running along the length of thigh, urging him deeper.

Elias needed no more encouragement as he sank into her, his pace steady as he pushed her bent leg higher, stretching her, opening her more.

Ursula's chest heaved as she rocked with him, the smattering of hair on Elias's chest tickling with each thrust. She threw her head back then, unable to keep their kiss going with the onslaught of feeling. This was no frenzied, quick coupling as he plundered deep into her.

He licked the sensitive skin below her ear, making her clench around him. Elias nibbled at her earlobe, worrying the skin just enough to make her breath hitch.

She came undone then, her climax stealing her breath as it ricocheted through her body.

Elias groaned again. He fisted the hand in her hair, his pace erratic.

"Ursula…I'm so close. I'm—"

Panic pushed at her bliss, and she looked at him with wide

eyes.

"Don't finish inside me."

Her hands were still tangled in his hair as he pulled back, and she shivered as the cool night air nipped at her damp skin.

"I just want to choose."

It was true. She knew the mechanics of baby-making, and while she loved all her siblings, spending her life herding a pack of children made her queasy with dread.

"It's alright." He leaned in and kissed the tip of her nose. "I understand."

Despite his assurances, Ursula found herself turning away to stare at anything other than those eyes.

Elias lightly pinched her chin between his thumb and index finger, angling her face to his own. "Look at me."

His eyes bored into her, pupils so wide she could hardly see the stormy blue. Sincerity shone through them, and Ursula felt the warm glow of her orgasm deepen. He understood. He understood without challenging or pushing her or storming away. He implicitly knew how important choice was to her.

Her eyelids fluttered closed.

"Ursula, eyes on me." His voice was raw as it rasped in her ear.

Elias's hand drifted lower, down the smooth surface of his stomach. Ursula kept her eyes fixed on his as he touched himself. It started as slow, purposeful strokes, like he wanted to draw out his pleasure. His other hand skimmed her jaw, her lips, and she nibbled at the pad of his thumb. He moved faster after that, his eyes never leaving hers until the last minute when he crashed his lips against hers and shuddered with his own release onto the bedclothes between them.

Elias dropped his head to the crook of her neck, his chest

pressed against hers as he took gulping breaths.

Ursula soaked it all in. His warmth, how she could feel every sinew as his body pressed along hers, the way his hand skirted up and down her side. She hardly knew him, but somehow lying tangled with him made her feel complete.

# 16

# Elias

Elias woke to a warm breath on his neck. His mouth was dry, and he realised he'd been snoring through the night. He closed his mouth, trying to regain some moisture and blinked his eyes awake, slowly taking in his surroundings. The gauche decor was an assault on the eyes in the morning half-light.

Ursula slept heavily next to him, a tangle of limbs and hair. Elias leaned over, hooked the inky locks behind her ear, and planted a soft kiss to her exposed shoulder. She looked so different like this, more wild and untamed. Ursula grumbled in her sleep and burrowed deeper into the covers, completely cocooning herself in the mound of blankets.

Elias edged out of the bed and retrieved his pyjama bottoms on the way to the adjoining bathroom. The lock clicked behind him, and he poured water into a waiting basin. It was stale and tepid, but it felt like an elixir of life as he gulped it down from his cupped hands and splashed it on his face. He felt tired and content, and as if on cue, a yawn rioted through his body. He crept back through to the bedroom, unsure of what to do—should he clamber back into bed, or leave Ursula to rest and retire to the settee?

This was answered for him when he re-entered the room. Ursula was sitting up in bed, her hair a riotous halo having slipped from the braid she'd had it in last night.

"You snore," she said drowsily, rubbing her eye with the heel of her hand. He felt his heart skip a beat as he watched Ursula in the weak morning light. She was sleep-rumpled and candid, and he'd never seen anyone more beautiful. Elias smiled to himself, and he felt like he was seeing her for the first time.

"Ugh, yes. Sorry about that," Elias replied, suddenly feeling very embarrassed and exposed. "Should we call for breakfast?"

Ursula shivered and pulled the covers closer. Elias looked at the fireplace to see embers smouldering there. They had forgotten to bank the fire last night, and it had burned to nothing.

She yawned, sleep still lingering on her face. "Oh yes, that sounds like a good idea."

Elias nodded, stood up, and rang the servant's bell.

"Could you pass my robe? It's on the back of the door," Ursula asked, the covers wound even tighter around her. She looked endearingly absurd, like a swaddled baby, with her face poking through the mound of fabric.

Elias walked across the room to the heavy cotton garment hanging beside his own, and he had to bite the inside of his mouth to stop a laugh bursting out of him. Even the sorry state of his own house coat couldn't dampen his feelings. He made a mental note to replace the threadbare rage once back home. Elias grabbed Ursula's down from the door hook and looped it over his arms. He was hit by an intoxicating, almost peppery fragrance that was wholly Ursula. He wanted to bury himself in it. To lap up that dark scent. To feel her pulse flutter under his lips, under his tongue.

Ursula stood from the heap of blankets as he approached and the smile faded from his face. She was clad in a gauzy nightgown made of layers of flimsy, gossamer material that draped over her body like mist. He'd never seen her, only felt the soft swell of her curves. He held the robe open and she turned, putting her arms through. His eyes raked down her back, glued to those curves he'd caressed last night.

"Thank you." Ursula tied the belt and pulled her hair back over her shoulder. Elias's eyes followed the dark tendrils as they fell down her back. It took all his might not to run his hands through the silky strands.

"I think I'll get ready in the bathroom," Ursula said, stifling a yawn as she tottered sleepily through the room.

Elias jumped to action when he heard the bathroom door click, grabbing his clothes and tossing them on. He had never seen the point in fussing over one's appearance, but his usual rush was hastened by the worry that Ursula would walk in and catch sight of his scars. She'd skirted around them last night with her hands, and he'd almost pulled away when she'd first touched them, afraid of the inevitable rejection that would follow. But it never came, and she never flinched as her fingers skimmed his marked skin. Regardless, he couldn't face her seeing it now. It had taken all his might to relax enough to let her trace the gnarled flesh in the dark. Seeing the scars in the light of day was out of the question.

Ursula was dressed, her hair gleaming, when she exited the bathroom. Any hint of her earlier tiredness was gone, and her eyes shone in the low morning sun.

The table was covered in an array of delicate pastries, boiled eggs, and two fillets of smoked fish. A large pot of tea steamed in the middle, the aromatic mist mixing with Ursula's own scent as she sat opposite him.

"Tea?" he asked, gesturing to the pot.

"Heavens, yes please." She beamed at him as he poured.

"Milk?" Elias quite enjoyed this little domestic tableau they had fallen into. He could imagine many more mornings like this.

"Not for me. I usually take two slices of lemon."

Elias plopped the yellow slices into her cup and handed it over. Ursula gave him a small smile in return.

"Please excuse my terrible manners, but would you mind if I read a bit over breakfast? I had planned to read more last night, but..." Her words hung in the air, and Elias caught the faint blush on her cheeks. Last night had not been what either of them had expected.

"Of course! In fact, I have some work to catch up on, anyway."

Ursula moved to retrieve her book, but Elias stopped her with a hand on her forearm. "Allow me."

Elias did have work to do, but he'd read the same page countless times and was sure it was written in orcish, for all he took it in. His eyes kept drifting instead to the woman across from him.

She had a book in one hand and the remains of a pastry in the other. There was an endearing wrinkle in her brow as she read the text.

She caught his gaze, a smear of frangipane on her cheek.

"Interesting read?" He gestured to the book.

She brightened at his words and placed her book on the

table. Elias glanced at the cover; it was a crime novel about a highwayman.

"I'm not sure," Ursula said, the wrinkle in her brow deepening. "I can't tell if the plot is very cleverly crafted, or so silly it defies comprehension."

"Ah, is it about a roguish highwayman with a heart of gold who is pushed to do dastardly things for the people he loves?" he asked, a hint of ribbing in his voice.

Ursula beamed. "Quite the opposite. It's about a young woman named Ruby who is driven to a life of crime after being seduced by a dastardly duke. She vows revenge and steals from him and his cronies. I'm assuming she gets caught at some point, but she's had run-ins with the duke several times and he hasn't recognised her. Surely, he would have detected it was her by now? They…know each other well." She blushed at the meaning.

Elias understood the inference and simply said, "Some men don't pay attention."

Ursula's eyes widened at the remark and she coughed, picking up her book again.

The rest of breakfast passed with much safer conversation about the weather and other polite chit-chat. Soon, the pair felt comfortably full.

They were making moves to leave the table when Elias reached over and swept his thumb across Ursula's cheek. She jumped back at the movement, but Elias just licked the digit and shrugged.

"You had something on your cheek. I didn't say before, as I thought it was charming. Although, I'm sure you would have gutted me if I'd let you walk around all day with it on your face."

"You fiend," she said, busying herself with neatening their dishes.

Soon, everything was in order, and the day stretched out ahead of them.

"I was thinking about a horse ride. It's cold, but the brisk air might be nice?" he asked. "I know you said you like to ride, but we could do something else like a walk or reading in the atrium."

"Riding sounds great. Carriages are fine, but it's nothing compared to having the wind in your hair," Ursula replied, a broad smile on her face.

A shiver passed through Elias as he imagined Ursula, cheeks bright and panting, her hair flowing behind her on a galloping steed.

Reality proved every bit as magnificent as his imagination, and Elias couldn't take his eyes off Ursula as they galloped along a stretch of road amongst the trees. It had taken her a while to get reacquainted in the saddle, but it was obvious how much she enjoyed the feel of the powerful horse beneath her. She leaned forward, urging her mount on with a silent command, her body moving with the beast as its hooves pummelled the ground.

The woods were a blur as they raced along the track. He should have made a bigger effort to take in the scenery, but the sheer pleasure emanating from the woman next to him stole all his attention.

They slowed to a cantor as the manor appeared into view again. The afternoon had been more fun than he had expected. He tried to point out different plants and expand on the manor's melodramatic history, but that soon faded as they pushed their mounts to go faster and faster.

"I think I'm in need of a good soak," she said. He could see that she tried not to wince as she descended from her horse. Elias rushed over to help her down, his weak side straining as she slid against him.

"Thank you," she whispered, their faces almost touching.

Elias edged forward. Ursula sparkled in front of him, windswept and breathing heavily.

A groom walked in then. "Ah, Mr. and Mrs. Clearbould. I see you've given the mounts a good run, eh?"

Elias ran his hand down the horse's side. "We tried to."

"Always like it when they get a bit of exercise," the groom replied. "Fresh air does us all good, eh?"

The pair nodded awkwardly as the young man took the reins from Elias's hand.

"Enjoy your day," the groom said, then tapped his hat and steered the horses away.

"You too," Elias replied to their receding forms. He picked at a loose thread on his coat as they ambled across the stableyard.

"I do have some papers to go over. I'll escort you to the room and try to find a quiet place to work while you bathe," Elias said, his voice coming out more strained like he'd have liked.

Ursula took his proffered arm, and the pair walked back into the manor.

Her fingers curled around his bicep like they had been made to fit around him, and Elias couldn't help but flex a little under her touch. He'd long ago lost the bulky muscles that came from a lifetime of playing sports, but his consistent running had kept his body strong, if not a bit more compact. Ursula tightened her grasp, and Elias smiled to himself as they walked up the wide manor steps. The soles of their shoes click-clacked against the polished stone.

Ursula sucked in a breath. "Do you really need to work?"

Elias chewed on it for a second. He wasn't sure how to answer. How do you convey that you feel you should work, that you are trying to emulate the man who taught you everything, but you'd rather do anything else. "'Need' is probably not the right word. 'Should' is more appropriate, but I 'should' be doing a lot of things."

Like undressing his wife for her bath and washing those long dark locks. He would never get bored of running his hands through them. His nostrils flared. He wanted to get lost in her rich, spiced scent again.

Ursula's steps slowed and she turned to look at him. "Oh."

She was still flushed from the ride, and her hair had come loose around her. Dark tendrils framed her face, and Elias stopped to take her in. "There's nothing that can't wait a few days."

Ursula smiled at him, and he knew he'd made the right choice. "You're sure?"

"Completely. There's plenty to explore here." He leaned in so close; he could feel her breath on his lips. "The library even has rolling ladders."

Ursula's eyes went wide with delight. "I've always wanted to try one of them."

He brushed a quick peck on her lips and tugged her after him. "Come on, the baths can wait."

# Ursula

They were back on the road to Cairden, and Ursula was feeling refreshed. Their stay at the manor had been short, just two nights away, but she had savoured the time alone with Elias.

She looked out the window, enjoying the terrain. The landscape was wild here, and seeing the stark change in the seasons still filled her with wonder.

The days they spent in the manor had been restorative, and Ursula didn't want to burst the bubble of tranquillity they had built. They had spent their time lounging around reading, going on brisk walks around the ground and eating in the lavish dining room. However, Ursula was itching to get back to Cairden and the little routines she now built her days around. She was starting to miss Mrs. Dyce's more homespun cooking and Maisie's bright chatter. She couldn't wait to tell the maid and Nurse Selwyn about her stay.

She laughed to herself thinking of all the times she had silently cursed her nurse growing up, desperate to get away from the woman's eagle eye. She imagined a younger version of herself rolling her eyes behind the woman's back at her silly comments and gossiping.

The days of being coddled were firmly behind her, as she was now someone's wife.

In some ways, the last few days had put her worries to rest; she had to admit that she was growing fond of Elias. His easy manner wasn't a facade, and it was obvious from his ready laugh that he actively looked for joy in the world. She had expected someone who was old money like him to be staid and buttoned-up. She had expected him to be like the society toffs she'd met in Currington. Instead, he had carved out time for her, taking an interest in what she liked.

Her cheeks reddened when she thought of their wedding night. He was the same then, attentive and encouraging. Her pulse fluttered at her throat, and she took a few steadying breaths as they rumbled up the hill towards home.

Nurse Selwyn was waiting outside Cairden Abbey when they arrived. Ursula could see her luggage stacked in the hall behind her. Unshed tears glistened in the older woman's eyes, and Ursula jumped from the carriage as soon as it was stationary, earning a tut and eyeroll from the driver. She missed Elias's curt response to the man as she crashed into her nurse's arms, cherishing her stout embrace.

"I thought you were going to be here for at least a few more days," she wailed, her voice muffled as she held the older woman close.

"A missive arrived while you were away. I'm to go and… support your mother a bit earlier than planned," her nurse replied, dodging Ursula's eye.

"She's in good health, isn't she?" Panic flared in Ursula, and she scanned her nurse's expression for any hint at the sudden change in circumstance. She swiped at her face in an attempt to remove all trace of her tears, even as new ones fell.

"Nothing I haven't seen before, my girl." Nurse Selwyn soothed, wiping at Ursula's cheeks like she did when she was little. "No need for you to worry. Each child is different, and this one is proving to be a menace. I wouldn't be surprised if it were a boy after all this. They do love drama, don't they?"

Ursula managed a weak smile, trying hard to believe her nurse's words.

"Please, don't leave," she said in a small, cracked voice.

It felt so wretched to ask, but she wasn't sure she could face this alone—whatever 'this' may be.

"Ursi, you will do fine here. You have a man who obviously cares for you and a chance to strike out on your own. Grab it with both hands," her nurse whispered back.

Her nurse patted her back a few times, and Ursula could feel the tears dry with each beat. She could do this. Bravery didn't just need to be sword wielding and dragon slaying; it could be small things, too. Things that looked ordinary from the outside but changed a person. She took her first step in her journey north and she would keep forging this new path, this new *her*. She had to do this, to make the best of it.

"Now I best be off. We've got a long journey ahead and I don't like travelling in the dark. There are still bandits in these parts," Nurse Selwyn declared to her leaving party as Ursula managed a real smile. She would miss the old woman fiercely, but she was right. This was her opportunity to strike out on her own. To shape the world she wanted.

Ursula gave her one last squeeze before saying, "Please write to me when you arrive at Bowside. I'd like to know you and Mother are safe."

Nurse Selwyn nodded and gave her a reassuring pat on the arm before shuffling to the coach that had been called for her. She would feel much better back down south; these weeks up in the north, though charming in their own way, had not swayed her otherwise.

And with that, she was gone. Ursula wished she spent more time with the older woman in the weeks since they'd come north. Instead, she had been consumed by thoughts about herself and her marriage.

It all felt so petty and selfish now. Ursula hugged herself tightly, like she could squeeze all the sadness down until it disappeared.

Elias reappeared beside her—he had hung back and spoken to the groom while Ursula said her goodbyes. She was sure he'd done it intentionally to let her have this moment alone with her nurse, and the kindness made more tears sting at her eyes.

"Are you alright?" His voice was soft, and Ursula was sure the tears would spring loose again.

"Fine. I'm fine."

Elias raised an unconvinced brow but didn't press. Maybe she would be fine if she kept saying it.

"I think I'll go lie down now," Ursula said. She let herself have one last look at the retreating carriage, one last look at her tether to her old life, then walked away.

Ursula sat in her room. The tears from Nurse Selwyn's departure had dried, leaving her eyes sore and gritty. She needed to clear her head, to blast away the cobwebs. How she missed the salty, sea air of home; it was the perfect antidote to a blue mood.

She let out a pitiless sigh. She had been so focused on getting out of Currington, it never occurred to her that she'd miss it when she was gone. How easy it is to be exasperated by your life when you're comfortable in it. To look for more because you don't appreciate what's in front of you. A searing pain burned in her chest, and she wished she could hug her sisters. She would pull them close and tell them how wonderful they are, even in the moments when they behaved like the most frustrating creatures on earth.

An idea struck as Ursula looked out of the window to the vast expanse of forest beyond. Today she would tackle the woods and not mope around indoors like some pampered pet.

Ursula scuttled about her room to fetch her cloak and shawl from where they were hanging beside the fire.

Sinjorro Zavaran's clothing had, indeed, kept the cold at bay, and she now had two new cloaks—one fur-lined for the winter, the other a deep green wool with the standard northern embroidery around the trim.

Her dress was in the local style, too—richly dyed and high-necked for added warmth, the arms and bodice loose for easy movement and extra layers. Still, Ursula wasn't ready to forgo her stays for the fabric bodices that she had been supplied. The familiar feel of them moulded to her shape like her own brand of armour.

She wrapped her shawl round her shoulders and slipped on the embroidered cape, ready to face the forest. Impulsively, she grabbed her writing pad and pencil as she passed her desk.

Ursula padded down the stairs and out of the front door, longing for the wide-open spaces of Currington. The bluffs there could be seen from her family home, and she missed the salty freshness in the air.

The thin air of high altitudes and the mulchy scent of the woods would have to do.

She turned right and followed the road from the front of the house until it became a thin gravel path snaking through the trees.

This was the route she could see from her bedroom window, and she had always wondered where the winding path led. Her footing was unsteady on the craggy earth, roots and stones seeming to appear out of thin air. Jittery excitement made her stomach somersault. She glanced back at the house before continuing deeper into the woods.

Maisie's warning from the teashop about the dangers lurking in these woods reverberated through her mind, but she pushed them aside. She needed to feel the fresh air in her lungs and the burn in her legs, anything to stop herself giving in to the well of sadness she felt. It would do no good to turn around, to curl up on her bed and cry. The only path to healing had been getting up, facing the world, and putting one foot in front of the other.

Flickering movement at the edge of her vision forced Ursula to stop, the hairs on the back of her neck standing on end. There was nobody there but the trees crowding around the spindly path.

Ursula picked her way down the trail, but her nerves stood to attention no matter how much she tried to shake her disquietude and focus on the pine trees that littered the land. It was like she was being watched, which was preposterous considering she was alone. She couldn't help but imagine there were others in bright autumn shades dotted across the landscape, their fallen leaves like a blanket on the ground.

The seasons changed abruptly here, the delineation between summer and autumn as stark as day and night. There was none of the slow slip into colder days and longer nights from her southern homeland.

It was almost a novel experience to feel the seasons so viscerally, and Ursula bent to pick up a leaf mottled with yellow and orange. She studied the pointed edges, unsure what kind of tree it came from, and slid it into her pocket.

Ursula wound on through the forest, trying to the best of her ability to push aside the tingle of apprehension down her spine. The scenery was so beautiful, she could almost forget the feeling of being watched or the way the trees pressed in on her inch by inch.

Eventually she came to a clearing, nothing more than a small circle of open ground with tufts of grass and a few scattered rocks. She sat down on one of the larger rocks and craned her head back. Her eyes drifted closed, and she could practically feel the forest breathing around her.

Ursula's hand drifted towards the leaf in her pocket, her fingertips tracing the veins along the pliant surface. It was dry and brittle, sat right in the middle of summer and winter. Of life and death. She took the handkerchief stuffed up her sleeve and spread it open on the rock beside her, laying out the leaf in the middle. Ursula folded the fabric carefully before placing it in her pocket, her hand resting over the spot where it lay.

She wanted to remember this moment, to preserve this sense of calm she felt in the woods and use it to remind her future self that she could do hard things. That the most rewarding moments came from when she was scared and mastered that fear. Her life may be small and ordinary, but she had taken the first step when she got in the carriage bound for the north and jumped into the unknown.

Ursula took a long breath and began walking again, letting her feet guide her.

Her hair snagged on another branch, and Ursula shrieked, shirked and kicked the nearest trunk. She didn't bother to notice or care if it was a tree attached to the offending branch. They were all to blame, the whole bloody forest.

She felt betrayed by the woods—how could this be the same place where her wedding was held? The forest had welcomed her then, and she had felt wholly protected by it. Now, it was like every twist and turn led to another maze of trunks to navigate. The path she followed had dwindled to a skinny, brown line through the undergrowth, barely wide enough for her two feet to stand together until it was swallowed up by the forest floor.

The sun had sunk low in the sky, and the mulchy, damp air had sunk into her bones. She had no idea what time it was, but night was approaching. She suddenly realised the very real possibility of having to spend the night in this awful place. Ursula tried unsuccessfully to stop her teeth chattering at the thought and pulled her cloak closer around her, determined to find her way out even if she had to walk all night.

What had started as an uplifting exploration of her new homeland had descended into hours of trudging in loops through the never-ending forest, getting more and more lost with each passing minute.

Her boots felt about two sizes too small, and they pinched and rubbed as if they were made of ill-fitting sandpaper rather than calfskin leather. Her face was tight and chapped from the cold, but it was her pride that was wounded most of all. Silly to go scuttling off and not tell anyone, to try and act like she was part of this place now, too. Silly to think that wandering off into the woods would make her forget her sadness in the first place. A cold lump burned in her throat, making her chin tremble as angry tears stung at the corners of her eyes. A large, embarrassing part of her wanted to flop onto the nearest thing that resembled a seat and cry. She really was a silly, silly girl.

Ursula pushed on, fear nipping at her heels with every step.

The trees loomed closer. Branches reached out like spidery fingers, snagging at her clothes and her hair as she passed.

Her muscles were taut, ready to strike and run. Cold panic engulfed her stomach, shrinking it to the size of a peanut. What would Elias make of her absence? Would he assume she'd left him? So consumed by Nurse's departure that she, too, fled home to the south?

Would he come after her if he believed she had?

She stopped, but the wood creaked and sighed around her like an old house settling. Ursula tried to take a deep breath, but her heart was hammering so hard all she could manage was a few jittery, weak gasps. She ran a shaky hand over her face and massaged her eyes until she saw stars behind her eyelids.

Finally, she managed to take a deep inhale. The forest smelled damp and loamy, and the chill air stung the back of her throat.

There was no one else here, no one to rescue her.

She had to do this herself.

Ursula looked around; there was no marker, no hint as to where she was.

Her eyes drifted upwards. The stars were starting to show now, making an early appearance in the twilight. She didn't know many of the constellations, save for her namesake, and her gaze raked over the dusky sky.

*There!* she nearly shouted out, or maybe she did—did it even matter in an empty wood? Ursa Major curved majestically next to Ursa Minor, its tail pointing her way north.

She could find her way. She knew it.

The woods shrank back a little as she ventured on, one plodding foot in front of the other.

"Right! That's it! I know you can hear me. I've had enough. Let me out!" She pointed wildly at the forest around her, her foot having caught on yet another tree root as she stumbled along. She knew she looked like a half-crazed hedge witch—her hair sticking out at all angles, the bottom of her dress caked in mud—but she didn't care. Ursula knew deep down that this was wood's fault, and she wanted to show it who's boss. "I've been tripped, poked, prodded, the hair snagged from my head. Enough!"

Ursula felt her bravado drain when she heard a twig snap. Her shoulders tensed, and an icy shiver ran down her spine as she looked for its origin. Her mind spun with images of bandits, bears, and scarier things that she wouldn't even dare to name.

Time suspended as she stared into the forest gloom. The trees cast lengthy shadows, the damp causing a rolling mist on the ground. Shadows danced and her eyes played tricks on her. It was like the trees bowed and bent, clearing a path to a looming form up ahead.

The shadow moved towards her and Ursula felt rooted to the spot, stiffer and more frozen in place than the tricksy floral around her. She willed her legs to run, to dash away from whatever danger stalked the woods.

was exaggerating for comedic effect."

"No," he said, his hands squeezing her shoulders for emphasis. "It's my fault. I should have been here."

"I wanted to be alone," Ursula saidfaintly.

Elias takes her chin in his hand, the pad of his thumb moving in tiny strokes as he tilts her this way and that. His eyes rake over her face until he spots something, fingers tightening then move slowly up to her hairline.

"You're bleeding." His voice was strained, and Ursula couldn't hold his gaze. Somehow, it was different to be this close in the low light of dusk, surrounded by the forest. It was like being in a strange mirror of their wedding ceremony, and Ursula, for one, found it much easier to touch and taste him in the dark of the manor.

"It's only a scratch," she whispered back.

His fingers skimmed the stinging skin on her forehead, then drifted back to the side of her neck, his warmth a welcome reprieve from the wood's cold. The wide expanse of his grip was as warm as a fire, and she leaned into the touch where it tingled against her skin.

Ursula took a tiny step forward. She itched to touch him, to kiss him, to take them back to the ceremony in the clearing. It was like the woods settled with Elias here; she could feel the trees exhale and stop their oppressive looming. She tipped her face up, angling herself into him even more.

Elias ran his thumb along the underside of her jaw and Ursula shivered against his touch, the heat spreading down her spine like molten fire. Did a husband's touch always inspire such sensations? Her entire body felt like it was singing, and she couldn't feel the sting from her cut anymore. The movement seemed to jolt him from wherever his mind had drifted, and he pulled the scarf off from his neck and wrapped it around Ursula.

"Let's get you back to the house.  There's a flagon of tea waiting for you, and I'm sure Mrs.  Clough has doctored it with enough brandy to make you feel better in no time."

Ursula smiled at him. Little did he know, he'd already done that.

# 18

# Elias

Elias snapped his ledger closed, sending dust plumes into the air. He coughed, swatting a hand to dissipate the cloud. That decided it; it was time to get some fresh air. He had been holed up inside for so long, cabin fever was setting in. He thought that going through the historic accounts would cause something to stand out to him, something that would point to the quarry's creeping demise. Instead, all he found was years and years of dwindling margins, yet the same productivity.

Strain knotted the muscles in his shoulders, and Elias rolled them to relieve some of the lingering tension. Resigned, he dropped his head back on the chair with a thump and let out a weary sigh.

Ursula's bride price would keep the company afloat for a while, but eventually they would sink.

He turned his head from side to side, stretching his tight neck as he breathed through his nose just like the *fakúr* in the East had taught him. Elias let his eyes grow hazy and gave over to the breath. The world melted away as he counted to ten.

The tension in his body eased, and his eyes focused back on the world around him. Trees swayed in the window, dancing on a stiff autumn breeze. He wondered what Ursula was doing now. He hadn't seen her since breakfast. In fact, he hadn't seen her much at all in the days since he'd come upon her in the woods. They met at mealtimes, but his mind was always on his work. He'd deluded himself into thinking that all would miraculously be solved if he just spent enough time poring over the numbers and looking into the state of affairs down at the quarry.

Instead, he'd spent more time with financial documents than his new wife.

Elias resolved to change that right now, rolling his shoulders one more time before he pushed off from his chair.

He stood on the threshold of the garden room, and a prickle of self-consciousness crept across his skin.

She was exactly where Mrs. Clough said she'd be—bundled up in one of the ancient rattan chairs, a book in one hand and a steaming cup of tea in the other.

Elias took a moment to savour the scene in front of him, the self-consciousness giving way as he watched Ursula. It warmed him to see her enjoy the often-overlooked place. He couldn't remember the last time he'd been down here himself.

He straightened, walked into the room, and gave an awkward cough to announce his presence.

Ursula looked up from her book, the end of her nose red from the cold. The cut on her head had healed to a tiny, thin white line.

"Oh, it's you!" was all she said in a way of greeting, but her face was warm and welcoming.

"It is." He smiled back at her and was at her side in a few sure strides.

The air was chilly, but fresh in the glass room. The overgrown plants lent a fairytale quality to the space.

Elias sank into the chair opposite her. "I would be very grateful if you would let me show you around Allerbrock."

Ursula blinked at him for a few seconds, her lips puckered to blow on her tea. She gave her head a small shake and placed the cup back on the saucer.

"I'd almost given up hope that you'd ask me." She beamed at him, a twinkle of mischief in her eyes. There was a time he would have stewed in this comment, berating himself for not being better or doing more. Instead, he allowed himself to just revel in her attention, to unfurl like one of the plants that surrounded them—happy to sit and bask in her glow.

"Excellent. I have something special to show you." And he truly meant it. "I'll meet you in the foyer in ten minutes. Is that enough time?"

Ursula shrugged off the blanket, then gave a little shiver and pulled it back around her. "Is this another race?"

Her amber eyes glinted at him, and he had to hold himself back from pouncing on her to kiss the smirk off her lips.

"Only if you want it to be." He jumped up and dashed over to the door, glancing back to see Ursula charging after him with a pile of blankets in her wake, before he sprinted into the hall.

They walked through the main door and down the hill towards the town centre. Elias loved to share this view, to watch people's eyes widen as they took in the scale of the town, the way it snaked down into the valley.

He could feel Ursula's grip tighten on his arm each time

they came to a particularly steep slope, and Elias let himself indulge in being her support as he inhaled the earthy, spiced scent she left in her wake.

"I'm still not used to the hills," she muttered, her gaze firmly fixed on the ground.

"Don't worry, you'll be galloping around them like a local in no time."

Elias was glad she couldn't see the laugh he was repressing with each step.

"The main square is just ahead," Elias said as they came to a stop, "and there you'll find our famous alder."

He could see Ursula's shoulders inch down from her ears to their normal position, the vice-like grip on his arm loosening as they stepped onto level ground.

They were at the end of one of the wide, straight roads that led to Allerbrock's town centre. Shops lined the streets here with rows of apartments above. The lanky buildings shone in the low winter sun.

Elias drew in a long breath and puffed out his chest. The wedding had caused time to slip through his fingers. Days had turned into weeks, and it only now occurred to him to formally introduce Ursula to her new home.

They sauntered down the broad vista, and Elias watched from the corner of his eyes as Ursula took in the town now that she was on firmer footing. Warmth settled in his chest at her reaction, and he ran his hand over the one she rested on his forearm.

They headed to the town square, which was quietly bustling with mid-morning traffic. A few food stalls were open selling fresh produce and quick eats, nothing like a lunchtime hubbub or furore of market day.

They tread on light feet, manoeuvring through the roots and thickets with ease.

Relief thundered through her when she saw a familiar pair of sapphire eyes.

Elias held his hand over his brow, like he was a sea captain catching a glimpse of shoreline.

Ursula wanted to scream and shout, to rush over to him, but all she could manage was a feeble raise of her hand.

He ran over to her then. Navigating the divots and mounds of the forest with such grace that Ursula forgot the cold in her bones for a moment, and just watched him in wonder. He seemed to attune to his body, to the landscape, like they were all working together.

"Are you okay?" he asked, his hands on her shoulders, eyes darting all over her body to ensure she was unharmed. She hoped his gaze wouldn't linger too long on her matted hair and stained dress.

"Yes, I thought today would be good to get some fresh air, but I'm afraid I've gotten rather turned around," Ursula admitted, her windburned cheeks flaming scarlet.

"I'll say! What made you come out here? Alone, too! You need to know the woods and the woods need to know you. They like to play with outsiders."

The word *outsider* clanged through her. It was a small, casual thing but reminded her that no matter how comfortable she felt now, this wasn't her home. Not yet.

Nurse Selwyn's receding carriage flashed in her mind. Perhaps she should have gone back, that the north would never really accept her.

Ursula looked down, the adrenalin from seeing Elias nose-diving into a black pit of embarrassment. "I thought Maisie

They sat on a low stone wall that edged the square. The river rushed behind them, swollen from the rain that was omnipresent in the colder months.

The alder sat proudly on the riverbank, offering a reprieve from piercing light.

Elias watched as Ursula's gaze wandered up the tall trunk to the golden canopy above.

"So, what's so famous about the tree then?" she asked. Her mouth was pulled to the side in an insolent pout, and again he wanted to reach over and kiss it off her.

Perhaps followed by more thorough discipline.

He could feel his blood thrumming in his veins as he shifted in his seat, giving his trousers a surreptitious tweak. Ursula's eyes scanned the tree from the root to the highest branch, and Elias looked on as her face filled with wonder. He leaned closer, watching her shiver as his breath caught the shell of her ear. He had planned on being a well-mannered tour guide, but all he wanted now was to be alone with his wife. To watch her tremble at his words, no matter how innocuous.

"It's where the town gets its name from. Like all good fables, it starts with a lonely traveller lost in the woods. As you well know, our woods are tricksy."

Elias smirked at the huff she let out, still not over the embarrassment of her foray in the forest.

"He realised his time on this plane was coming to an end and sat under the alder tree, ready to await his fate. The alder is known for its power, its connection with land and water, and was so moved by the traveller's bravery and pure heart it decided to bestow its power on him. The traveler lay against the tree trunk for three days and nights as his strength returned, and he pledged to dedicate his life to serving nature

once he fully recovered. News spread of a hermit and a healing tree, and soon enough a town sprung up around them."

Elias leaned closer until the very tip of his nose brushed the sensitive skin beneath her ear. Ursula sucked in a shaky breath, her eyes still glued to the tree.

"It is rumoured that touching the trunk can ease one's pain, be it physical, emotional and everything in between. But this can only happen once, so you must choose wisely."

She slowly turned to look at him. The sun picked out the gold in her amber eyes and lit lustrous streaks in her ebony hair.

"Have you ever touched the tree?"

Elias's smile faltered for a second. "No, some things are meant to be felt."

He thought about it when he first came back a year ago. When the enormity of what had changed since he left crashed over him like a wave, and he never thought he'd ever surface for air. He probably wouldn't have if it wasn't for Susannah and the boys cajoling him out into the world.

Susannah suggested he get a hobby in some dim hope that he'd do something like rugby again, but Elias couldn't face playing the sport now. His body wasn't the same; it felt more fragile now and he didn't trust it to survive being slammed around a muddy field.

He decided to sort through his father's things then, to breach the final border between them. It was in this slog through the paperwork he'd found out about the state of the quarry and the long-forgotten betrothal contract. It was this that knocked the edges off his grief, spurred him into action, and put him on the path he was today.

Ursula looked around the square, happy to slip into silence

and take it all in.

"Alder wood is special, you know."

"Oh? How so?" Her tone was teasing as she leaned back, bumping shoulders with him.

"It's the only wood that gets stronger in water." He looked back at the tree, his arms propped behind him  Ursula was neatly tucked around him like a cat. "It takes something that would wear away anything else and uses it to be stronger. The alder proves that we can become better through difficulty."

"So, it's magical? Like in the story?"

"Maybe." He tipped his head to the side. The alder always felt like a melding of worlds, where science and magic could exist in tandem. "You should see the lines of heartbroken maidens that flock here after an acting troupe has been through town."

"Thespians," Ursula replied tartly, then swept her gaze over the sleepy square. "It is a nice story, though. The town does have a unique feel."

Elias nodded. Allerbrock did have a special atmosphere, the Pale City surrounded by forest and hills.

"Yes, it does," he said proudly. "There's magic in the north, even in the humblest of places."

"Maisie showed me," Ursula said with finality, and Elias stopped.

They may share a landmass, but the customs in the south were rigid with little room for romanticising. His schooling had taught him that.

Elias cleared his throat and stood, extending his hand to Ursula, who placed hers in it and rose with practised grace.

"There's somewhere I think you will like much more than an old tree with a sad story." Elias placed a hand on the small of Ursula's back, directing her where they should travel. He could have sworn she gave a slight jump at the touch.

They wound through the streets, the town more vibrant and bustling as morning crept into the afternoon. People filtered around them as they moved through the crowds quietly beside one another. They soon turned a corner to see a charmingly haphazard building in front of them. It had a wide oval window beside a set of unwieldy double doors, a sign hanging precariously above. It flapped in the breeze, wafting the patrons as they entered.

"A bookshop!" Ursula let out an undignified squeal. "How did you know?"

"You're never far from a book, and I thought you might enjoy it."

It looked more like an oversized hermit's hovel than a bookshop—squat compared to the lanky buildings on either side. Ursula said as much, and Elias replied, "Don't be fooled. People cherish books here. We need something other than the bottom of a bottle to keep us occupied on long winter nights."

Images from that night in the manor flashed through his mind, and he bit the inside of his cheek as a distraction. He placed a hand on Ursula's lower back to guide her safely in, admitting to himself that he missed touching her in their walk from the main square. She leaned into his touch, letting him guide the way even though he was sure she wanted to sprint off.

"So, what do you like to read? Just mysteries?" Elias asked as they stepped through the heavy doors.

"You remembered!" She smiled at him, her eyes dreamy and faraway. "I'll read anything, within reason, but especially like a good mystery, one that keeps you guessing until the end. Do you like to read?"

Elias thought for a second. Reading had never come naturally to him. "I've never been one for much reading myself. Was always off gallivanting and making trouble, but then this happened." He held up his left hand, overtly showing her his missing fingers for the first time. He was about to hide it in a pocket again when Ursula grasped it, tugging him further into the shop.

"I have been known to pick up the odd history or biography that we have in the library at Cairden in recent years. Although, I must confess, most of what I read are tracts about trade levies, engineering advances, and porosity of stone. Not quite as scintillating," Elias blustered, feeling flushed from her touch.

"We're in the right place, then," Ursula said, beaming. "I'll see if I can find a Lambert Lawson mystery for you. They are thrilling! All of his books are set in a far-flung court, with lots of murder and intrigue. I warn you, though, they are addictive. You may find yourself staying up all night just to find out who bumped off the king or was caught in bed with the princess."

Elias's mind whirled, and all he could squeak out was a weak, "An exciting prospect, indeed."

She sped over to the counter, asking where the mystery section was.

"Back left corner," a bored assistant said, not lifting their head as they gestured in the vague direction. Pointed ears poked out of lengths of strawberry blonde hair. *Typical elf. Always so aloof*, Elias thought as Ursula rushed past him. He followed her retreating form through the avenue of shelves.

Ursula looked back over her shoulder, her eyes shining and

face alive with glee. Elias reached out and pulled her to him.

They landed against one of the shelves with a muffled bump, and there was a perceptible wobble from the stack of books behind them, but he didn't care. The whole thing could crash down, and he'd barely notice.  He'd wanted to kiss her so many times today, and seeing her joyful face at something he suggested tipped him over the edge. All he could think about was her lush rosy lips, and he wanted to taste the excitement on them.

She was flush with his chest now, pressed tightly against the whole length of him.

Ursula let out a little shriek when he squeezed her waist, but didn't move away.

"What are you doing?" Her voice was a breathy whisper.

"Something I've been thinking about all day."

Elias's hand ran down her side, and Ursula shuddered under his touch. He squeezed at her hip as she pressed herself against him, moulding even closer to his body.

"Oh, why didn't you then?"

She jerked her hips, and Elias drew a hissed breath in through his teeth.

"I don't think people would approve of what I'd like to do to you in the town square."

"And what's that?"

"This."

He hooked her leg around his waist, his hand skirting up the tender flesh of her thigh.

"This."

He moved his hand underneath the soft swell of her back side, enjoying the feel of her flesh between his fingers as he lazily played with the lacy fabric that edged her underwear.

"This."

He toyed with her earlobe in his teeth, savouring the sound of her panting breath.

Ursula shuddered, her chest pressed against him and held onto the bookshelf behind them. Her knuckle turned white with the force of her grip.

"But most importantly, this."

Elias wound his other hand into her hair and tugged her against him. His mouth clashed with hers in a deep, bruising kiss.

Ursula looped her arms around his neck, running her hands through his hair as she pulled him closer. His hard length pressed against her stomach, and he caught her moan in his mouth, driving deeper with his tongue.

He had started this, but he couldn't stop now. He wanted her desperately.

Elias trailed kisses down her neck and along her collarbone.

"Elias, please," Ursula whispered in his ear. Her voice was soft and urging, and all he wanted to do was take her here and now.

His hand moved below the silken fabric of her underwear, blood rushing in his ear with each minute movement.

"Yes."

Her voice was like a caress down his spine.

His fingers edged closer, brushing against her damp hair. Ursula clung to him, her hips moving in tiny, entrancing thrusts. Her hands roved through his locks and nearly tipped him over the edge. He could have spent hours like this— kissing her, touching her, tasting her.

Elias moved his hand again, giving over to her wetness. He might have moaned; he wasn't sure as Ursula went stock-still.

He pulled back, dropping his hand. "I'm so sorry, I shouldn't have—"

Ursula covered his mouth with her hand and shook her head. Her eyes were as wide as dinner plates.

A shuffling noise came from the next row, and they jumped apart like a couple of teenagers caught necking after midsummer.

Ursula was positively aflame in front of him as she rearranged her skirts. Her rosy lips were now a deep red, like glittering rubies in the low light of the shop.

She stared at him, chest heaving and eyes burning. He wanted to throw caution to the wind, to kiss her again, to skirt his hand along the soft skin at her neck, the weight of her skirts as he rucked them up—but they came for books, and books they would get.

"C'mon," he said as he held his hand out, "show me those stories you've been telling me about."

She slipped her palm against his and tugged him along.

The pair of them were lingering near the counter at the front of the store a few moments later, Ursula asking the surly elf a barrage of questions. *Serves them right!* Elias thought. The elf had always been testy and unhelpful in the few times that he had been to the bookshop before, and having a deluge of questions flung at them by an enthusiastic patron was like the universe righting itself.

"There you are!" Ursula appeared with another stack of books and looked down sheepishly to the pile of books on the counter. "I'm sorry, I couldn't resist."

The bored assistant rolled their eyes as they tallied up the total. Ursula went for her purse, and Elias swatted her away. She looked at him squarely and spoke in a kind yet determined voice.

"Let me buy them. The money belongs to both of us now, after all."

Elias relented with a fond shake of his head. It was true; what had once been individual was now collective—or *his* own, if he was the miserly sort. He didn't know how they conducted finances down south, but northerners liked to pride themselves on their ability to share and work in common.

Ursula's voice chimed again, dispelling his musings. "But if you want to be heroic," she said, "you can carry them up the hill. I doubt I'll make it back as is."

He huffed as he picked up the now-wrapped books, the weight reminding him of his army training. Ursula moved to protest, her face contrite again, but was silenced by Elias's easy smile.

"Who would I be to disagree with my wife? Although, I may have to throw in the towel mid-way and get a carriage."

"Oh, come now, I'm sure you'll manage well enough. You can put those muscles of yours to good use."

Ursula touched his arm for emphasis and Elias flexed his bicep underneath.

"See?" she said with a smirk, and Elias felt as powerful as ten men. He wanted to throw her over his shoulder and haul them both back up that hill.

Instead, he shifted the books higher in his grasp. "Dare we do another race?"

Elias galloped ahead leaving Ursula in the shop doorway gaping like a fish.

"You fiend!" Ursula shouted and dashed after him.

# 19

# Ursula

Ursula was busying herself with the household books in her study. She was glad to be able to contribute in her own way to the running of the house, although Mrs. Clough ran such a tight ship, she doubted how much she was actually needed.

Things had been so sedate since she'd come to Allerbrock. A few of the local society ladies had called in on her in the few weeks since the wedding, but Ursula had found them dull and self-interested. She much preferred spending time with Maisie or wandering around the town—hills notwithstanding.

Once all the figures were totted up, Ursula sat back in her chair and looked around the room as if another task would magically manifest in front of her. Maybe she could organise the bookshelves or rearrange the furniture? The study was next to her bedroom, and while it was not a big room, it had a large window and enough space for a fireplace, desk, chair, and bookshelf. Much like the room she was sleeping in, it had belonged to Susannah who had emptied the shelves when she married and moved, leaving Ursula the opportunity to fill them in her stead.

Although, she didn't need any more excuses to go to the bookshop. It was becoming a second home; even the prickly shop assistant, Kieran, was warming to her.

She had to admit the study was fast becoming one of her favourite places in Allerbrock, and she could while away the hours reading in the room's cosy walls. After a lifetime of sharing, it felt like a space she could make her own.

Ursula took out her writing set and started drafting a letter home. Regular correspondence with her family was an unexpected upside of her move. Letters had become a weekly occurrence, often firing back and forth almost daily. There was always a scandal to share or a sibling to moan about. Her mother's letters had been unusually restrained, talking about books she was reading and euphemisms about her confinement. Nurse Selwyn had written a huge diatribe about her journey home that had made tears of laughter run down Ursula's face.

She would never have known about the realities of life at Bowside were it not for her sister, Miranda. They had been chalk and cheese since birth, which was further exacerbated by being just over a year apart in age and constantly lumped together. For every word Ursula swallowed, Miranda said them loud and proud, happy to spit in the eye of authority. It was like she deliberately went out of her way to make a fuss, and it always rubbed Ursula the wrong way. Was it so hard to behave like people expected?

The words turned in her head. Had she not shucked off some of this stiffness herself since being in Allerbrock? Had she not seen glimmers of what it was like to live your life for yourself?

Ursula picked up her pen, determined to write home and close the gap between herself and her sister. Her pen scratched across the page in wild loops, the words tumbling out of her almost too quickly to catch on the page. Turns out that all the warring siblings had needed was a few hundred miles between them to become close—irony at its finest.

There was a light tap at the door, and Ursula opened it to find Rodger, Elias's valet, standing there. "Letter for you, madam."

She accepted the dispatch from him, surprised by the heavy gilded envelope. Rodger left the room with a nod, his manner as formal and quiet as ever.

Ursula's brow creased as she perused the missive, its weight and ostentation completely out of the ordinary.

She broke the seal and inspected the contents. The inside was even more decadent, with loops and whorls in glistening gold. It was an invitation to a Yule party at Susannah's: a three-day celebration to mark the solstice in a couple of weeks.

Ursula couldn't stop the thrill that ran through her; the prospect of a party was a rare treat. The last one she had been to was her own wedding, which already felt like a distant memory. A few nights of dinner, dancing, and music were exactly what she needed in the bleak winter months.

She gathered up the paper and made her way down the corridor to Elias's study, still a bit wary of encroaching on his space. It was a place she deliberately hadn't spent any time in, for no particular reason other than the intrinsic notion that she shouldn't.

Once she was standing at the broad door, Ursula mastered her nerves and gave a firm knock.

She could hear him rifling through papers on the other side.

When he eventually shouted for her to enter, she squared her shoulders before pushing on the round brass doorknob.

Sure enough, Elias was sitting at his desk, a mountain of documents splayed out in front of him.

He looked up after a pause and gave a double take. "Ursula! I thought it was Rodger. You have such a commanding knock."

She swallowed, trepidation bubbling inside her as she thought of what to say next. Elias just smiled, and her stomach decided to do a tiny flip now, too.

"We've been invited to Susannah's Yule party the week after next."

"Ah, the famous Lockston winter revel. You'll need your dancing shoes, if I remember correctly. It's been a couple of years since I've gone, but they were always spirited affairs."

"Sounds wonderful," Ursula responded sincerely. "I'll make arrangements with Mrs. Clough and see that the staff take the time off. They'll want to spend the solstice with their families, I'm sure."

"That's very considerate of you. Yule is normally a subdued affair here."

Unsure if she should leave, Ursula stood there awkwardly in the doorway and gave the room a surreptitious scan. It was a conventionally masculine space, all dark wood and oppressive colours. There was a domineering stone fireplace on the opposite wall, and the sword hanging above it glinted in the light. The walls were oxblood red with dark panelling up to the midpoint. Yes, this was the epitome of a man's domain, and all Ursula could think was how much better it would look with the heavy drapes thrown open and a fresh coat of paint.

The seconds seemed to crawl by until Elias finally piped up. "Perhaps you could organise something for Yule this year?

Decoration has never been my forte."

She perked up at the prospect of a project, albeit a frivolous one, and was determined to bring cheer this festive season.

"I'll get started then…" She trailed off, unsure of what to say next. Standing in his study, she realised how much she missed her husband's company while he worked and felt an impulse to extend their time together. "Will I see you at dinner tonight?"

"Depends if I can get through this." Elias gestured to the paperwork in front of him, his attention already drifting back to his work.

"Would you like a hand? I used to help my father all the time." Ursula tried to keep her voice steady, to not reveal how excited she felt at the opportunity to work with him.

Elias stopped, thinking for a second before his face split into a brilliant smile. "I'd like that."

Ursula returned the look and walked over to his desk.

From a distance, the papers had looked like an unruly heap, but up close they were positively overwhelming  Books dating back years, judging by their yellowed colour, sat jumbled with new reports and accounting. Everything was in chaos.

She came beside him and leaned over the ledger that lay open on top. Her eyes scanned the book, but all she could concentrate on was the heat emanating from Elias. Ursula swallowed, trying not to let her eyes rake down the expanse of skin from his ear to shoulder.

Elias seemed completely unbothered by her presence until she saw him shiver.

"Chilly?" she asked.

"Yes?" He looked up at her, and she wanted to dive into the deep pools of his eyes.

Ursula straightened, glad to put a bit of space between them. "I'll throw another log on the fire, and then we can get to work."

She mustered herself as she moved around the room. The wonder of Elias's eyes could wait. She had a task to complete, no matter how much her cheeks flushed or heart beat a timpani in her chest.

Ursula went back to her spot at Elias's side, only this time making the conscious decision to stand just a fraction further from him.

"First off, we need to get this sorted into chronological order." She gestured to the mess of papers. "Then, we organise everything into categories—accounts can go here, order forms here, invoices by the letter opener and payroll there."

Ursula pointed to various spots on the desk, already feeling far more confident than when she walked in. Decorating for Yule was one thing, but this was far better—something she could sink her teeth into.

Elias jumped up and started moving around the documents. She felt like a general about to wage war. Yes, this was far better than choosing baubles for a holiday.

She plucked the ledger from the top of the pile and examined its pages, grabbing one of the battered fountain pens, too.

"Aha! Here's your issue. Look—that's been counted twice, and you haven't carried this over."

She scratched the pen over the page in small, emphatic strokes as if her hand was trying to keep up with her brain.

"Oh, the decimal point is in the wrong place for this—unless this is the actual price. In which case, you have been had, my friend."

"Done!" Elias looked at her proudly, the papers now piled

in teetering towers behind him across the whole expanse of the desk.

Ursula looked at the haphazard mountain of work ahead of them and swallowed. "I think we should have food sent up here. We're in for a long night."

# 20

## Ursula

Elias was reading beside her on the rickety rattan settee in the garden room, wrapped up against the cold. He had moved from one of the armchairs to the settee a few days ago. There was no presumption in the choice; it felt natural. Obvious, even.

They had started to while away the hours after dinner here as night fell earlier and earlier. Candles were haphazardly arranged on available surfaces and lent a golden glow to the place, softening its run-down edges.

His hand rested on her foot that was buried under the blanket wrapped around her like it was something they had always done.

Ursula felt a shiver run through her. The familiarity sparked something warm and gooey in her chest. She hadn't been touched like this since Nurse Selwyn had left. It was a touch of comfort—of someone who knows you. A touch of *home*.

She sank further into the sofa and repressed an audible sigh. Ursula had forgotten how much she needed this.

"I have something to show you," said Elias abruptly, making

her jump.

Ursula looked at him; his nose was shiny and red in the chilly room. He looked as bright-eyed and fresh-faced as a child running back home after conquering a particularly large hill while sledging.

Part of her wanted to be annoyed at him for breaking the serene atmosphere, but he looked so excited, she couldn't help but get swept up by his enthusiasm.

"Alright," she said, "let's go."

Ursula set her book on the occasional table beside her and shrugged off her blanket, neatly folding it in a square before dropping it over the back of the settee. Her skirt was creased underneath, and she gave it a few solid swipes in the hope of smoothing the wrinkles. Perhaps a dishevelled appearance came with the territory up north, with so much heating and layers to contend with.

When she looked up, something was dangling for Elias's hand.

"It's a surprise, so you'll need to put this on." The silk scarf fluttered as he moved towards her.

"Why?"

"I don't want you peeking." His voice was laced with mirth.

"Fine." Ursula took the scarf from him. She tried to give an exaggerated, peevish sigh but her traitorous lips kept smiling. This was a new, more playful side of Elias, and she basked in it.

"Happy?" she asked, hands on hips.

"Very." Elais's voice was filled with mirth, but there was an undercurrent of something else—something wilder. The warm, gooey feeling from earlier dropped into the pit of Ursula's stomach.

He moved behind her, placing his hands on her shoulders and briefly running his thumb along the back of her neck. Her skin tingled at the touch, and she would have leaned into it were it not for the guiding nudge he gave her. She put a faltering step forward and stopped, scared of the step into the unknown.

"Do you trust me?" he said in a half-whisper.

"Yes." Ursula gave a shaky laugh, trying to master her own body. All she could think about was the same words on her wedding night.

After a beat, Elias simply said, "I'll guide you."

And she surrendered to him.

He had deftly moved to her side and held her hand in his. The hand at her waist was a beacon guiding her.

Ursula could feel his touch like a brand. They had just about navigated their way out of the room when Ursula lost her bearings. Her thoughts started to wander as she was ushered by Elias, instructing her when to take steps or turn. His hands never left her, and she wondered what would happen if she asked him to keep them there.

She had been plagued by thoughts of him—the kiss in the bookshop, their night at the manor, the warm pulse of his hand when he touched her. She wanted all of it and more.

They ascended the stairs, and Elias dropped her hand as he steered her to the handrail. She wanted to snatch his back, to feel his warmth on her skin. Instead, she followed Elias's instructions, his hand at her back still showing her the way.

Soon they were walking down a corridor, but Ursula had no idea what floor they were on; the stairs seemed to go on forever. She tried counting them but gave up halfway through.

They finally stopped, and Ursula felt her mind snap back to

the present.

"We're here," Elias whispered. His fingers skimmed over her as he untied the scarf.

Ursula gasped—they were at the door to his parent's room.

She had never been inside this room. It had been briefly pointed out on her tour with Elias, but she had never wanted to press about it. He could talk about it when he was good and ready.

"Why are we here?" Ursula asked, awe and confusion in her voice.

"I thought…" Elias cleared his throat, nerves etched on his face. "I thought you might like to move here. That this could be our room."

He turned the handle, and the door swung open. They walked inside to see a room richly decorated in navy. The furniture was in the same unpretentious style of her bedroom, although on a grander scale.

"I don't know what to say." Ursula blushed.

Elias reddened in response and dropped his gaze. Ursula stared at the fan of dark lashes across his cheeks. She wanted to kiss them. Kiss *him*.

"I understand if this is a little presumptuous and it will take weeks to complete, but I know that couples share a room in your mother's homeland. I thought you could decorate here, to make it your own. If you like…"

The space between them felt like a gulf. She rushed towards him and flung her arms around his neck.

"It's a wonderful idea, Elias. Thank you so much!"

His blush deepened as their eyes locked. His gaze skittered down her face and landed on her lips. She thought he was going to kiss her, but instead he dropped his forehead to hers.

"I'm glad you like it. I was worried you'd think it was morbid."

She thought about lying next to him every night in their bed. She pictured sharing a space with him, folding their lives around each other. It thrilled her.

Ursula inched closer so her nose could skim his cheek. She could feel his breath against her skin, feel the way it stuttered when she moved close. "Look at me, Elias. I like this very much."

His eyes met hers, and he had such a genuine look of admiration that the gooey feeling went positively molten as it coursed through her body, landing in her chest and warming her like kindling.

Ursula lifted her chin up and licked her lips, an invitation on them. She could see Elias's eyes drift to them again, and she hoped he would bridge the gap this time. Instead, he stilled, not pulling away but also not advancing.

"Elias, thank you. Truly."

This broke his reverie, and he finally moved. His hands cinched around her waist, anchoring her to him.

Ursula slowly worked her way to his mouth, leaving feathery kisses in her wake.

She could hear his heart crash against her own as she spread her palms on his chest, her hands looped around his lapels in a vain attempt to pull him closer.

His kiss was timid when their lips first met. Ursula wrapped her hands around his neck, tangling them in his hair. She wanted to feel all of him, to explore.

He pulled her close then too, his hands crawling up her back and pulling her against him. Ursula let out a soft moan then, feeling his tongue against hers. His kisses were languid and assured as they trailed down her jawline and made her want to melt into him.

Elias swept his hands up and down her back, holding her against him. The feeling of their bodies touching, his hands trailing along her spine, made Ursula's skin feel too tight, like her skeleton wanted to jump out of her body. She was flushed and dizzy, like a simmering pot about to boil over.

She pulled at his hair, wanting something to grab onto, and Elias gave a guttural moan that sent heat pooling in her abdomen. Ursula squeezed her thighs together, needing something to ease the pressure building there. She tugged at his jacket, pushing it down his shoulders. It fell to the floor with a dull thud. Her hands raked over the cotton-covered muscles, tracing a line from his shoulders down his spine and enjoying being able to see and feel him.

A loud crash echoed from the hall.

"Sorry!" Maisie's voice floated through the closed door. "I was just refilling the coat scuttles and had a spillage. Er, probably best to give it a few minutes before you leave the room, but I'll have it cleaned up in a jiff. No need to worry!"

They both froze, eyes wide and still tangled in each other's embrace. Elias rested his forehead against her shoulder and shook with silent laughter.

"That's fine, Maisie. We were just taking some measurements of the master bedroom," Ursula called out, voice only wobbling slightly with mirth.

He looked up at her with a raised brow, his face still flushed and lips rosy. Ursula wanted to kiss the smirk off his face.

"You are a terrible liar," Elias whispered. His hand skimmed down her body and gave her backside a playful squeeze.

Ursula had to bite her lip to stop the laughter erupting out of her.

They heard Maisie noisily complete her task and walk away with deliberate footsteps.

When Ursula looked at Elias again, his eyes had lost some of their jocular shine. Instead, he stared at her earnestly.

"I hope you know how much this means to me."

His right hand was now at the base of her spine, fingers working in slow circles. Ursula didn't know if he meant the room, the kiss, or both. It felt like something very delicate was hanging between them, and she didn't want to disturb it. She needn't have worried, as Elias silenced her thoughts with another kiss, and she felt the world slip away again.

# 21


# Elias


Ursula sat opposite Elias at his vast desk in the study, various ledgers and parchments open between them. There was an air of quiet contentment as they both worked.

Elias sat back and watched Ursula. He liked to sneak a peek at her like this—face stern with concentration, completely in her own world.

She had delved deeper into quarry business than he ever had, blooming with every bit of new information, every penny saved, every win—no matter how minuscule. It was becoming very apparent that he was superfluous, but it was rather freeing and enjoyable watching Ursula in her element. It was so different from the clawing inadequacy he had to fight every day. He hoped she would rub off on him, guide him through the maze of paperwork that he stumbled through.

Elias pinched the bridge of his nose. They had retired here after dinner but he was losing focus as the night wore on.

Ursula didn't seem to be losing any vigour towards her task as she lifted paper after paper, frantically making notes.

Occasionally, she mouthed along or spoke out loud, a habit Elias was finding increasingly endearing. He tried focusing on the page he was reading but found himself listening instead for any tiny sound Ursula made.

"We must visit the quarry once the weather picks up. I think it would be good to meet the men and get a handle on things. Also, there are a couple of issues I'd like to go over with the foreman. His rotas leave much to be desired, and the machinery is ancient. I can't believe you still use manual winches—there's been steam power for years."

"The foreman does the best he can. My father laid off a quarter of the staff when I was away." Elias froze where he was, unable to look Ursula in the eye. He treaded lightly around the subject, not wanting to condemn his father, who had made some drastic changes to staffing in the years he was in the east. "I've hired some new staff, but they're all a bit wet behind the ears."

He could hear Ursula straighten the papers in front of her. "All the more reason to go."

Elias was sure she'd have the telltale frown on her face if he looked. He snuck a side glance and couldn't help the broad smile that bloomed on his face.

Ursula was staring at her page, her brow furrowed in deep concentration. A tiny laugh escaped him, and she looked up from the papers.

Ursula patted her cheeks. "What? Do I have something on my face?"

He shook his head. "No, I'm just grateful to have a wonderful spouse with such business acumen."

A delicate blush dusted her cheeks, but she glowed from his words. He vowed to himself then that he would praise her more often.

Ursula slumped back in her chair and let out a sigh. "There are still a few more things I need to arrange, and I haven't even started on our bedroom. My eyes are so tired, the pages are swimming."

He liked it when Ursula referred to the bedroom as theirs. He was sure his parents would have approved.

"Perhaps we should retire then?"

His voice was huskier than he intended, and while tiredness still nipped at him, it was followed by that hot, fluttery feeling in his stomach that he got around Ursula. It was happening more and more, like when the light caught her dark hair and made it shine like polished wood. Or when she gave him the serious look she was now, straight-backed and ready to take on the world.

"Yes, that's a good idea," she replied, her voice unsteady. Her eyes were dark, and he wanted to reach across the desk, loop his hand around her neck, and pull her to him.

He could have sworn she wanted it, too.

She let out another sigh, but this time her breath shook as she stood.

"I'll just tidy these." She hurriedly arranged them back into piles, but Elias stopped her hand with his own.

"I'll do it. You go to bed."

Elias didn't move his hand away, but neither did she. He swept his thumb along the back of her hand, and Ursula inhaled another shaky breath. Her gaze flicked between their joined hands and his eyes. Those amber eyes bore into him, and Elias felt pinned to the spot; he couldn't have moved if he wanted to.

She swept her tongue along her bottom lip in the same way

she had in the dark hallway all those weeks ago, and Elias felt his blood crashing in his ears. All it would take was one tiny movement to get Ursula in his arms.

Ursula cleared her throat. "Yes, bed. Bed is a good idea."

She slowly pulled her hand away from his and left the room.

Elias sat in his study a while longer, staring into space.

Normally he could work for hours in Ursula's presence, time passing by in congenial silence. But something flared in Ursula's eyes tonight, and he didn't dare wish it was the same thoughts that had been building in his head for weeks.

He could have sworn he saw yearning in her gaze this evening, and it fanned the want that already coursed through him. He wanted to haul her against him, to finish what had started in their prospective bedroom, but he didn't want to push. They had not been intimate since their wedding night, and a part of him still worried that her intention was only to ratify their marriage. It was silly, he supposed, but how could a woman as beautiful and accomplished as Ursula truly be satisfied with an arranged marriage to some highland yokel like him? How could he possibly know if she felt the same pounding need in his presence as he did in hers?

Elias rubbed his temples, trying to spin out time and figure out his next move.

His eyes caught the book on the desk, and he seized it up on his way out of the room.

Elias gave a light tap on the door and felt the breath leave his body when he heard her stir within.

"Yes?" she said in a light voice.

Elias shuffled in, barely able to see in the shadows from the banked fire.

Ursula lit the lamp next to her, the light scarcely lifting the inkiness of the room. He watched as she studied him, pulling the covers closer as she shifted into a sitting position.

Elias felt his resolve falter as he looked at Ursula in bed. She had on another one of those ridiculous, gauzy nightdresses. His mouth went dry, and he doubted he'd ever be able to see chiffon again without losing his mind.

He cleared his throat. "I, uh, hope I didn't wake you. I meant to give you this earlier, but it slipped my mind..."

He moved towards her, his limbs slow and lumbering as he placed the book on her nightstand. He was very aware that all his blood had fled his brain and left him dizzy and awestruck.

She gestured to a deserted book on her bed like it had been cast away in a fit of frustration. "Oh, thank you. I couldn't sleep and was sick of this one, anyway."

Elias nodded and advanced towards the door.

"Stay." Her voice was a small, timid thing.

Elias froze, his back still to her. He knew if he turned around it would change everything. Their eyes met through the gloom.

"Stay," she said again, with more force this time.

"Do you mean it?"

"Yes. Stay. I'd like it if you stayed."

# 22

# Ursula

Elias turned to her, his eyes blazing.

They were dark—almost stormy—and even though his gaze never left hers, she could feel their burning path over her skin. The pale light in the room danced over his sculpted features, and Ursula's fingers itched to run her hands over them and through the messy waves of his hair. To tug him down onto her and watch him as he came undone.

"There's nothing I would like more. I have thought about nothing else since our wedding night."

Goosebumps erupted on her skin as Ursula repressed a shiver.

He was very still, like one of those jungle cats that she had read about in her stories, ready to pounce.

She realised then that he was letting her lead here, letting her determine what would happen. She swallowed, unable to contain the blush on her cheeks. Her face burned as she whispered, "I'd like you to take off your clothes."

Elias gave a small nod and started to take off his jacket. It slid off his broad shoulders, crumpling in a heap at his feet.

He pulled at his shirt next, tugging the cotton free from his trousers with his right hand and slowly undoing the buttons, each one exposing more of his milky skin. Ursula sucked in a breath when she saw the uneven flesh of the jagged scar that splayed across his chest.

He stopped then, and Ursula kicked herself. She hadn't paid attention the night they were together, too caught up with how he felt underneath her fingers, against her skin, to notice. She wanted to run over to him, to show him how much he affected her and how she would never miss something like this again.

His hands paused at the hem of his shirt as he stood there, a dark, detached look on his face.

"Don't. I think you're magnificent." She looked him square in the eye. "All of you."

Elias cast one more predatory stare and shucked off the rest of his clothing, leaving them castaway in a heap on the floor as he stood before her in just his drawers.

His eyes burned into her, but there was a teasing lightness there now.

Ursula knew a challenge when she saw one.

In return, she clasped the hem of her nightdress and pulled it over her head. Elias's eyes roamed over her body, and she saw his briefs tighten in response.

A slow smile crept on her face as she arched her back ever so slightly. It was wonderful feeling this powerful. Exhilarating being this free.

She would never have done this before: told a man what to do, decided how *she* wanted things to progress. But there was something about the way they worked together—worked *towards* something. It was liberating the way Elias trusted her, believed what she had to say. It was like he saw her, and she wanted to show him every part of her in return.

Ursula signalled for him to join her with an inclination of her head. Elias did as she asked and slowly came to kneel beside her.

"I want you to touch yourself."

Her voice was direct, and Elias huffed out a throaty groan in response. His hand drifted to the waistband of his briefs, pushing the material down to his muscled legs.

Ursula bit her bottom lip at the sight of him. It was so different seeing him rather than relying on touch alone. His body was sturdier than she realised, and the candlelight flickered over the rise and fall of his lean muscles.

Elias gripped his hardened cock, deliberately toying with himself in painfully slow tugs.

Ursula slammed her legs together, suddenly aware of her own arousal. Elias gave a throaty chuckle at her squirming. She quite liked this little game they were playing.

Her gaze drifted up and down Elias's body, and she hungrily followed his hands as they moved faster and faster. The tip glistened as he swallowed another moan.

She looked at his face then, serious and contorted with pleasure, and their eyes locked for a moment. His breaths started to stutter, pupils so dilated that his dark sapphire eyes looked black. Ursula held his gaze as she pushed the bedclothes away, letting them rumple at her feet.

She ran a hand along her collar bone and over her breast. Elias groaned again, pained and insistent. Ursula let her hand drift lower, slowly wending its way down her torso and over her stomach. Elias's eyes followed as hers had done, and she moved her legs wider.

He froze then, his breathing so shallow it was as if he had run up the hill from town. She let him look, feeling positively drunk on his attention. No one had ever looked at her like this, with such fixed concentration.

Her hand moved lower still, parting the coarse hair and running her fingers through her wetness.

Elias let out a guttural groan. "Can I touch you?"

Ursula nodded, a shiver running through as he moved between her thighs and nudged them wider. She'd never been so exposed before.

Elias tentatively spread his hand above her knee, trailing up the length of her thigh, over the curve of her stomach, before following the same path as her hand along the line of dark hair that led below. His hand moved across her skin in lingering, electrifying strokes, like he wanted to remember every arch and curve.

She bucked and trembled under his touch, trying to ease some of the pressure building within.

She had never been touched like this—so reverently, with such care.

His hand was still working himself, the strokes now matching the unhurried caresses across her body. She closed her eyes, giving over to the overwhelming feelings flowing through her.

Elias hesitantly moved his hand lower through the damp curls between her thighs. Ursula gasped, the meagre touch heightening the ache within. He lingered there, his unhurried fingers moving up and down across her clit.

Ursula sucked in a shaky breath. It was all too much, and yet, somehow, not enough. Her hips bucked against his hand as she chased her own release.

She felt so flushed, she was sure she'd melt the candle at her bedside.

Elias shifted, his fingers pushing inside as his thumb made maddening circles against her clit. Ursula threw her head back, eyes closed as her body tightened around his fingers. The mounting pressure in her stole all the breath from her body.

He kissed her then.

A light, searching peck on her lips as she held him against her, her hands driving into his shoulders.

Elias kissed her deeply, his tongue pressing against her own.

His hand moved then, a furious plunge to a deep beckoning coil. Ursula sobbed into his mouth. She knew her body flooded his hand, that her climax was tantalisingly close. That she would soon be completely undone.

Ursula clutched his shoulders as Elias kissed the corner of her mouth, tracing a line of butterfly-soft pecks across her cheek.

"Take what you need," he breathed in her ear, and she rode his hand as she cried out, her release erupting through her.

Elias grunted against her, his face buried in her hair and breath hot against her neck. His body snapped like a bow as he came.

They lay there in silence as their chests heaved, eyes closed. Ursula turned to him, the movement disturbing the equilibrium between them.

Elias opened his eyes to meet hers and lifted his fingers to his mouth, sucking her wetness off them. Ursula's eyes widened at the sight, her breathing still laboured.

"I can only assume from your response that your lover never did that," he said somewhat smugly, a shy smile on his face.

"No, never," Ursula replied truthfully, thinking back to those times with Hugh. They had been tender and caring, but there had been no heat between them—not like this.

"Have you ever tasted yourself?" he asked, his voice barely louder than a whisper.

Ursula shook her head, still trying to return to earth after everything that had happened.

Elias leaned forward, brushing a demure kiss on her lips. The taste was sweet and musky. She started at first, then melted into his embrace. Their kiss deepened as they fell back against the bed, limbs entwined.

They fell asleep in the same position, a hair's breadth between them.

Ursula woke with an arm casually thrown over her waist, the weight a comforting but unusual presence. She stretched out her legs, her toes skimming her bed partner's shins.

Her mind was slowly waking up, and she started to recall the previous night's activities. She moved away, clamouring to find something to cover herself with, but the hand around her grasped her side before she could bolt from the bed. Ursula opened her eyes to Elias's face, his hair rumpled and eyes half-closed.

She pulled the bedclothes that were bunched around them up to her chin, her reserve careening back in the light of day. It was still early, but the faint light in the room was enough to keep her previous abandon under wraps.

"Good morning," he said, his voice croaky and sleep-soaked.

"Morning," murmured Ursula in reply.

Elias ran an unhurried hand up and down her back, and Ursula could feel the familiar heat building in her core. "How did you sleep?"

His hand settled at her waist again, his eyes more focused now. "Well, and you?"

"Good, thank you."

She looked at his face, so close that she could see the flecks in his eyes like slivers of a gemstone. There was a scar in his left eyebrow, a tiny nick that she'd never noticed before. Her fingers traced the pale, raised skin, and Elias froze.

Ursula snatched back her hand, worried she had stepped over an invisible boundary.

"I never noticed this before," she said apologetically.

"It's one of my most important battle wounds," he said with a mock serious face.

Ursula blushed, feeling flustered by his candour. "You don't need to tell me about it. I'm just being nosy."

"This scar was the result of a fight over a wooden horse with Susannah when we were children. Needless to say, she won the battle, but I won the war."

Ursula softened, glad she hadn't brought up some deep, dark piece of his past by accident.

"So, you were always a good strategist, huh?"

"Oh yes, the best." Elias laughed, his head tilting towards her as his nose softly brushed against hers. "I immediately ran to my parents, blood dripping down my face. Even though I had started it, Susannah had two weeks with no dessert. The perfect crime."

"So, it turns out I married a criminal mastermind?"

"I'm afraid you did, dearest. Now, you better be careful because I might corrupt you." Elias pulled her closer to him, his hand skimming her lower back.

Ursula couldn't help but melt at the endearment.

"We'll see about that." She tipped her head up to catch his

lips in a kiss.

Elias pulled her closer as the kiss deepened, his hand travelling down to cup her backside.

Ursula let go of the bedclothes, her mounting warmth dispelling any lingering bashfulness. Her hands stroked the nape of his neck, angling Elias closer to her. The feel of his chest brushing her own elicited a moan.

Elias trailed kisses along her jawline and down her neck, each touch getting more frenzied as he moved down her body. Ursula arched into the movement, his hair caressing her as he shifted on the bed and moved between her legs.

Ursula stroked the skin across Elias's shoulders, enjoying the feel of his taut muscles. She parted her legs, thoughts of the morning spent in bed stretched ahead of them.

A loud knock wrapped at the door and they both froze. Maisie's voice trilled "Morning!" as the handle started to move.

"No! Don't come in!" Ursula shouted. "I'm, uh…not feeling well!"

"I've got tea, that should sort you out." The handle swooped down.

"No, Maisie, really. Don't come in! My stomach is upset, and it's not pretty!"

"Oh, right then. I'll leave you be. I've popped the tea down, so you can get it at your leisure," Maisie replied quickly, her footsteps retreating from the door.

Elias burst out laughing, his head still resting on Ursula's stomach. He planted one last kiss before sitting up.

"Stop it, you. I didn't know what else to say!" Ursula's face twisted with embarrassment.

"We're married, Ursula. The staff will expect to see us

together eventually." Elias grinned.

"Not like this!" She motioned to their nakedness. "Anyway, I like it being just us at the moment," she added coyly, unable to match his gaze.

"The staff always know more than they get credit for. Haven't you noticed people have been very heavy-footed around here of late?"

Ursula looked at him quizzically; she'd never really thought about it.

A mischievous smirk played on his face. "I'm not suggesting we invite her in, just that we be a bit more open with our affections to one another. They say three's a crowd, but I could always be persuaded otherwise."

That comment earned him an exasperated gasp and a cuff with her pillow. Elias caught the missile mid-air.

"Oh, so you want to play rough?" His eyes burned into her, a wicked gleam in them.

Ursula shrieked as he dove for her, catching her mouth with his.

# 23

# Ursula

Maisie stacked a pile of books in front of her, noting down the titles and authors without her usual sparkle. They had been like this for most of the morning—hunkered down in the stacks. The bare trees outside offered no respite from the low sun as it blazed through the bevelled glass windows, blinding them when caught at the wrong angle. Ursula looked at the young woman opposite her, shoulders hunched as she scribbled across a sheet of paper. A creeping anxiety took root in her stomach. Something was wrong—Maisie was never this quiet.

She sat back on her heels and looked around the room, wishing there were less books to organise. Instead, she was met by the same sight as before—piles of books heaped at odd angles on every available surface. Ursula had hoped this project would help pass the time between downpours and teeth-chattering gales as autumn unceremoniously gave way to winter, but she had bitten off more than she could chew.

The library at Cairden was a cavernous space that always looked a little neglected despite the staff's efforts to maintain it. Dust littered every shelf, and the books were musty and mottled with damp. Ursula could have sworn they left a grimy film on her skin.

Maisie sighed, and her shoulders seemed to droop even more. Her face was a bland, expressionless mask that made Ursula's gut twist into even tighter knots.

Something was definitely wrong.

"Maisie—" Ursula's words were cut short by a coughing fit.

"Here now, Mrs. Clearbould. Let me fetch you some water!" Maisie dashed over to the battered pewter ewer across the room and poured Ursula a generous glass. "Take small sips." The young woman's voice took on a commanding bent as she gave Ursula the water.

Ursula could feel her face burn brightly as she tried to calm the tickle in her throat, one cooling sip at a time. Dust motes danced around them as if to taunt her.

"Thank you, Maisie," she managed to croak out after her glass was practically empty. She pushed a stray lock from her forehead and downed the remaining water in a giant gulp. "I'm just going to come out and ask—is something the matter? You've not been yourself lately."

Ursula tried not to squirm at the sound of her own crackly, weak voice. She could just imagine Elias's face when she explained to him how she'd lost it thanks to some pesky dust.

Maisie startled, her eyes downcast as she fiddled with the pile of books in front of her. "No, it's nothing. Just have a lot on my mind."

"Maisie, you know you can confide in me if you need anything."

The girl relented under Ursula's sympathetic gaze. "I meant to tell you when I first found out, but there never seemed to be the right time…"

"And…" Ursula coaxed, hoping for the best.

"I've been asked to apprentice Miss Malvina, the town apothecary. She heard about my family's abilities and proposed I come in for a trial. We're elementals, you see, and Miss Malvina thought it would suit with the herbs and things she uses. I haven't given her a reply yet, though!" Maisie stammered.

The freezing nerves she had felt started to thaw into a bittersweet ache right in the middle of her chest. Maisie was such a constant to her in Allerbrock, it was painful to imagine her days starting without their chats and little rituals. Ursula tried to school herself to not be selfish, but all she wanted to do was keep her close.

"Maisie, that's wonderful!" Ursula exclaimed, plastering a smile on her face. "I think you would be a perfect fit."

It was true—Maisie had such exuberant charm, customers would surely end up buying all and sundry in the shop.

A riotous blush spread across the girl's cheeks at the compliment. "Thank you, Mrs. Clearbould. I was ever so worried about telling you. Mrs. Clough already knows, but she said I had to tell you myself. I'll work my full notice and all…"

Ursula smiled again, the ache in her chest lessening as Maisie talked, her face becoming as bright and animated as usual. They both stood and brushed the accumulated grime from their skirts as best they could. Ursula took the moment to pull Maisie into a swift hug.

"Please don't take my happiness as a slight. I will miss you very much, but it seems your talents are wasted here." Maisie reddened more at Ursula's words. "And excuse my ignorance, but what is an elemental?"

"I suppose Mr. Clearbould hasn't told you much about the magics up here, what with him losing his, but my family can move the elements. Shape them to what we like."

Ursula tried to keep her face neutral, but she felt like the ground had opened beneath her and she was tumbling down fast.

Magic was a part of this land. She'd known that before her journey north, but Ursula had to admit to herself that she'd never delved too deep with it. It was easier to keep it at arm's length, like at her wedding or in the tearoom. Magic made her uneasy, something she'd never admitted to herself until it was in her family. In her marriage.

Sweat prickled across her skin as she tried to keep a seal on the riot of emotions whirling in her. The bittersweet ache now curdled like ice burning through her. She felt like an idiot for not knowing that Elias had kept this from her, for moving so far from home to a place and never learning about it. Hot tears stung at her eyes. Part of her had always hoped that the marriage would never take place. Now it had, Ursula realised she liked Elias so much more than she ever could have dreamed. But he was holding back, even after she gave him the tools to ruin her.

She trusted Elias, but he didn't trust her.

"Oh, so that's what you showed me in the tearoom?" Ursula asked. She tried to keep her voice steady as her thoughts were consumed by one thing—Elias was magical.

"I have an affinity with air and a touch of earth from my mother's side." Maisie puffed up with pride as she waved her hand in front of them, causing a stack of books to fly from the ground onto the shelf.

Ursula jumped as they clattered onto the bookcase in a neat row. She had always thought of magic as parlour tricks or nonsense prophecies from crones, not like the tangible force in front of her.

"How does it work?"

The desperate, incessant edge in her voice made her want to bolt from the room, but she just stood there, rooted to the spot with the silly grin glued to her face.

Maisie didn't seem to notice and gave a casual shrug. "I honestly don't know. I was just born this way. My mam's mam had it, hers too. It goes as far back as we can count in our family. The men have some magic, but it's strongest in the women. The way my sister goes on, you'd think she was the only one who could control fire. Mam says if she was made of chocolate, she'd eat herself."

The young woman smiled shyly, plucking at the fabric of her sleeve. Ursula felt foolish for pressing Maisie for information when there was only one person she should be questioning.

She swallowed, the tumult inside her wanting to break out. "So, how long do we have you until?"

Maisie looked sheepish again, avoiding her gaze. "I haven't confirmed yet, but Malvina hoped I'd be able to start with her at the beginning of next month."

January was only a few weeks away, and they had Yule in between. The thought of spending all those days away in someone else's house, with someone else's friends and family, suddenly sounded awful. A dizzy tiredness hung over Ursula, and all she wanted now was to lie down. She looked at the mess all around them, the monotony of rearranging the library would give her something to focus on—and an excuse to miss dinner. The cold shard in her chest twisted, and Ursula knew she was kidding herself. She was well practised in pushing her own feelings aside for others.

"Why not go and talk to Malvina now, then take the rest of the day off? It's better than working here with me and some dusty books." She patted Maisie's arm, hoping some of her zest might rub off on her.

Maisie returned the gesture with a bright smile. "Only if you're sure?"

"Of course! Now hurry along, I'm sure you have plenty to discuss with her." Ursula shooed Maisie to the door, keen to be alone.

She toppled against the door when she could no longer hear Maisie's footsteps. It was like all the air had been wrung out of her, her chest heaved as she tried to catch a steady breath. Her mind was oddly blank, like every emotion had piled in and cancelled each other out.

Eyes squeezed shut she counted to a hundred, then again, then again. Until she could no longer hear her pulse thrum in her ear, and her brain quietened enough to string a thought together.

Ursula stood slowly and straightened her skirts, a nervous gesture she had never been able to shake, then plastered a serene look on her face and left the library.

She had no idea how to deal with this information, but she was the lady of this house now and determined to act like it.

# 24

# Ursula

The lead up to Yule was a flurry of activity—meeting vendors, bartering with tradesmen, and decorating the house.

Cairden was now decked out in rich greenery, the surfaces wreathed in foliage and festooned with berries and dried fruit. It was like they were living in part of the wood, something that would have sent an icy chill down her spine a few weeks ago but now just felt right. Ursula liked the staircase best; she loved how the heady smell from pine filled the air every time she passed by it. It made her feel so connected to the house, so proud that she had made it look more alive.

Ursula was glad of the reprieve. Her days were swept away from under her, and her evenings spent reviewing the quarry's paperwork.

She would occasionally catch Elias looking at her askance, his eyes narrow and mouth in a half-frown. He knew something was wrong, but there was never a time to ask.

The hurt had settled in her like a bruise she could only feel if touched. Ursula avoided prodding at her feelings, filling each moment of the day until she could fall into a dull, exhausted sleep.

Their packing was nearly complete, and the house buzzed with excitement as people prepared for the celebrations. Maisie was in her room putting the final touches to her outfits for the Lockstons.

"Oh, Maisie, you don't have to do that. Go home and rest before the revelry begins. I can see to this." Ursula batted Maisie's hand away from her luggage, which was almost fit to burst. She wondered if the girl had snuck in another couple of outfits.

"I had to make sure everything was just so. I won't settle until I know it's all there," Maisie said, refolding a dress that definitely wasn't in there this morning. "Are you sure you don't want me to come? You know I'm the only one who can do your hair."

It was true. Ursula's attempts paled in comparison to Maisie's careful braiding, but it would be too selfish to drag her along. Ursula wasn't even sure what the celebrations would be like. From her talks with Elias, she had the impression they would be riotous and busy with the staff at Lockston Hall relegated to shadows during the merrymaking.

"Absolutely not. Enjoy this time with your family. I couldn't live with myself if you missed out on some fun, the winter here is punishing enough. Plus, Susannah's there if I need anything. There's a goose and some wine in the kitchen to take home with you as a small token of our appreciation."

"Thank you, and Happy Yule," Maisie replied, smiling and looking as if she wanted to move in for a hug.

"Happy Yule, Maisie." Ursula smiled in return and gave the girl a quick squeeze. "Now, hurry on home before I change my mind."

The feeling of the carriage rattling along the icy roads took Ursula's mind back to the night of the wedding. So much and nothing had changed since that night. The tiny ember of hope she nurtured flickered.

Elias sat opposite her with a stack of documents in his hands. His eyes were trained on the window as he looked out at the landscape that passed in a frosty blur beyond. Everything sparkled under the icy blanket, but Ursula couldn't tear her eyes away from Elias.

They had both shared such vulnerable parts of themselves; why would he choose to hide such a monumental truth from her?

Elias had given her a glimpse of a real partnership, but he had hidden something so huge from her that she felt once more like a chess piece being moved around to fit someone else's whims.

The bruising hurt throbbed, and she twisted her hands in lap.

"Susannah was right. You are always working—and in a carriage, of all places. How can you keep the words straight on these bumpy roads?" Ursula laughed, but it was a strained, needling sound.

Elias sighed. "It's true. I'm a boring, old workhorse." He winked at her and put the papers down. "You've seen that state of things. I keep thinking that a brilliant idea will strike if I just try hard enough, but I will try and put work aside for the next few days. The emphasis is on *try*."

Their eyes locked, and Ursula could feel a genuine smile bloom on her face—the first one she had felt since the day in the library. "I'd like to see that. I'll wager you won't last the day."

"You're on! What are your terms?" Elias retorted, his eyes crinkling. It was such a lovely sight to see him so warm and relaxed, she could almost forget what she knew and go back to how they were just a few weeks before. It was nice to give over to this, to push everything else from her mind.

Ursula thought for a minute, tapping her finger against her lip with a theatrical flourish. "Let me think… let me think…" She quirked a smile at him. "Elaria's sticky buns every day for a year."

"A year! Come on, how about a month?"

"Six!" Ursula volleyed back.

Elias stuck his hand out, his face awash with mischievous glee. "Fine, six it is. You have yourself a deal!"

"I'm not shaking on anything until I know your terms. When you have as many siblings as me, you know to wait to find out what people want first!"

"You are a hard taskmaster, indeed." Elias chuckled. "If I win, you wear your hair down every day. No more of those fancy braids. I like your hair more…natural."

He sucked his breath between his teeth. "Hair like yours, all long and inky and sleek, deserves to be free. Flowing around you like some untamed goddess."

Ursula was a bit taken aback by his comment. The men she had grown up with never paid attention to intricacies of women's appearance, and she assumed Elias didn't either.

"Is that all? Oh, you have yourself a deal!" She gave his hand an enthusiastic shake. "I'm sure Maisie's hands will be glad of the rest while she works her notice."

Elias titled his head, his eyes tender and sympathetic. "How long until she finishes?"

Ursula's heart skipped a beat and she rubbed at her chest. She could feel hope bloom again, easing the hurt that lingered. If she focused on these moments, maybe she could force it away for good.

"Two weeks. She'll be gone by mid-January."

"We'll need to find a replacement." His voice was soft, encouraging.

"I know, I know. Can Mrs. Clough do it?"

Elias reached across the carriage and gave her hand a squeeze. His face was so open, his voice so soothing it made Ursula tear up.

"Don't worry, she'll just be down the road."

His thumb swept across the back of her hand, and Ursula's heart skipped again.

She cleared her throat, trying to ease the lump that had formed as Elias gave her one last reassuring squeeze, then sat back.

"So, what should I expect when we get to Susannah's?" Ursula asked. "Mrs. Clough gave little away. You know she's a bastion of discretion."

"Oh, Mrs. Clough worships the ground Susannah walks on. She'd never disclose anything, no matter how innocuous," Elias teased lovingly. "The house is very grand—one could even say palatial. It makes Cairden look like a shed. Cal has money coming out of every orifice. His parents gave him the glittering pile when he got married. I told you Susannah was born under a lucky sign."

"Oh, they don't give off that impression." She thought back to seeing them before the wedding with minimal staff in toe. They had been such hands-on parents, not at all like how she expected the people of their station to be with their children.

"Cal has always been humble, sometimes to his detriment. He lets people—including my most wonderful sister—walk all over him. There will be some characters at this shindig. It's why I've avoided them the last few years."

The carriage rattled and rocked over a particularly icy patch and Ursula held onto the seat for dear life.

"How did Cal and Susannah get together? You mentioned they were young, but was it some romantic tale of secret trysts and love letters?"

"Probably!" Elias laughed. "You've met Susannah. She'd love something melodramatic like that. There was a bit of a row, but nothing monumental. Our parents had been close, and we all basically grew up together. It can be difficult living up here, and it means you make fast friendships. I don't think any of them ever dreamed of Cal and Susannah ending up together, though."

A sombre look touched his eyes. "I think Cal's family wanted more for him, not some tradesman's daughter." Ursula let out a tiny gasp. It was like hearing one of her biggest fears come to life. She could imagine the sniffy women of Currington saying the same thing about her—that she needed to marry a northerner to edge closer to a society match. Elias stared into her eyes, his chin dipped. "Their words, not mine…They dote on the children, though, and Susannah just goes along acting oblivious and being herself."

"Will his parents be there?" Ursula asked, again hoping Elias was exaggerating for effect. She knew first hand how people like that looked on those who had to work to live, even if they reaped the benefits.

"Most likely. You'll spot Cal's mother, Estelle, a mile off. She usually has a face like thunder."

Ursula barked out a nervous laugh. "I know exactly the type."

Elias smiled at her, and they fell into a comfortable silence as the world passed them by.

He cleared his throat and fidgeted in his seat. "I wanted to thank you for decorating Cairden. It's not looked so festive in years."

"It was my pleasure," she said, surprised that it was true. She had enjoyed putting her stamp on it.

The coach took an abrupt turn, and Ursula braced against her seat, worried they had a wheel caught in the snow.

"Ah, now we make our ascent up to Lockston Hall. Prepare to be dazzled," Elias joked, his eyebrows lifting.

Dazzled, she was indeed.

Ursula couldn't believe her eyes; it was the biggest house she had ever seen. It was so large she wasn't sure it could even be called a house. A palace, maybe.

It even made the manor they had stayed in after the wedding look plain.

The house sat at the top of a hill, bright in shining white marble. The main building stretched out with expansive wings swooping round in a curve on either side.

Large topiary lined the driveway up the hill and fanned out in front of the facade, their shapes alternating between tapered triangles and round baubles.

There were friezes adorning the exterior depicting each of the Gods, gold accents picking out the key scenes and throwing light on the glittering snow.

Ursula could feel her mouth gape, unable to stop herself.

"Told you," Elias muttered before springing from the carriage, the door held open by a footman.

He held out a hand for Ursula, who managed to school her features into a semblance of normality despite her eyes remaining wide with wonder. Elias placed his hand on her lower back, a movement she was coming to hold dear. The heat that emanated from him always grounded her, fought off any chill that crept up her spine and settled in her chest. She leaned into his touch, and he felt like a shield from the overwhelming grandeur.

The pair walked up the steps that led to the house, and Ursula knew Elias set a slow pace so she could take everything in. Susannah and Calvin stood at the top, wrapped in furs and welcoming guests as they arrived. They were surrounded by footmen, and Ursula blanched at the sheer number of staff they had on hand.

"Your home is spectacular. It looks like an ice palace from a fable," she said to the couple earnestly.

Susannah pulled her in for a tight hug. "You have Cal's great-grandfather to thank for that. Subtilty was not his forte."

Cal blushed a little, the opulence obviously not something he basked in.

"Don't mind me. I like to run my mouth off." Susannah gave her hand a reassuring squeeze. "It's lovely to see you both. You look like two turtle doves all nestled in from the cold." She dropped Ursula's hand and turned her attention to her brother. "You'll be in the blue room. I'm not wasting Darrow's time showing you to your sleeping quarters. You know your way around well enough."

Susannah looped her arm around Cal's waist and looked up to him. Her husband leaned down, settling a kiss on her brow. "We are playing sentry here for the foreseeable future."

They said their goodbyes to the hosts and made their way

into the house. Elias placed his hand on Ursula's back again, and she was grateful for his steadiness.

The inside of the house was just as impressive as the facade. They were met with a glinting fairyland come to life with garlands, swags of fabrics, and candles on every surface. The smell of pine, cinnamon, and cloves drifted through the house, making the colossal space cosier.

She followed Elias as he wove down the corridor, trying to make a mental note of when he turned various corners and wishing she had a trail of breadcrumbs like in the children's tale.

Finally, they arrived at a wide white door, and Ursula felt as if they had tracked back halfway to Cairden with all the walking.

"This house is not for the faint-hearted. Literally," Elias said, his breathing heavy.

He pushed the door with a sweep of his arms, and it flew open to reveal a huge, beautifully decorated room.

Ursula timidly stepped inside, glad for somewhere to rest. She tugged off her cloak as she perched on the large, canopied bed.

"Why is everything here so arduous to get to? I feel like we've been walking for miles. Honestly, if it's not at the top of a hill or at the bottom of a valley, it's along the world's longest maze of corridors."

Elias sat next to her, and part of her wanted to reclaim the distance that had fallen away on their journey over. She couldn't bring herself to move, liking the way the heat of his thigh felt against her own.

Elias shuffled in his seat, his fingers clumsy as he worked the buttons on his coat. "We northerners are gluttons for punishment."

Ursula batted his hands away and undid the tiny top button that seemed to be giving him the most trouble.

"Thank you," Elias said. His thigh pressed close to her, and Ursula could feel his scalding heat along her leg. It was like she'd been lit on fire, and all she wanted to do was melt.

Ursula shifted away, needing some space between them. Her eyes drifted around the room, properly taking in her surroundings for the first time. It had the same tranquil charm as her room in Cairden, and she knew it must have been decorated by Susannah.

"I don't think I'll ever get used to these hardy northern ways." Ursula smiled at him, but Elias had lost the glint in his eye. She felt that bruising hurt throb again.

Ursula jumped to her feet, determined to focus on the tasks at hand and not be distracted by her thoughts. "Time to unpack, I think."

# 25

# Elias

He watched Ursula bustle around the room. A lazy smile tugged at his lips; he didn't realise how much he'd missed just being in her presence. Recently, they had been like ships passing in the night. Ursula was always off doing something—arranging the workmen for the bedroom renovation, organising the decorations around Cairden, or working with him in his study. Although, he had to admit that those hours spent sifting through the various facets of the quarry's administration with Ursula were the high points in his day.

He still had the niggling doubt she was avoiding him, and her throwaway comment about never fitting in in Allerbrock made the doubt take root. It was like a metallic taste of panic at the back of his throat. Elias swallowed, hoping to suffocate it.

Ursula handed him a neatly folded stack of clothes. A crisply ironed dress shirt sat on top, which was no doubt Rodger's doing. The poor valet was forever bemoaning Elias's lack of finesse and how difficult it was to get out the various creases and spills his clothes acquired.

"I'll let you put away your own unmentionables." Ursula's voice had taken on the vacant tone he'd grown used to over the last couple of weeks.

He nodded, not sure what to say to bring back the convivial atmosphere of their coach ride over. He'd loved it when she leaned in close to him upon arrival, the way she fit right against him. The wild spice of her scent sent him giddy.

They sorted through their belongings, working quietly beside one another. He let himself imagine that this was their bedroom, that it was just a normal day in their lives together. His daydream was interrupted by a knock at the door.

One of Susannah's many servants stood holding a thick folder in his hands, which he silently deposited with a nod. Ursula turned at the noise, interest piqued.

"Have I already won the bet?"

The flash in her eyes was such a welcome sight, it was like water in the desert. He pushed his doubts further down. This would be fine. *They* would be fine.

"Alas, no. I am still very much winning that." He handed her the richly decorated dossier. "Looks as though Susannah has a full itinerary laid out for us."

He saw another flash of excitement pass over her features as she opened it, and the acidic worry ebbed even further.

Ursula's eyes widened as she scanned the paper. Susannah always liked to throw extravagant bashes with countless activities. It was enough to make anyone's head spin.

Ursula looked at the clock on the wall, gasped, and looked at the paper again.

"How are we supposed to get ready in that time? Dinner is in two hours! There are so many guests it will take half the time to get a tub filled, and I need to wash the travel off me before—"

Elias beamed, knowing full well he had an ace up his sleeve. He beckoned Ursula to follow him into the adjacent bathroom.

"Watch this." He guided her to the bath, a smirk playing at his lips as he pumped a small lever at the far end. There was a pause before the water descended through a shining metal pipe and began filling the tub.

Ursula looked at him with a quizzical expression. "I hope you don't expect me to have a cold bath. I'm not one of your soldiers."

Elias gave her a gentle tug on the arm as she turned to leave. "Please, just touch the water. You'll see."

Her expression softened at his touch and smiling face, but her brows were still twisted in consternation. She moved to the water and carefully placed her fingertips in the spray. Her eyebrows shot up in surprise as she whirled around to look at Elias, sending a shower of droplets in her wake.

"It's warm," she said, disbelieving.

"I told you there's magic in the north. Although, this may also have to do with the Lockston's incredible wealth as much as anything. The house was built over a hot spring, and Cal's grandfather worked with a band of engineers to draw the water up from the source. It's the only house I know of that has hot water running through it. Apparently, the secret died with him, but I'm still working on trying to get it out of Cal."

A delicate blush dusted the apple of her cheeks, but Ursula straightened her back and looked him in the eye, mischief twinkling in them.

"Well, this will make things a lot easier."

Elias dropped his hand. He was sure he should leave, but he

found himself wanting to stay with every fibre of his being.

"I'll leave you to get ready."

The door clicked behind him, his mind whirling with thoughts of Ursula bathing.

He stomped along the winding garden path that had been cleared of snow; the cool, crisp air a welcome contrast to the heat within him.

The gardens at Lockston Hall were vast, and the intricate web of trails through them offered Elias the respite he needed. His near-constant thoughts of her were bad enough, but hearing the water lap against Ursula's skin in the next room would have driven him insane.

Still, he knew he needed to head back soon to get himself ready for an evening with Susannah's insufferable friends. He only hoped this air of unease between him and his wife would resolve itself before the festivities began. Whatever was causing Ursula's apprehension, mindlessly wandering was doing him no good.

Elias took a deep breath, the bracing air grounding him as he turned back to tread the familiar path to the house.

# 26

# Ursula

Ursula sat in the small sitting room that was attached to their assigned bedroom. She drafted a letter home, extolling the virtues of the unbelievable house she was staying in. She'd never seen grandeur on this scale and knew it would titillate her sisters to hear about it.

She suddenly heard the door to the bathroom open and stilled, the buzz of Elias getting ready filling her ears. She turned her attention back to the letter, meticulously describing the house's furnishings in a bid to stop her mind from wandering down dark paths.

Elias coughed to get her attention, but she was already well aware of his presence in the room. Ursula wasn't sure when she had gotten used to the cadence of his walk, but she bet she could spot his tread in a crowd.

She shifted in her chair and looked at him. He looked devastatingly handsome in an understated way, dressed in a richly decorated jacket of slate grey that brought out the silver hues in his blue eyes. His hair was still a bit damp from his bath and curled around his ears endearingly. He still had a dishevelled air about him with the top buttons on his jacket undone and a kerchief casually knotted around his neck.

"Ready?" he asked as he held out an arm for her.

"As I'll ever be," Ursula replied, moving towards him.

They left the security of their rooms and travelled down the labyrinth of corridors towards the rest of the party.

The dining room was as decked out as the rest of the house. The table glittered with candles and frosted glass decorations, a long garland of greenery snaking down the middle.

Ursula tried to count, but there were easily thirty seats. She took a deep breath in; this was a dinner unlike any she had attended before. She clung to Elias, overcome by the proceedings. He placed a reassuring hand over hers, and she melted into his touch. The warmth radiating from him was almost enough to chase away the cold detachment that had hung between them all afternoon.

Almost.

Susannah swept over, her eyes gleaming like the candles that lined every surface as she gave them both a kiss on the cheek. She had changed into a dress of embroidered ivory, her red hair in stark contrast to the pale gown. She looked every part an ice princess.

"Don't you both look wonderful!" Her voice was in the sing-song pitch of the perfect host. She looked at Elias, her face stern, eyebrows pinched together. "I've sat you next to Tilda and Jacob, so no need to fret. I know what you think of my nearest and dearest."

His grip on her hand loosened as some tension drained from him.

"You're somewhere near the middle." Susannah gestured to the table before getting pulled away by another guest.

They shuffled to their positions. Elias pulled out Ursula's chair, and his hand skirted over her shoulder as she sat.

Ursula fiddled with the stem of her wine glass. "You're awfully quiet tonight."

"I find these large affairs often rob me of speech. I've never had an aptitude for small talk with strangers," Elias replied.

Ursula looked around the table at the other guests laughing and chatting comfortably. "I'm normally fine, but I've never attended a gathering of this magnitude."

"This is nothing. The big dinner tomorrow night is at least double this size."

Ursula swallowed and sipped from her water glass.

"Look, there's the *real* lady of the house." Elias nodded to the top of the table where a pinched-faced woman dripping in diamonds sat. Her salt and pepper hair had been pulled back into an elegant chignon and topped with a twinkling tiara.

"So that's Cal's mother? You would never know from meeting him," Ursula whispered back.

Estelle Lockston looked around the room with such a bored expression, it was as if she was watching paint dry rather than at a dinner party. A thickset, ruddy man was beside her, chatting animatedly to the person next to him and turning to shake hands with everyone who passed by.

"I think we have Cal's father to thank for that."

"Thank the heavens." Ursula held up her glass and Elias clinked his against it.

"You wore your hair down," Elias said quietly.

"You won the bet," Ursula replied, catching his eye. "Unless you slunk off to do work without me noticing"

"I won fair and square." He gave her a small cocky grin that made her stomach flip. "I went for a run, just needed to stretch my legs."

"Elias! Fancy seeing you here!" A ruddy-cheeked woman plonked down next to him. "Can't believe we've got you back in polite society."

"Polite? You? Now, that's an understatement," replied the man next to Ursula.

"Jacob." He held out his hand for Ursula to shake. "And that's Tilda. Don't let the braying voice fool you—she's as bad as she sounds."

The woman burst into peals of huffing laughter, and Ursula could only surmise her blush was due to a tipple before dinner.

"Lovely to meet you," Tilda half-shouted as she leaned past Elias to kiss Ursula's cheek.

"So, this is your beautiful southern wife? Susannah has been singing her praises, and I can see why. What a delicious creature."

"Hush, Tilds, you'll scare the girl," Jacob countered. "Ignore her, she's half-drunk and looking for trouble."

"It's not that I look for trouble. Trouble finds me," Tilda barked back, a wicked grin on her face.

"A likely story," Elias replied, a knowing look in his eye.

Ursula missed what Tilda said in response as the wine was poured, but she saw her place a hand on Elias's arm and wanted to swat it away. It was petty and jealous, but Ursula could never imagine being so exuberantly herself as Tilda. Was this what Elias was used to? Confident women who said and did what they liked? The bruised hurt from earlier flared, and she took a large gulp of wine to push any thoughts from her mind.

If hedonism was the name of the game, she might as well play.

Jacob was a pleasant enough dinner companion, regaling stories that bordered on the sordid, name-dropping people she didn't know but sounded important and clueing her in to the gossip surrounding various guests round the table.

Ursula laughed at the appropriate times and let herself be ferried along in the conversation. Her wine glass was always miraculously full no matter how much she drank, and soon enough she felt the heady buzz of the alcohol in her veins.

The food was a lavish treat, with one course after another of luscious delights. Meat so pink and rare it melted in the mouth, fish that flaked off the bone, perfectly risen soufflés and candied fancies fashioned from sugar.

She ate and drank her fill, aware that she'd hardly spoken to Elias all evening. She had felt his eyes on her and their arms occasionally brushed against the table, but every time she went to speak to him Jacob started another story, and the moment passed.

Eventually the meal was over, and Ursula felt the world tilt. She was well and truly soused, wobbling like a foal as she stood.

"Joining us for cards?" Jacob asked Elias. "It's been a while since I rinsed out your coin."

Elias eyed Ursula. "Not tonight, Jacob. My ego and purse will be there for the taking another time."

He slung a protective arm around Ursula, and she fought the urge to fall back into it, to let him look after her.

"Ah, I see you have other things to attend to," Jacob leered, his colour high from the wine.

Ursula's spine straightened at the insinuation. "Don't decline on my account," she said stiffly, enunciating her words to halt any tell-tale slurring. "It's alright, go if you want to."

Even as the words left her lips, a traitorous part of her hoped he wouldn't. Hoped that he would choose to stay with her.

"We've had a long day and need rest," Elias said with finality, guiding her from the room.

Ursula wasn't sure what she expected his response to be, but her heart fluttered at his decision.

Ursula was just about ready to collapse as they reached their rooms. Her head was spinning now as Elias gently sat her down on the bed.

"Are you alright?" He kneeled in front of her, his eyes clouded with worry.

"Why?" Ursula asked.

"You hardly spoke to me all night, you're drunk as a skunk, and I have a horrible feeling you've been avoiding me."

Ursula dropped her gaze, unable to face him. Her head swam at the movement, and she swayed in her seat. Elias placed his hands on her legs, anchoring her to the spot.

"Ursula, please. Are you alright?"

She let out a long breath, feeling like such a coward. Why couldn't she be more like her mother—strong, courageous, outspoken—instead of hiding her feelings away?

Elias's thumb moved in a slow, comforting sweep against her leg, and she finally looked at him.

"Why didn't you tell me about your magic?"

Her voice was a low whisper, but Elias looked so surprised she might as well have shouted in his face.

"How do you know?"

He froze, about to pull away when Ursula grabbed his arm. He flinched at her touch but relented, sitting back on his heels.

"Maisie told me by accident. Why didn't you?"

"It's gone. I didn't see the point." His voice was small now.

Ursula slipped from the bed onto the floor in front of him.

"But it's a part of you, and you didn't tell me. Even after I told you…" She couldn't finish her sentence, her eyes drifting back to the floor.

"Ursula, look at me." She did, her head still swimming as she met his stormy gaze. "I didn't tell you because it's in my past. Because we've only known each other a short while and…I didn't tell you for the same reason you didn't ask."

She could feel her brow crease at his words.

"But I'm your wife."

He gave her a half-smile. "I'm your husband. A husband you didn't choose. A husband you have a lifetime to learn, if you want."

Ursula edged forward.

"I do. I want to know everything. Your favourite colour, how you take your tea, the name of your childhood pets. I want to know it all."

He leaned forward and kissed her then, a light, searching kiss that promised many more.

"Don't worry, we'll get to know these things in time." He gave her a peck on the tip of her nose. "Now, let's get you to bed."

Ursula cocked her eyebrow at him.

"Not like that, you've got a mighty hangover coming, and you need as much sleep as you can get."

He helped her stand, his sure, steady hands turning her around before undoing the fastenings at the side of her dress. The fabric fell in a heap at her feet, and she pulled back the covers to climb into bed still wearing her shift.

Elias walked around to the other side of the bed and shrugged out of his clothes, leaving them where they fell. He pulled her close against him, his voice soft against her ear.

"Blue, with just a splash of milk, and Colin. Our dog's name was Colin."

Elias turned and blew out the candle, and Ursula couldn't help feeling that something monumental had shifted as she drifted off to sleep.

# 27

# Ursula

Ursula cracked an eye open and immediately wished she hadn't. Her head was a soupy mess, and all she wanted was to sleep the day away. She rolled over and buried her head into the pillows, instantly regretting it as her stomach lurched into throat. The bedding was cool against her clammy skin, and she was thankful Elias wouldn't see her in such a mess—or rather more of a mess than last night. Even though she'd woken up alone, the bruising ache she'd been carrying the last few weeks eased as her head pounded.

Ursula lay there until her organs went back to their respective homes and winced as she let out a long breath. Her breath tasted like a dead badger—or what she imagined it would taste like—and she bet it smelled just as bad.

She sat up, inching towards the edge of the bed at a snail's pace. Remnants of last night swirled in her head—the flare of anger, Colin the dog, and white-hot jealousy as Tilda pawed at Elias. Ursula scrubbed at her face like she could wipe everything clean and start fresh. Her stomach did another tumble in response, and her whole body shook.

Ursula struggled to her feet, donned her robe, and padded to the bathroom. She splashed water on her face, scrubbing at the skin. Her skin was pallid and blotchy, and her eyes had a hazy, unfocused edge to them. Ursula splashed her face again, hoping to regain some colour from the bracing water.

She went into the dressing room and carelessly pulled on whatever clothes she grabbed first for the day.

Elias popped his head round the door of the little sitting room and gave her an uncertain smile.

"Morning. Just about."

"Morning," she replied in a distracted voice, her drink-soaked brain picking over what he said. "…just about? What time is it?"

"Gone eleven, I think, " Elias replied. His smile deepened as he walked over to her and pulled her into an embrace. Ursula sunk into his arms and rested head against the crook of his neck.

"Wait! It's after eleven?" Ursula replied, jerkily looking from the clock on the mantel to Elias and back. A wave of nausea washed over her as her head swam, and she let out an irked huff. His arms around her were the only things keeping her upright. "Why didn't you wake me?!"

An impertinent look flashed on his face, and Ursula knew whatever had changed between them last night was for the better.

"Oh, I tried. You were dead to the world. I might have thought you slipped into a coma if it weren't for the snoring."

The blush came then, and Ursula understood why her mouth felt like sawdust.

"Did you sleep alright?" His voice was level, but there was

concern in his sapphire eyes. They glistened like an oasis in a desert, and she wanted to drink them in.

"I'm going on a ride with Cal and the boys. They have some new Yule ponies and want to test them out. Would you like to join?" Elias asked.

Ursula considered for a moment. The open air sounded appealing, even if the thought of bobbing around on horseback sent her stomach into somersaults.

"That sounds wonderful." She gave him a quick peck on the cheek and picked up the itinerary from the occasional table it had been discarded on. "I don't see horse riding on the list."

"Ah, it's off the menu. I'm getting some special uncle treatment." Elias smiled. "Are you ready to go now?"

"No time like the present."

The promise of fresh air sounded more appealing by the second. Her haphazard clothes would have to do. She didn't have enough brain power to plan a different outfit before heading out.

"Fantastic." He paused and leaned down to sweep a kiss across her cheek.

Elias stayed close, his face inches from her own. His hand was now wrapped around her elbow, and she moved closer to drop a light kiss to his lips. It was little more than a peck, but he flushed all the same. The clock chimed quarter past, and Elias dropped his hand.

"We should get to the stables. The boys will be chomping at the bit as much as the ponies."

She picked up her cloak and shawl, praying that there would be tea to steady her shaking body.

The labyrinthine corridors of Lockston Hall were finally starting to make sense as they wound through them to the main foyer. People were milling around as music poured out of one of the many drawing rooms. Heat pumped out of the huge roaring fireplaces dotted around Lockston Hall. The combination of the sheer number of bodies around and the residual alcohol in her blood made a queer, sticky sensation erupt across Ursula's skin.

"Down here and to the right. You'll see the paddock once we round the corner."

A frigid wind blasted them as they hurried down the wide marble steps, and Ursula felt like she was taking the first proper breaths of the day. Her clammy skin cooled as they followed the snaking path around the house.

The gardens around Lockston Hall seemed to go on for miles, but they soon heard the laughter and babbling of the boys growing closer.

Cal was in the paddock with the children, each of them perched on a small piebald pony led around by a stable hand. Felix bobbed along on his mount, safely held in his father's hands, and Nicolas was exclaiming to all and sundry that his pony kept trying to bite the poor lad leading it around. The stable hand couldn't have been older than fifteen, and Ursula chuckled as the boy dodged the pony's ferocious teeth.

"This is exactly what I needed," she said to no one in particular.

"Me too," Elias replied, grasping her hand and pulling her along the path.

They propped themselves against the paddock's fence and watched as the ponies made another circuit. Elias rubbed his hand up and down Ursula's back, and the steady rhythm quelled the queasiness bubbling inside of her.

Cal manoeuvred Felix's pony over to them by the fence,

and the toddler held out his chubby arms to his uncle. Elias scooped him up and set the boy on the fence to watch the antics of his older brother. Nicolas urged his pony to go faster and faster, and the stable hand leading him was quickly doused in sweat.

"Uncle El, ride with me!" The boy's tiny voice was full of command as he shouted across the paddock.

Cal offered Elias the reins. "Go on, you can take Felix's. The ponies are sturdy enough."

Elias looked at Ursula and motioned for her to take his spot behind Felix. She shifted over, worried what the toddler would do once his beloved uncle left, but Felix just sat there. His chubby baby bulk was soft in Ursula's hands. Elias gave her a warm smile and clambered over the fence with practised grace before hopping onto the pony's back. Ursula and Cal burst into peals of laughter as his legs dangled down the pony's sides, nearly touching the ground.

"You've got an excellent seat, El!" Cal bellowed.

Elias threw his head back haughtily and trotted over to Nicolas's side, which sent the group into even more fits of laughter. Even Felix joined in the mirth, clapping happily.

Warmth spread through Ursula as she watched Elias with his nephews. It was like he came alive around them, and it sparked something in her. The feeling was heightened when Felix leaned into her and looped a chubby arm over her shoulder.

They stood like this for a long time, watching Elias and Nicolas ride around the paddock, dodging the young boy's pony as he tried to chomp everyone in sight. Felix bent in towards Ursula, his downy hair soft against her cheek as let out a huge yawn. Cal called the riders over, and before long they were all toddling back to the house. Nicolas talked excitedly about his exhilarating ride to the group while Ursula cradled the sleeping toddler. Despite being a recent addition to the group, she felt every bit a part of the family as they all headed inside.

Ursula let out a contented sigh once they got back to the room. She was windswept and pretty sure she stank of horse, but felt a thousand times better than she had when she woke up that morning.

Elias slumped down onto the bed, his face bright from the biting cold.

"Elias—" she began, but faltered. He looked up at her, his sparkling eyes tinged with worry. "I don't think I can face dinner tonight. There were just so many people last time, and all the wine…"

The spectacle of last night's dinner loomed large in her mind. It was childish but she didn't want to fight for his attention, to have her words drowned out by louder voices. She wanted to keep Elias to herself tonight and extend their day together as long as possible.

His eyebrows darted up in surprise, but his face shifted into a roguish grin. He jumped up from the bed and grabbed Ursula's hand, tugging her along behind him again.

"Follow me," he said over his shoulder, his eyes full of mischief.

They dashed down a winding, stony staircase that was either abandoned or for servants. The cacophony of pots and pans clattering in the kitchen and the servants' voices shouting as they readied for dinner grew louder as they went.

"Mr. Clearbould! What on earth are you doing here?!"

someone bellowed as they turned a corner. Ursula crashed into Elias's back as her feet skidded on the well-trod flooring.

"Don't mind us, Mrs. Patterson. We will be out from under your feet in no time. I'm just showing my new wife the hidden wonders of Lockston Hall."

An oven glove narrowly missed Elias's head as he ducked down the corridor away from the kitchen.

"That best be all you're showing.  We're preparing food here!" the cook shouted after them.

Ursula giggled as they wove past staff rushing to feed the throngs of dinner guests upstairs but was relieved when they rounded another corridor into a semblance of quiet.

"You didn't tell me we were going to disturb the kitchens!" Ursula said with a chuckle.

"Don't worry, we'll be out of their hair in a moment."

He shot her another wicked smile as he led them to a storeroom.  He shoved an assortment of cheese, crackers, dried fruit, and chutney at Ursula before dashing off into another cupboard.

She looked down at the growing pile in her hands and cocked an eyebrow at her companion. "What are you getting?"

"Wine, of course!" Elias popped out of the door, two bottles in hand.  "Do you think it's enough?"  He jiggled the wine, earning a huge smile from Ursula.

"Beyond the shadow of a doubt," she said.

It was like being a child again, exploring the world with fun as the objective.  Her heart hammered an exuberant tattoo in her chest as she trailed after Elias, feeling giddy as they wandered down corridors and through doorways. They were on a scavenger hunt together, and she was struck by the fact that he was the sole person she wanted by her side for every adventure from here on out.

"Here we are!" Elias proclaimed at the top of a set of spiral stairs.

He pushed open a creaky door to reveal a musty, abandoned room. The sparse furniture was covered in sheets, and the faded yellow wallpaper curled down from the ceiling in the corners.

Elias set the wine down and patted his pockets. A metal matchbox rattled in his hand, and he lit a couple of half-used tapers on the tarnished candelabra.

Dust plumed in the air as they moved through the room, and she supposed it was kind of romantic in a ghostly sort of way.

"This used to be a parlour or a sunroom or something," Elias said, taking his jacket off for them to sit on. "I think it has faded glamour."

Ursula followed suit and placed the food on the ground.

She sat next to Elias and looked at him out of the corner of her eye. The soft light of the candles picked out the red in his hair and gave his skin a golden glow.

Yes, this room was romantic. Creepy and romantic, Ursula decided.

A popping noise caught Ursula's attention. Elias had laid the food out, using the cheese wrapping as a platter. He was working the cork out of the wine with a penknife, and his fingers left prints on the dusty surface.

"I just realised we have no plates or cutlery or glasses. We'll have to share." He took a swig out of the bottle and held it out to Ursula. She reached for it but stopped her hand before making contact.

"Unless you want your own bottle?" Elias shrugged.

"I don't think that's wise," Ursula said, putting the bottle to her lips and taking a long draught. The wine was rich, smooth, and deliciously decadent. A tiny moan escaped her, and she heard Elias give a small chuckle as he tackled the block of cheese with his penknife.

Ursula watched him as he cut jagged, bite-size chunks from the cheese, and her stomach gurgled in response. She just realised she hadn't eaten all day.

"Hungry?" Elias looked at her, and all thoughts of food vanished from her mind.

Yes, she was ravenous—in more ways than he knew.

She feared she had conveyed her thoughts aloud to him as the penknife slipped in his hand, catching his thumb. Elias hissed and sucked on the wound.

"Let me see?"

"It's nothing," he mumbled, the digit still in his mouth.

Ursula gave a stern look, and Elias held out his hand. There was a shallow cut along the pad of his thumb, but it had already stopped bleeding. Ursula looked for something to wrap it in, but Elias waved her away.

"It's fine, honestly."

Ursula gave him a withering look and shook her head. "Alright, but let's swap. It'll stop both of us getting into mischief."

Elias accepted the bottle from her, drinking a couple of long gulps before setting it down.

Ursula sliced the rest of the cheese, popping a few stray chunks into her mouth as they fell away from the block. It was pleasingly sharp on her tongue. She sifted through a wax paper parcel that held thinly cut cured meat and arranged them in a neat fan on the flattened paper.

"It's good, isn't it?" Elias asked. "It's a local sheep's cheese. Tastes great on its own, but earth-shattering with something sweet."

Her mind snagged on the term 'earth-shattering', and her eyes snapped to Elias. He piled a cracker high with chutney and cheese and held it up to Ursula. She knew she should take it from his hand and daintily nibble on it. She knew she shouldn't look him in the eye as she leant forward to take a bite. She knew she shouldn't deliberately graze her teeth across his finger.

But she did it anyway.

Elias sucked in a breath as her teeth scraped against his skin, his hand still hanging in the air between them with half the cracker in his grasp.

Ursula was momentarily overtaken by the flavours in her mouth. He was right; the sticky chutney married perfectly with the tang of the cheese. It was simple food but surpassed anything they could have served upstairs.

Being here with Elias on this little adventure felt right, and it reminded her of all the times they had fleetingly carved time out for each other in the last few weeks. These small moments felt like they were building to something big, and it sent warmth radiating through her body. It was like sinking into a hot bath after a long day in the saddle, easing the aching parts of her.

She took the rest of the food from Elias, who caught her gaze for an instant before he bent down and retrieved the wine for a quick swig. Ursula thought she saw a smirk playing on his lips, but the flickering candles cast too many shadows for her to be sure.

Ursula followed his lead and fiddled with the food. "How

did you know about this place?"

Elias sat back against a shrouded settee, his head rolling back against the seat.

"Many years of exploring around with Cal. This is the Lockston's winter retreat, and we'd spend hours gallivanting while our parents were off doing whatever they did. These Yule parties are a long-going tradition, although Susannah has really upped the ante in recent years."

He took a swig from the bottle and passed it to Ursula.

She looked around the room again, happily chewing. The wallpaper was covered in elaborate designs with exotic animals and plants. Chimaeras sat next to monkeys, and dragons were framed by huge palm trees and orchids. There was a faint sheen that caught in the candlelight, showing where gilded threads had run through it even though most of them had been rusted by time.

Ursula could see a young Elias hiding out in here, running around like a rascal with the same impish look on his face as he'd given her earlier when she suggested they skip the formal dinner. She could imagine Nicolas following in his uncle's footsteps and doing the same thing. A soft smile bloomed on her face. He was her nephew now, too.

"It's charming, in its own way."

Elias gave a little chuckle and devoured another mouthful of food. "That's one way to put it. We always told ghost stories here, although I'm sure Susannah and Cal also used it for their rendezvous. The moon is especially striking from this vantage point."

Ursula looked out of the enormous window. Sure enough, the moon sat square in the middle, shining like it was a painting just for them.

She took a long drag of the wine, taking her time to bolster her courage. A question burned inside her that she needed to get out. Somehow, sitting here in a half-dark deserted room with only the moon as their witness gave her the resolve to jump. The last few weeks had shown how brave she could be.

"Can you tell me about your magic?"

The question hung in the air, and a tingling cold crept over her as he remained silent. She wished she could take it back, to not push. That was the way she had been raised, after all— to watch and wait. Yet some part of her thought this would be different. Elias was so warm and open and genuine, she thought he might finally be ready to trust her with this.

Ursula kicked herself for ruining the little world they had built here.

Elias let out an inscrutable sigh, and she wished she'd talked about the moon instead.

"I was a healer," he said after a few breaths.

Ursula leaned back on the sofa beside him, the coldness receding as her shoulder touched his and he leaned into her. She handed him the wine bottle, and he took a long sip before passing it back. They continued this back and forth, propped against the old furniture. It was easier to talk with their eyes fixed on the night sky.

"Have you always had it?"

"In a way, I suppose, but I only noticed it when I was ten. A friend fell from a tree, and I went to help him. Suddenly, his bent wrist straightened."

He blew out a long breath and held out his own arm out, as if picturing the broken bone snapping back into place before his eyes.

"I was terrified he was going to tell, terrified everyone would find out. As it was, he was more scared of his parents finding out we went apple scrumping without permission, and so we swore each other to secrecy. It was like that for a long time. I didn't do much with my magic. I should have trained to become a healer, should have worked for the Core, but I kept quiet until the call to war came."

Ursula nodded, another question bubbling up from the dark recesses of her mind. A question that she tried not to think about, one she never thought she'd ask.

"So why did you go, then?"

Elias paused again, and she braced for his reply. The icy tendrils closed around the hope that still flickered in her.

"Because I was scared and arrogant." He sighed deeply, the next words scarcely louder than a whisper. "And I didn't know what would be waiting for me."

Ursula couldn't look at him, but she could feel his eyes on her.

"My life was mapped out for me. I'd take over the quarry after my father, and I'd hate it. I knew I'd be terrible at it, and so far, I've been proven right." He gave a mirthless chuckle. "I thought adventure in the east would give me purpose, but all I got was a few itinerant years roving the desert and a blasted hand. It took coming back here and accepting my future to realise what I'd missed."

"And what was that?"

She knew she was angling for a compliment, pushing him to say what she hoped.

"Why, you, of course." He said it as if it was the most natural thing in the world.

"But you'd never met me," Ursula said, a small, satisfied smile on her face. She was sure she was glowing like the moon in the sky.

"And maybe if I had, I'd still be whole."

Elias held up his scarred hand again, and Ursula wrapped hers around it.

"You are whole."

"Not really." He looked down at their joined hands. "I don't have my magic."

Ursula looked at his face, the tightness around his mouth, the lines between his eyebrows. She couldn't fathom what it must be like to lose something so intrinsically part of yourself that you didn't even know where it came from. It must be like losing the ability to breathe, to laugh, to cry.

She gripped his hand a little tighter to let him know she was there, and hoped that this tiny movement would show that she always would be. "Where did it go?"

Elias let out another sigh. "I don't know. The army healers thought it was still here." He rubbed at his chest. "That I have some block and need a way to overcome it. It's all very vague and useless, really. They think what happened with my friend unlocked it in me. He was hurt and in danger, and my instinct was to help him. It was like I knew in my bones I could make a difference."

"You still can," Ursula said. And he had; he had made a difference to her, to her life.

"I like that you think so." He kissed her knuckles. She was surprised his words were so calm now and looked into his stormy blue eyes.

"Now, Ursula, tell me about you?"

28

Elias

"What would you like to know?"

Ursula's shoulder was flush against his own. His skin tingled where they touched, even through the fabric of his shirt. It was like every single one of his nerves was singing just for her.

The sparse candlelight danced across her bronze skin, making her look like a statute from a museum instead of a living woman. Not his wife.

The word took on a whole new meaning, and Elias had to remind himself to breathe. Through circumstances beyond his control, this woman in front of him had become his spouse. Hiding with her in here, away from the hustle and bustle of the party upstairs, felt like one of the best choices he had made in a life marred by bad ones. She fit into his life so perfectly, it was hard to believe it wasn't fate.

He wanted to soak her in, to stay here and bask in her glow like the candelabras that sputtered next to them.

"Everything."

A single word that held so much meaning. It was true—he

235

wanted to know everything about her, very part of the last few years he could have had. Everything he missed.

He watched her intently, noting the way she swallowed nervously but still held his gaze. "Tell me about him."

The words tumbled out of Elias's mouth before he could stop them, but he didn't regret saying them. That they had been burning in the back of his mind ever since their wedding night.

Ursula's gaze wavered, and she plucked at the fabric of her skirt. He wanted to scoop her up, to pull her to him and whisper to her that he wouldn't judge. He just wanted to know who he shared her heart with.

He wanted to be as important to her as the man who preceded him.

Instead, Elias placed his hand over hers. Her fingers were cool to the touch, and he wished he'd had the foresight to bring a blanket to the abandoned room.

Her eyes dropped down to their hands for a long minute, and Elias followed her gaze. His breath froze in his chest. He hoped he hadn't pushed her too far, that she wouldn't shut down like she had in those long weeks before their journey here.

Then, miraculously, Ursula turned her hand, inching her palm to touch his. Her skin was so soft, like silk pressing against his palm. Long fingers tangled with his as she drew their hands together. He wanted to share his warmth with her, the urge to pull her close nearly overtaking him.

"His name was Hugh." Ursula's voice was low and matter-of-fact. Like she was recounting a school lesson and not some deep, tortuous memory.

Elias swept his thumb across her knuckles. He liked the

way they fit together, her hand equal to his own.

"I met him when he moved to Currington after his wife passed." She looked at Elias now, the deep amber of her eyes dancing in the flickering light. "He was a widower and a father."

Ursula swallowed again, and her mouth trembled in the corners. Elias passed her the wine, and she took a perfunctory sip.

"He was at one of the local dances. It might have been Beltane or Litha—I can't remember, exactly. I just know it was a warm day, unseasonably so. The Assembly had erected ice sculptures at the dance. Big statues of the Gods with sickly, sparkling wine running down them." Elias chuckled at her teasing tone.

Her face warmed then, eyebrows quirked upwards. "It was quite the spectacle. Believe me." She took a bracing breath before she continued. "I had gone out for some air. That's one thing you get by the water—there's always a sea breeze, even when the sun feels like it will melt the skin from your bones.

He was there on the patio, looking out onto the sea. He was sipping a glass of the horrendous wine, grimacing with each taste. I suppose I laughed then, and he looked at me."

"Careful Ursula, this is all sounding too romantic. I might not be able to heed the rest," Elias quipped, his thumb still moving in languid strokes across her skin. It was true. It sounded like the beginning of a sweeping saga where the princess meets her true love, only to be thwarted by the forces around them.

"It does, doesn't it?" She gave a light laugh. "We got to talking then. He had returned to live with his parents so they could help with the children. He'd been in the capital for years, working his way up at the Chamberlain's office. I think he was quite proud of that. Anyway, he knew of my father, which is par for the course back home, and we talked a little more about inconsequential things.

"He called around the house the next day to see my father, but I bumped into him on his way out, and he walked me to town. I think he kissed me then, on the coastal path. And it kept happening—his visits, our walks—until he asked to marry me."

Elias stopped dead. He suddenly felt far away from his body, like he was watching this scene from above. He had expected a torrid affair, maybe some pretty words, but not a marriage proposal. Ursula squeezed her hand in his, and he drifted back into himself.

"I told him about our betrothal, about how I thought it could be easily broken. That it was a harebrained scheme made by two men looking for a way to join their families and their businesses, and that the Council could surely nullify it. And he seemed to take it in, to understand…but then the visits slowed."

Elias blinked slowly, fierce black worry gnawing at him as Ursula continued.

"He'd write the occasional letter saying he was tied up with business or family matters. I stopped looking for him, stopped waiting around to run errands when he came by. One day, my father told me he had gone back to the capital and had married some young heiress."

Part of him wanted to thrash Hugh for the hurt he'd caused Ursula, but a bigger, more puerile part of him wanted to hug the man for being so foolish as to cast a woman like her aside. He had made the mistake of nearly letting Ursula slip through his fingers without ever meeting her, but Hugh was a clod for having her and letting her go.

He vowed then that he would never make that mistake again. There would be no more secrets, nothing hidden between them.

"I realised then that he wasn't the man I thought he was. That he liked respectability more than he liked me. I was just a tool to him, a shortcut to get where he wanted to be in life. I wouldn't be here if he had been a better man, and now I couldn't be more grateful for it."

Her voice wavered at the last part, and euphoria swept through Elias like a king tide.

"I've always thought respectability was overrated." He ran his finger along her jaw and hooked his hand at the nape of her neck.

"Me too," Ursula replied as her mouth crashed into his.

The fierceness of her kiss stole Elias's breath, and it took him a beat to catch up with the moment. His hand gripped at her neck, anchoring her to him as Ursula clutched at the lapel of his jacket and him down onto her. Her skirts swamped them, and her hair fanned out on the rumpled jacket below.

Elias clung to her as his hand skated into the dark mane, fingers lacing around the long tresses. He wanted to devour her, to claim her, to prove that he would never choose another path again.

Ursula wrapped her long legs around him as she had done on their first night together. For the umpteenth time he wished he could see her, touch her, magic away the layers of fabric between them. She worked the buttons of his shirt until it hung open and loose from his body. He grabbed her wrist, pinning it to the floor.

"Not this time," Elias growled. The sound was gravelling and commanding.

This would not be slow and romantic. This would not be languorous touches and soft caresses. He ran his hand down her neck, past the swell of her breast, down to the hem of her ruffled skirts.

Ursula writhed beneath him, hips colliding against his own—wanting, *needing*. He pushed her skirts higher, fingers skimming the soft skin of her thighs as he hooked a digit around her briefs and tugged them down in one savage sweep. The silken garment circled her ankle. She hissed then, sucking the air between her teeth as the cool night air touched delicate skin.

His hand lifted from her wrist as Elias moved down her body like a man possessed.

"Stay there. Do not move."

He crouched between her thighs, pushing them wider and exposing her to him. She was wet and glistening, but not enough—he wanted her soaked through and wrung out.

Elias lined her thighs with feral kisses, biting as he went. Her bronzed skin darkened as he moved upward.

Ursula bucked against him then, and he held her hips firm. He was determined to show her how he felt, determined to blot out all thoughts and memories of anyone but him.

His mouth circled her clit, sucking at the tender flesh, and Ursula moaned in response. He couldn't see her face behind the mass of material, but he knew she had thrown her head back, her eyes screwed shut with pleasure. He pushed her legs wider still, spearing her wet cunt with his tongue. She tasted like ambrosia sent from the Gods, earthy and musky and a heady scent of all her own.

He swept his tongue over the length of her, her wetness in his mouth almost too much. He wanted to drown in her, to pull those sounds from her soul. Ursula's breathing stuttered, a quiet moan escaping her lips as he circled her clit again in urgent strokes.

His hands held her hips against him, so tightly he was sure they'd leave a mark. He sucked again, nibbling at the sensitive skin. Velvety hair brushed his cheek, and Elias groaned. He wanted to be in her, to take her roughly. But this was more important.

Her hips rolled against him.

"Elias…Elias…I'm going—" He pushed his tongue inside her again, the pad of his thumb working frantically at her clit as she exploded against him. He felt every quiver, every shake as her climax ripped through her.

He didn't stop—he had a point to prove. Elias moved back to her clit, his tongue caressing with soft, incessant flicks as his fingers lightly toyed with her drenched pussy. He could feel her draw to the edge again, ready to fall off the precipice once more. He pushed harder, his fingers driving a steady rhythm only matched by his tongue. She clawed at his hair, unable to stop the onslaught. He pushed harder still, wanting to shake the very foundations of her soul.

Ursula came again, a loud cry ripping from her throat as she crashed into an all-consuming orgasm.

He calmed then, letting her come back to earth with slow kisses along her thighs to soothe the marks he had made before.

Ursula's breath was deep and halting as he kissed her, the taste of her still on his tongue.

"I bet your widower never did that." Elias tried to keep the arrogance from his voice as he pulled Ursula flush against him.

"No. No he didn't," she whispered as she laid her head on his chest.

He ran his hands through her hair, down her back, and along her sides. He wanted to learn every part of her, every groove and divot, and add it to the catalogue of 'Ursula things' he kept in his brain. He liked to pore over it at night, to take these titbits out and look at them from every angle like a scholar studying a rare and precious piece of art.

She sighed into his shoulder. "Call me Ursi. All my family does."

Elias felt like he'd been kicked in the chest as all the air fled his lungs. He was her family now. They had been married as strangers, but now they were creeping towards something deeper. Something lasting. A smile burst on his lips, and he pulled her close to kiss the top of her head. He felt like he could burst, could float away. The woman in his arms was the only thing keeping him tethered to the ground.

"Only if you call me El."

She looked up at him, her amber eyes dancing in the candlelight. Elias knew he was in the place he was supposed to be. He inched his face forward, his mouth a whisper from hers.

"How about Eli?" Her voice was breathy against his lips.

"I like it. No one's called me that before."

He kissed her then. Hard and bruising.

Then the music above them swelled, the sound of chairs scraping the floor and the clamour of voices so loud it was deafening.

Ursula pulled back. "I suppose we should go."

"If we must," he sighed into her mahogany hair.

243

# 29

# Elias

Elias felt like a tempest as he tore through the room, flinging on his clothes in a blur. The bedroom walls pressed down on him, and he had to fight to keep his mind on the task at hand instead of letting them drift to earlier. If he thought too much of Ursula's silky bronze skin, he'd never leave.

"Ready?" he shouted.

He usually gave little consideration to his attire, but suddenly found himself tinkering with his cuffs and trying to straighten his necktie. Ultimately, he had to admit defeat, and his appearance was only marginally less haphazard than usual.

He joined Ursula, who was pacing in front of the mirror in the dressing room.

"I don't know what to do with myself. I've been at this for ages." She gestured with a long, thin brush in her hand. Elias stalked over to her, drawn in by her eyes that sparkled like there was a fire within. Her face was still awash with the glow of her climax. "I tried to sit down and do it, but I didn't want to crease my dress."

And what a dress it was.

It was red with a neckline that skimmed her collar bones and made of a lustrous material that gleamed in the light. It should have looked demure, but the silhouette followed the lines of her body in a way that made Elias's pulse quicken.

Ursula made a tiny, sharp inhale under his gaze and he couldn't stop himself from making a self-satisfied smirk in response.

"You look wonderful," he said simply, offering his arm as they left for the party.


They halted once they were just outside the ballroom, and the double doors were swung open for them by two flamboyantly dressed footmen. The party was in full swing when they arrived. The room was aglow with candles, and a gargantuan chandelier of fresh greenery hung in the centre above exuberantly dancing couples. Others milled about at the edges, talking, drinking, and flirting.

Elias felt compelled to close the distance between them, to keep her away from the appraising looks Ursula garnered when they entered.

He placed a hand on her lower back and nearly withdrew it, surprised to be touching skin rather than fabric. A sideways glance confirmed that her dress was, indeed, backless, a thin gold chain hanging between her shoulder blades. Elias groaned, and he doubted he could stand straight at this rate. Her hair had been swept over one shoulder, and he had to fight the urges to cover her up or possessively paw at her.

Ursula turned to him and smiled, tilting her head up. The rosy glow on her cheeks was so beguiling he wished they had never left their hideaway.

Instead, he found himself asking, "Would you like to dance?"

His hand never left her back as he guided her to the throng of dancers, and he was sure Ursula could feel the heat radiate off him. It moved in slow, unconscious circles as they pushed through the crowd.

The guests surged, and the pair suddenly found themselves chest to chest in the middle of the dance floor, the closeness stealing his breath.

Ursula kept her eyes low, and Elias placed his hand under her chin, his thumb skimming along her jawline. He wanted to speak to her, to whisper about how wonderful she looked—how wonderful she *smelled*—but the band started a lively waltz, and they were carried away by the sway of people.

It felt as though time had stopped as they spun around each other. Elias only half-heard as the music shifted from one song to the next, and he'd been so caught up in the moment he nearly missed the tap on his shoulder.

"Mind if I cut in?"

The voice was soft and familiar. Cal stood beside them, his face flushed and awkward.

"Susannah said I should dance and be a 'proper host', whatever that means. You don't mind, do you, Ursula?"

She smiled back at him, looking luminous in the wash of candlelight. "Of course. It would be my pleasure."

Despite the deep trust and admiration Elias felt for his brother-in-law, he felt at once like sending Cal away with a growl. His hand tightened on Ursula's waist, and she patted affectionately at his chest.

Her touch was like a balm, and he could feel the tension leave him inch by inch.

"Thanks, El," Cal said as he took Ursula's hand in his. "Watch out, Ursula. I have two left feet."

"Don't worry. I do, too."

"Didn't look like it there when you two were cutting a rug."

Ursula let out another sparkling laugh, and Elias wanted to snatch her back, manners be damned.

"Oh, that's all Elias." She beamed at him over Cal's arm.

Cal burst out laughing. "First I've heard of that."

"Enough of this! You two better start dancing or else it'll be a wrestling match, Cal."

"Ok, ok," he replied, and the pair spun away as Cal quietly counted the steps under his breath.

Elias felt sore and prickly as he walked over to a footman standing with a huge tray laden with drinks.

Susannah sauntered over a second later, having just deposited her last dance partner at the edge of the dancefloor. She looked smug and a little tipsy, her eyes unfocused and her pale skin pink in the heat of the room.

"It's wonderful having another woman in the family. It saves my toes a mashing and means I don't have to send any thank you cards to anyone else he mangles during a foxtrot." She turned to Elias. "No need to look quite so stormy. It's just Cal."

"I think I need some refreshment anyway," Elias grumbled.

"Uh-huh," Susannah said with a smirk on her face. She picked up another of the drinks from the tray. It was pink and sparkling, and it looked so sweet it set Elias's teeth on edge.

"Relax. It's a party, and she's your wife."

He just stood, watching Ursula move around the floor with Cal. Their movements were stilted, but they were in fits of laughter.

"Precisely my point."

He turned to Susannah, but she was already being pulled in the other direction by some friend who he's met countless times yet couldn't remember the name of.

He stood stiffly at the edge of the room, listening to a woman drone on about the party and how much fun she was having. He nodded when he thought he should, but his eyes kept drifting to the dance floor.

His neck craned as his gaze followed Ursula around the room. She was on the arm of a far too gallant youth, whose eyes roamed over Ursula's form like she was a succulent lamb and he, the wolf.

A hand on his arm pulled him back to the present. "As I was saying, the Hertidges's ball is something else. Last time they filled the ballroom with orchids from the east."

Elias nodded silently.

The woman beside him ran her hand up his arm and wrapped her fingers around his bicep. He flinched, trying to shake her off.

"There are lots of dark corners for dark deeds," his companion cooed.

Elias nodded again, barely registering the words. His eyes followed the flash of scarlet as it moved across the floor.

She tugged this time, licking her lips and arching an eyebrow when Elias finally turned to her.

"Excuse me, I have to find my wife."

The woman squeaked in shock, her mouth a perfect circle as he pried her hand off his arm and stalked back towards the dancefloor.

He knew exactly where she was. The crowd parted around him until he had a clear path to her, bronze skin luminous against her red dress.

Seeing her like this made something deep stir within him—breathless, flushed, skin glowing. His eyes narrowed as he saw her dance partner slowly run his hand down her back, and Ursula smiled after a beat.

He was striding across the room in no time at all.

"I'm cutting in." He had the same raspy voice as earlier, and Elias wondered what had come over him. He imagined his face held a rather stormy expression, and Ursula drew in a quick gasp as he pulled her in close. He could feel every plane of her body against his own.

His head dropped, and she angled towards him, her breath against his cheek.

"Do you like it when we dance like this?" His voice was low and silky.

"Yes," she breathed, unable to say more. He spun her out in time with the music, curling her back into his embrace.

"What about now?" His hand snaked down her back. The movement was a deliberate possession—he would not share her anymore tonight. It made her eyes flutter closed, and Elias smiled.

Elias left his hand at the bottom of her spine, fingers splayed as his pinkie caressed the spot underneath the fabric of her dress.

Her skin was moist with sweat, and it sent a shiver through him. All he wanted to do was taste her again, to lick the moisture from her skin.

"Why did you smile at him?" The fire in his blood made his words sharp. This was the first time he had seen someone touch Ursula so intimately, and the memory was more than he could bear.

"At whom?" she asked, her voice airy and distant.

Elias pulled her closer, wanting to anchor her in the moment with him. "Your dashing dancing partner."

Ursula's eyes snapped to his, confusion furrowing her brow. "Him?! I didn't smile at him."

"You did. I saw you."

She rolled her eyes. "I didn't smile at him. I smiled about something else while he was there."

"What were you smiling about?" His voice had lost some of its hardness, the tone more curious now.

Ursula dropped her gaze. His hand caught her under the chin, stopping her retreat.

She let out a small huff, her body relaxing more against him. "I was thinking about our dancing at the wedding. I find our mutual inability charming."

"Charming, eh?" They swayed to the music. "Do you think we are charming now?" He grazed his hand along her spine before pulling her even closer, a devilish smirk on his face. He knew exactly what he was doing to her.

Ursula cleared her throat. "No, this is something else."

Hazy dawn light crept through the windows, casting a grey pall over the last vestiges of the party. Stragglers stumbled around them, but Ursula and Elias had never left each other's side, dancing in each other's arms long after the music had stopped.

# 30

# Ursula

Ursula stared at the ceiling. It was deep into the night, but sleep evaded her. She wasn't sure if it was leftover adrenaline from a night of dancing or something else that was keeping her awake.

Elias was fast asleep next to her, his breathing deep and even.

She cast a sideways glance at him—how was he not tied up in knots? It felt like every single one of her nerves was jangling, and the incessant heat in her abdomen would not go away.

Ursula closed her eyes and tried to will herself to sleep.

Time crept by, and she could hear the clock on the mantel count every second that passed.

All she could think about was Elias holding her close, his gentle touch on her back and his breath against her skin. She thought of his lips against her, the way his touch was just this side of reverent, like he was holding himself back from completely devouring her. She squeezed her legs together and tried to force her brain to calm down, to force her pulse to stop hammering through her and let sleep take over.

A jolt sent the bed lurching, and Ursula's eyes flew open. Elias was writhing on the bed, his whole body trembling. His head thrashed from side to side as he moaned unintelligibly.

Ursula bent over him, unsure what to do. He was jerking so much she couldn't get close to him. Reaching out an unsteady hand, she threaded her fingers through his mangled left hand.

She stroked his arm reassuringly, the grip on his hand still firm as she spoke soothingly to him. At first, her words were nonsense platitudes, unconvincing as Elias struggled against her. His muscles were bunched tight under his tunic.

"This is a story my mother told me when I was scared at night. It's from her homeland," she whispered into his ear. "There once was a shy musician who could pick up any instrument and play it as if they had for a hundred lifetimes. The mandolin was their favourite, and they played it as if the Gods were in their fingertips."

Tension rolled off him, and after a few seconds he stopped twisting against her. Ursula kept up the steady brush of her hand, her voice soft and melodic.

"They made the most beautiful music when they were alone but froze like a statue any time they had to play in front of another soul. The musician loved the local carpenter and wrote song after song about them, but they never could muster the courage to play them a single note."

Ursula kept the even rhythm of her words, elongating each stroke of her hand until he was still.

"The carpenter vanished one day. Their tools were left hanging as if they had never been used, and the magician knew something bad had happened. The carpenter's tools were as much an extension of themself as the mandolin was for the musician. They hunted through the carpenter's workshop and found a tiny scrap of black paper snagged on a nail by the door. The only person who used black paper was a fearsome magician who lived in the centre of a vast maze."

Slowly, Elias came to, his gaze groggy as he tried to focus on his surroundings.

"Where…Ursula is that you?"

He reached for her face, his movements slow and groggy as Ursula leaned into the touch. His words were heavy and sleep-laden, as though he would slip back under at any minute.

"Yes, it's me.  I'm here," she whispered, giving him a reassuring squeeze. "We're at Lockston Hall and you were having a bad dream."

Elias had such a wary look in his drowsy eyes. "I like your story. Can you tell me how it ends?"

"I will.  Just rest.  I'm here, and I won't let go," Ursula murmured as she settled back on the pillows, their hands still entwined.

He nodded, rolling closer to her as his eyelids drooped and his head nestled into her shoulder.

"The musician was sick with worry and tried to tell the local people what had happened, but no one believed them. Why would the most powerful magician in all the land need a simple carpenter? But the musician was resolute and set out to save their love.

"They walked and walked for days until they got to the humongous maze.  It was so large that it had never been charted on any map, but our musician was special.  They didn't just rely on sight to guide them, but sound, too. They could hear the rustle of a mouse in a thicket or when the wind foretold of rain. They could even hear roots moving below the earth. And so, they listened. They listened so hard they could hear the carpenter's heartbeat, which was a mirror to their own."

Ursula felt her heart swell as she looked down on him, his face much younger in slumber, the lines around his eyes smooth. She battled the urge to place a kiss on his cheek, instead waiting until his breathing was steady to drop a quick peck.

"That's nice. What happens next?" Elias mumbled as he slid an arm around her waist. Ursula looked askance at his slumbering figure.

"The musician walked and walked, listening to the wind through the hedge and following their lover's heartbeat until they got to the centre of the maze. The carpenter was there, being forced to build the magician a great archway that would take them to another world. The magician cackled with evil glee, planning to open the portal and unleash a horde of monsters on the land and take it as their own.

It was then the musician knew what to do. "Cover your ears, my love," they said to the carpenter, who did as commanded, and they played all the songs they had written for them that they would never hear. The magician fell then—the music was so pure, so full of love that it made their black heart stop. The musician and the carpenter went back to the town and made mandolins side by side for the rest of their lives."

Elias buried closer to Ursula, his fingers tracing tiny circles at her waist.

"I want to go home tomorrow. I want our bed…" The end of the sentence was lost to sleep as it claimed him.

Ursula settled into the embrace, a smile playing on her lips as she finally drifted off.

The house woke around them, and Ursula could hear the patter of feet along the corridor outside of their room. No doubt the servants were in peak demand this morning from fragile party guests.

Elias stirred beside her, his arm still looped over her waist. It sent a thrill through Ursula that there would be many mornings like this to come.

"I see you've woken up bright-eyed and bushy-tailed." Elias's voice was thick with sleep, reminding Ursula of last night. Had he remembered anything he said?

"I had a very tiring night," she said as she rolled to face him. Her thoughts were consumed by their time in the dusty room—the way he had taken her, toyed with her until she was a quivering wreck, and then danced all night.

"Tiring, indeed." He raised his eyebrows wickedly and stretched. She missed the weight of his arm over her, the press of his body next to her, but that was soon forgotten when she watched his lithe torso bend. She could see every muscle, every scar. Her eyes roved over his body, and Elias caught her staring.

"You've never asked about them."

Ursula looked at his face, stunned. "I never thought to. It seemed too personal."

"And yet you asked about my magic." His tone was light, almost teasing. She could feel the fierce blush on her face, but it was true. She had asked, and perhaps that was the most personal thing of all.

"Will you tell me then?"

"It was at the front lines. We had not long arrived at the desert and were making our first assault. A new recruit broke ranks, petrified of the unknown, of the army of colossals we faced. I tried to help him, as a healer does, but he was too lost in his own storm, and I bore the brunt."

Ursula traced her fingers over his chest, staring in wonderment at what he had survived. "And the lad? What happened to him?"

"He was a caster, but his stunt rendered him unreliable, and they sent him home. I went to the infirmary to wait out the rest of the war."

Her stomach dropped at that—the sights he must have seen. She couldn't imagine the broken bodies sent to be healed after enduring a giant's wrath.

Elias seemed to notice her thoughts and reached over to his bedside table, retrieving a small vial.

"I can't forget what I've seen, but this helps." He passed her the small brown glass bottle, which was half empty. "Malvina, the apothecary, made this for me. It's a tincture with St. John's Wort and other remedies. It helps keep me on an even keel."

She looked at the tiny vial in her hand, surprised that something so small could be so powerful.

"She sounds like a great herbsmith."

Elias chuckled. "I'm pretty sure she's a witch, but don't tell her I said so. She'll want to dazzle you with her powers herself."

Ursula handed Elias the vial, and he dropped some of the tincture under his tongue. They settled back into bed after that. Her head rested on his chest, listening to the steady beat of his heart.

Their coach moved at a snail's pace along the bumpy mountain roads. Freezing rain fell in dark sheets all around them, battering against the side of the carriage and shaking it violently. The blankets and footwarmers Susannah had given them were barely keeping the cold out, and Ursula felt sorry for Kelman, their driver, who was undoubtedly soaked to the skin.

Elias sat opposite her again, although he had no papers in his hands this time. He had obviously taken her quip about working too much to heart. While she loved their evenings together working on the quarry, the business was not in good shape. She had the nagging feeling that they would have to sell after all; there had been a steady decline in profits in the last decade. There was a distinct lack of modernisation, and while costs of living had creeped up, the quarry's productivity had not. Her bride price could only go so far, and she doubted it would cover their living expenses as well as all the improvements the quarry needed.

Guilt churned in her gut. Her father's profit hadn't been affected by the quarry's slowing business, and she wondered at what cost.

"Cold?"

He looked unfazed by the stormy weather or the chilling temperatures, and she wondered once again if she'd ever get used to the northern climate.

She smiled at him. "Always."

"Let's see what we can do about that." He jumped up and reached her seat in a single stride.

Elias lifted his arm, and Ursula sank down into his embrace, tucking her blanket around them both.

"Better?"

"Much." It was. The heat radiating off him was more comforting than an open fire.

"How long until we're home?" she asked, an undisguised note of pleading in her voice.

Elias pulled out his pocket watch, the metal glinted in the low light of the carriage. "Oh, we have a few hours yet. Unless we get stuck, then we can get cosy and bunk up with Kelman."

Ursula prayed to all the Gods that they would make it home in one piece.

Elias smoothed her hair in long, loving strokes, massaging the knots in her shoulders that had formed on the journey.

"Rest now. It'll make the journey faster."

It was like a command, and Ursula found her eyes drooping with each swipe of his hand.

＃ 31

# Elias

The journey was never-ending, but hope bubbled in him when he felt the familiar incline into Allerbrock. They just needed to crest the hill, and they would be back at Cairden. Back home.

He wanted to grab Ursula, to throw her over his shoulder and lock themselves away for days.

He'd woken up feeling the most refreshed he had in years. Normally he would be up and out, running off the vestiges of a nightmare. But he had fallen back to sleep so quickly, it was like it had never happened. He had the faintest memory of the melodic cant of Ursula's voice, but he couldn't be sure if it was merely part of the dream.

Kelman deserved a hot toddy and a raise for the way he ushered them through the storm. He would never have let on to Ursula how worried he was about the weather; storms rarely ended well this far north. It was his own selfishness that had driven them into this lousy weather. His own desire, his *need*, to have Ursula all to himself. He hoped he wouldn't regret it.

His heart rejoiced when the old road gave way to cobbles and the carriage thudded its way in front of Cairden. Ursula roused then, her head rising from where it had been resting on his shoulder as she slept like it was something they had always done.

He planted a kiss at her hairline, and Ursula turned to him and planted a soft kiss at the corner of his mouth. Elias could have happily sat in the carriage and just basked in her, but he was desperate to get her alone. To feel the soft stretch of her against him.

He willed his blood to cool down as the carriage rambled to the front door. They had been on the road for hours longer than planned, and Ursula deserved to warm up and stretch her legs, not be whisked off to bed.

The coach rocked as Kelman disembarked, and Elias knew it was time to move. He had just reached for the door when it was wrenched from his grasp, and Mrs. Clough's small worried face appeared.

"There's been an accident at the quarry!" She bounced from foot to foot. The hand that held her soaked shawl against her was clenched into a fist, the other flapping wildly.

"What's happened?" He strode from the carriage towards the house, and Mrs. Clough followed with Ursula closely behind.

The flagstones were slippery underfoot, and Elias dreaded to think what could have happened at the quarry under the weight of all that stone.

"A boy. I don't know who, but they've been pinned under a boulder. They tried to get in before the weather turned, but the wind broke the winch and trapped the poor lad." Mrs. Clough's voice was thick with emotion, and Elias patted her on her tiny shoulder.

She shook under his hand, and his stomach dropped. Only something serious would affect the unflappable housekeeper like this.

"Get by the fire, Mrs. Clough, and make something for you and Kelman to warm up." He looked at Ursula. "I'm going to the quarry."

The rain dripped off the end of her nose, and she swept it away with the back of her hand. She still had the blanket from the carriage wrapped around her.

"Then I will, too."

His mind exploded. There was no way he could let her join him in this. "Absolutely not." He didn't care how curt he sounded. He couldn't face the idea of anything happening to her.

Ursula's eyes narrowed as she held firm. "We are equals, Elias. We share our lives, and I am going."

He wanted to argue, to push her to join Mrs. Clough by the fire, but her steely gaze pinned him where he stood, and he knew he'd lost.

"Fine, but make sure you've got sturdy shoes on. We can't take the horses out in this."

Ursula just nodded and went to her room to change. Elias followed after her, sprinting up the stairs two at a time. The wind howled in their faces, the rain hitting like a thousand tiny needles. They had been walking in silence, the noise from the storm stealing any chance at talking.

They had passed through town, seeing a ring of women assembled by the alder. One woman sobbed as she held onto the tree's bark while the person behind her stroked her back. He hoped that her pain would be taken away, whatever the outcome.

Elias pointed to the quarry ahead, the white rocks stark against the forest. Even the storm couldn't dull the luminous stone.

They followed the path down. The rock was slippery underfoot, and they held onto the sharp ridges cut into the stone. The descent was painfully slow, and Elias focused on putting one foot in front of the other instead of the possibility that they were too late.

A group of figures huddled in the distance, their dark forms severe in the pelting rain.

Elias's stomach fell. Everyone was too calm, too still in the dark. He lost his footing, and his hand scraped against the jagged rock.

"We're nearly there." Ursula held onto his forearm, pulling him towards her and keeping him upright. She sheltered him, guiding him through the storm.

The boulder wasn't big—it couldn't have been more than three feet across. The men crowded around in a semicircle, a tarp held over the injured boy like a makeshift shelter. The foreman, Billy, was the first to speak.

"Mr. Clearbould, we didn't think you'd make it!" the man shouted in the tempest. "We sent for the healer but he's away down river to the Wilson cottage. She's due twins, and her pains came early. We're waiting for old Lynn to come over from Nether Barrow. We know not to move him, but time's running out."

Elias nodded, his eyes glued to the young lad under the stone. His tear-streaked face was unearthly and ashen, and he whimpered as the men moved around him. Declan, one of the men who had worked here since he was that age himself, held onto the boy's hand. The young lad gripped it like a lifeline, his knuckles white under the strain. You would think he had the strength of ten men from that grip, but his breathing was shallow and tinged with the ominous rattle that signalled the end. Elias doubted a healer could do much now.

"How long since the accident?" His throat felt raw, the wind swallowing most of what he said.

"Been about three hours. We tried to pin the winch down, but the wind caught it."

Elias laid a hand on Billy's shoulder. The poor man didn't look much better than the injured boy.

"You've done what you can." The words felt flat on his tongue.

Ursula moved beside him, and the man started.

"Billy, this is my wife, Mrs. Ursula Clearbould. I was hoping you'd meet under better circumstances."

The foreman doffed his soaked cap at Ursula. "Pleased to meet you, Mrs. Clearbould."

"And you, Billy." Ursula placed a supportive hand on the man's arm and turned to Elias. "I need to speak with you."

She sounded harried, and her face was drawn. Elias followed her a few steps away from the men. "You need to heal the boy."

"What?" He flung the word at her.

"Use your magic." Her words were hurried and emphatic, and Elias just stared. "Elias! I know you can. You need to heal the boy."

"What does a southerner know of magic?"

Ursula flinched, but didn't back down. She eyed him with unyielding determination.

He wanted to retreat back into himself, to the man he'd

been after his accident. When it had been easier to pretend his magic didn't exist, when it was just him in the world. But that wasn't the case now. He had people who depended on him, and the responsibilities that had once scared him now filled him with purpose.

Elias blinked slowly, water rolling down his face and pricking at his eyes. "Ursula, my magic is gone."

She gave him the same resolute stare, her silence as pointed as her gaze.

"I'm here to support my workers. We will need to pull the boy out and tie off his leg. I doubt we can save it, but it's the best we can hope for."

Ursula grabbed him on each bicep, her hands just as insistent as her words. "You can do this, Elias. The boy needs you. He'll be pulled from the stone regardless. You can save him, save his leg."

"What makes you so sure?" Elias whispered.

He looked back at the men, at the young, pallid face on the ground and reached inside himself as he had done so many times before. But there was nothing—no spark, no warmth.

Ursula yanked him to face her, hands on either side of his face. "Elias, I know you well enough now to know you will only make peace with this if you have tried everything to save him. Even the impossible."

"How can you say this?"

Ursula ran her thumb across his cheek. "Because you're my alder. I don't know how, but being with you has healed a wound on my heart so deep I didn't even know it was there."

"Hugh was an ignor—" She cut him off with a quick shake of her head, and her hands squeezed him nearly to the point of pain.

"Never mind him! I'm talking about you, you fool!" Her eyes were wild in the darkness. "You gave me something I never thought I'd have in a partner—someone who saw me for who I am and not what I could give them. Do you even know how much all those hours in your study mean to me? You believed in me, and now it's my turn to believe in you."

She ended her speech with an abrupt, fiery kiss that hit Elias like a thunderbolt.

Ursula was right—he needed to do something. For himself as much as the boy, who was fading fast. At the very least, he could tourniquet the wound. He'd lose the leg, but he'd live. Malvina would have the herbs to stave off infection.

They moved back to the group, and the men shifted uneasily. They knew what was to come, what lurked under the stone.

Elias cleared his throat loudly, trying to catch their attention.

"I was a healer in the Giant's War. Follow what I say."

He outlined his plan for the men to lift the stone and drag the boy out. He hoped his leg was still intact enough for him to work on.

Most of the men nodded silently, and one voice grumbled about waiting for Lynn, but they pushed on, fishing out a metal lever to lift the rock.

Metal ground against stone, and Elias and Billy hauled the boy from under the rock. The young lad shrieked in anguish and thrashed against them.

Billy held the boy against him, and Elias ripped the lad's blood-soaked trouser leg. The metallic scent of blood hit him, and Elias bit the back of hand with a muffled gag. Mangled flesh lay below the tattered fabric, and a huge gash ran down the boy's shin exposing the muscle and sinew. Pulverised fragments of white bone stood out among a sea of red. Blood pooled underneath the boy and crept along the stone, seeping into every crack. The skin that could be seen was blue-tinged, and he knew it would be cool to the touch.

Elias exhaled through his nose, letting the horror wash over him as he focused intently on his task. He ripped a length from the soiled fabric in his hands and looped it around the top of the boy's skinny thigh.

Elias counted his breaths and was about to tie the knot tight across the boy's leg when a pair of hands seized his own.

Ursula was crouched behind him, her soaked hair pressed against his cheek. Her scent wove through him, not damped by the downpour.

He could feel her breath against the shell of his ear as her chest heaved against his back.

"Heal him, Elias."

He tried to snatch his hands away, to finish what he started, but she planted them on the boy's leg as blood and gore covered them.

"I believe in you. I lov—"

Blinding heat surged through him, singeing away at his nerve endings. Elias was sure he was on fire.

Time seemed to stand still in the all-consuming blaze, and his vision blurred as whiteness took over.

He heard the pop of bone and sinew knitting together; heard the sound of someone retching in the distance. He could feel Ursula's hands on him as images of her swam through his mind—Ursula racing him at the manor, Ursula in the red dress at Yule, Ursula dragging him through the bookshop, Ursula bright-eyed and nervous on the first day they met.

Then the world went silent.

# 32

# Ursula

A tiny spot of blood welled where she had nicked her finger. Ursula sucked on it and stared at the embroidery hoop in her hand. She had picked it up for something to do when even her beloved books had offered no solace. There was enough uncertainty in her life now; she couldn't stomach reading about it.

Her foot tapped wildly as she snipped at a few threads and tried to ease some of the web of tangles loose, but all it did was cause the fabric backing to bunch. She let out a loud tut before throwing it back into the canvas sewing bag by her side. Nothing could take her mind off the slumbering figure in the bed beside her.

Elias's chest rose and fell in a methodic beat like a metronome marking out time in the day. Ursula listened to see if the pattern faltered, if he groaned in pain or gasped awake. Anything to let her know the man was still in there.

It had been three long, horrible days since the accident at the quarry, and all she could feel was dull panic. What food she could stomach tasted bland, jokes fell dead on her ears.

It was like she was watching herself from up high, bobbing along with the tide.

A headache bloomed at her temples, and Ursula stood and stretched, feeling days' worth of knots along her spine cry out. She'd had Elias brought into their new bedroom rather than his own room, determined to sleep next to him in their bed. Her hand feeling his lungs move in his chest was the only thing that allowed her to sleep at night.

The healer had come to Cairden instead of the quarry and had looked up at her with sad eyes from under his bushy eyebrows when he spoke. Half of what he said had washed over her, but his parting words had wormed their way into her soul.

"Nothing can be done for magical exhaustion, Mrs. Clearbould. Time will tell."

She'd gone over his words again and again, hoping Elias would come back to her.

The days since the accident had all blended into one, but visions of that night still plagued her. The way Elias's prone body had looked so frail and waxy as the men from the quarry bundled him onto a cart. How his head bounced over the rutted ground, and she stripped off her rain-soaked cloak to place beneath him. The rain that pummelled them with each step, pinpricks of ice that turned Elias's lips a ghostly blue. She'd kissed him, trying to bring some life back into him. Just like in a story, resurrected by true love's kiss.

But it did not work—Elias still lay in a sickening sleep.

Ursula crossed the room and sat on the edge of the bed. She fidgeted with the bedclothes, smoothing down invisible creases and running her fingers through his unruly hair. He hadn't moved since they'd laid him here, but somehow his hair stayed defiantly messy no matter how much she'd tried to tame it.

Ursula smiled to herself, tears clinging to her eyelashes. "Elias…Eli, you really do have impeccable timing. I told you I loved you, and you vanished. This is the second time you've left me high and dry, you goat."

Her voice wavered, and Ursula coughed, trying to clear the lump in her throat. "I hope you can hear me in there."

She leaned down and planted a kiss on his forehead.

"I nearly went to the alder, you know?" Ursula hung over him, whispering into his ear. "But you're right: some things are meant to be felt. What I feel right now is because I love you and I won't give that up for anything."

In those awful moments before the boy's leg had knitted together in front of them, she had known then. The ember of hope she felt on her way north burned like the sun, fuelled by all the tiny moments leading up to it.

Her love for Elias wasn't a sweeping thing; it was quiet and had snuck up on her. She hadn't even recognised it until it was taken away. Ursula looked down at Elias's placid face, and a fat tear splashed onto his cheek. She swept it away with her thumb. His skin was warm now, not icy and waxen, and her heart did a little tumble. He was still there. She had to believe it.

A firm knock wrapped on the door, and Ursula smoothed down the covers again. She had tried very hard to keep her emotions under wraps, to work through everything logically. She may not have left Elias's bedside for more than a few minutes, but she'd worked hard to keep the reins on everything after the accident.

Mrs. Clough managed the house while Ursula managed the

quarry. She would have missed meals and sleep were it not for her housekeeper nudging her forward with tea and toast and kind words.

Ursula's head shot up towards the person who entered the room. She had expected to see the small, green, kindly figure of her housekeeper with another teapot or bowl of broth.

But it was Maisie who stood there with a basket of cloth packages in her hands. Her face was warm and smiling, but her eyes had the same sad tinge of every visitor.

"Malvina sent me with some new remedies to try. I've got some tulsi, lemon balm, and slippery elm to brew. I'm going to pop down to the kitchens and get this going. Do you need anything?"

Ursula shook her head. Maybe it would be better if she ran over to her friend and sobbed on her shoulder, but her silly southern upbringing and the grinding panic froze them in her throat. Like a lump of bread too big to swallow. The one thing she needed was just out of reach. Instinctively, she covered Elias's hand with her own, looping her fingers around his limp grip. "No, I'm fine."

Maisie's mouth twisted like she was holding in words, but she only nodded before leaving the room.

"How are you holding up?"

"I'm fine." The words came out sharper than planned. It was the same script she'd been saying for days, and the words had lost their meaning long ago.

Maisie crossed the room and sat on Ursula's vacant chair, looking at her with concern in her eyes. The few weeks she'd been working at the apothecary had obviously given her a new insight into people.

"Are you sure?"

"Yes, I'm fine." Ursula swallowed again. "I wrote to Susannah yesterday. She's going to come through tomorrow, I think."

"Family's important at a time like this."

The words ricocheted through her. They were her family now, too. Susannah, Cal and the boys, Maisie and Mrs. Clough. Elias. She had forged a life here with the people around her, and instead of replacing the loved ones she left back south, they all added to it.

Tears stung again, but some of the weight of the last few days lifted. If she could just focus on the positive, maybe it *would* all be fine.

Maisie raised an eyebrow. "Who's looking after you? You don't have to pretend with me."

"Mrs. Clough has been brilliant, and you know how much Malvina's been visiting to help keep an eye on him."

Both their eyes fell to Elias.

"That's good, but I'm going to ask again. How are you?"

Blood rushed in Ursula's ears. All the emotion she'd been pushing down for days caught in her throat. She stumbled over the words. "I…I don't know."

It was like a dam breaking. Huge gulping sobs ripped through her body, and Ursula laid her head in her hands as they flowed freely.

She was trying to be strong, to be useful, to keep the quarry afloat. Elias would want that. Everything he had done was to keep the quarry and his family's legacy going, but now all of that was washed away by the aching, gnawing terror that this was it. That he would never come back to her, and she had lost him before he was even properly hers.

The blind panic that she tried to keep out through ordered

work snapped at her like wolves felling a stag. "What if this is it?"

Maisie sat down on the chair and reached for Ursula, who grabbed onto the girl's delicate hand. Her own paw dwarfed it, and her chest ached to think about how perfectly it fit in Elias's.

"I have a feeling. No, I know he'll wake." Maisie's voice was strong as iron.

Snot ran down Ursula's face, and she wiped it away with the back of her hand. "How can you be sure?"

"I can't put it into words, but I do know that anything can happen in the north. Especially miracles."

Maisie dropped her hand and pulled out a handkerchief embroidered with an M surrounded by thistles. Ursula blew her nose, knowing her friendship with this young woman had irrevocably shifted. Even if nothing else positive came from this time, knowing she was surrounded by people who cared for her plastered over the cracks in her heart. In a strange twist of fate, she had found belonging here.

Maisie's hand on her shoulder shook her from her reverie. "I've asked Mrs. Dyce to freeze the tincture I made. Let's see if Mr. Clearbould will swallow any."

Ursula placed her hand over the girl's and nodded. She had tried to make this better through willpower, now she had to give over to faith.

# 33

# Elias

Elias woke with a cold tingling on his lips.

He followed the sensation along the seam of his mouth with the tip of his tongue, his lips rough and chapped.

He felt desperately thirsty, his throat dry and aching.

Elias pushed at the bedclothes—or at least he tried to, but he couldn't move. His body was too heavy, as if it were filled with lead.

"Don't move. It's okay, just stay there," a soft voice whispered in his ear. "You need to rest."

The tingling sensation appeared again, and he realised that ice was being brushed over his lips.

A warm hand was pressed against his cheek, and he leaned into it. His eyes felt like they'd been stitched shut, and he used all his might to open them. The world came into blinding focus. A face peered above him, surrounded by a dark canopy. His vision shifted, and familiar tawny eyes stared down at him.

"Welcome back."

Ursula's voice was a soothing croon, and Elias felt a weak smile bloom on his chapped lips, splitting the delicate skin.

"Water." The word came out as a pathetic whisper.

Ursula cradled his head as she held a glass to his lips, and he managed to swallow a few meagre mouthfuls before he sagged with exhaustion.

"How long?"

The words felt sharp and rusty in his throat.

Ursula's teeth worried her lower lip, making the colour deepen to red. He wished the sight stirred the usual lust within him, but it only made him heady in the worst way possible. The room lurched, and Elias worried he would lose the contents of his already empty stomach.

She reached for a cloth from the bedside table and dabbed at his forehead and neck. The coolness brought him back from the brink.

"Please, Ursi…how long?" The words rattled out of him, the effort of talking stripping any remaining moisture from him.

Ursula fiddled with the cloth in her hand. "Nearly three days."

Relief flooded Elias as the words sank in—he had not been out for weeks. His gaze once again found Ursula's face, darting around every feature. There were soot-dark shadows under her eyes, and her skin was pallid, but she had never looked more beautiful. He would spend the rest of his life giving thanks to all the Gods for bringing him back to her.

"Only three days. You had me worried I was out for a week." He gave her another limp smile.

"I thought you had gone." Ursula's voice wavered on the last word, and she crumpled onto Elias, holding him tight.

Her hair spilled over them both, blanketing them in the silky strands. Elias rubbed at her back, feeling his strength return with each passing second.

"Now, now. I'm alright." He successfully pushed the covers away this time as he sat up.

There was a pause as Elias drew in breath, and his eyes flickered around the room.

It was familiar, but different. Better.

The walls were still navy on the bottom, but a dado rail now split the wall in half. The color on top was a pale, welcoming blue.

Light filtered in through white brocade curtains that were pinned back on ornate leaf hooks.

Elias grabbed Ursula by the waist and pulled her close. He nuzzled into the side of her hair and brushed a light kiss by her temple. She smelled of herbs and nursing, but also that unmistakable scent so decidedly her own. He wanted to throw her down on the bed and breathe her in for eternity.

"Thank you so much for this," he mumbled into her hair, not quite ready to let go.

Ursula held him close and pointed behind them. "You've not seen the best bit yet."

Elias turned. The furniture was the same, the stain had been lightened, and the utilitarian shapes had been carved with woodland motifs. What had been a wide expanse of plain wood now housed a perfect depiction of the Alder. Roots and branches reached out, the river running by it.

Elias looked closer, his eyes darting all over the carved wood. "Is this what I think it is?"

She looked down coyly, her foot scuffing the carpet. "I wanted to honour your family, your history—who came before and who's to come, like in the ballroom."

Elias looked back again at his parents' initials carved into the wood. His and Susannah's were positioned below, his nephews on the next line, and blank space for future generations of Clearboulds underneath.

He could feel his heart swell. Ursula had changed a dark, neglected space into something bright and hopeful. It straddled two worlds, celebrating both the past and the future.

Elias circled her wrist with his hand and pulled her down onto the bed. A squeak of surprise passed Ursula's lips as she tumbled onto the mattress beside him and settled into his arms.

"I think I'll be able to allay everyone's worries and let them know you are perfectly well now. Malvina has been around every day to check on your progress. You better watch out. She might pinch you for her apothecary next."

Elias tilted her chin up and looked into those deep amber eyes. He held her gaze, trying to find the words to say how he felt. Instead, he kissed her—a soft, tender brush of his lips.

"You have given me something I didn't even know I needed. How can I thank you?"

"You don't have to thank me, just do this…" Ursula licked her lips and drew him down for another kiss.

# 34

# Elias

"Please, just let me help."

Elias reached over to the dwindling pile of papers in front of Ursula.

She batted his hand away without even looking up from her work. "Don't you dare. You're supposed to be resting."

He let out a frustrated huff and sank back into his seat. They had dragged the old armchair over from the fireplace when his complaining had gotten too much. "I've been sitting here for three days, and you've not let me do more than answer the odd question and pour some tea. Please, Ursi, give me something to do before I go mad."

Ursula paused and looked up at him with a sceptical brow. "You are here in a purely advisory capacity, Mr. Clearbould."

It was true. Ursula had flown through the aftermath of the accident at the quarry by visiting the boy's family—who he now knew was called Evan—speaking to the Allerbrock Times to stop blame being assigned where it shouldn't, giving the men involved time off to recover, and all the while researching new equipment. Productivity would be down, but everyone

277

knew that the town needed healing after the accident more than the quarry needed profits.

When he had written south all those months ago, his focus had been on survival of the quarry, of carrying out his father's dreams and making the memory of him proud. It was all different now. Now he had his own family, a partner in life to face adversities with.

"Alright, Mrs. Clearbould, but you have to let me advise on something more than when tea is called."

Ursula looked up and smiled at him as if she could hear his mind working. "Fine. I need you to look over this new business plan anyway."

She walked around the desk with a thick buff-coloured folder and perched on the edge as she held it out to him. His pulse raced as he looked at the brilliant woman he married. He had always dreaded such work, slogging through it for hours by himself. Now he was excited to see what she had planned. How could one person upend his life so thoroughly without him even noticing?

"Well," she waved the folder at him, "are you going to actually look at this after all your bellyaching?"

Elias feigned a pout. "I can't reach, you'll have to come closer."

Ursula stood, and he drank her in, savouring each inch as he eyed her from head to toe.

"Closer."

She tutted and rolled her eyes but took a tiny step forward. "Closer."

A flush crept up her neck, and Elias licked his lips as she moved nearer.

"Closer."

He uncrossed his legs, and she stepped between his thighs.

"Perfect." He took the folder from her hands and launched it across the room. His other hand snaked around her waist, and he pulled her down into his lap. "Absolutely perfect."

Ursula frowned at him, arms crossed. "As I said, you are supposed to be resting."

Elias wrapped his arm around her, enjoying the feel of her lush curves in his hand as he pulled her further into his lap.

"Ursi, I've been resting for over a week now. I'm fine."

He nuzzled her neck, and her pulse fluttered under his lips. She may be putting on a stern front, but she wanted this as much as he did.

"I've had to deal with you in bed next to me every night. I'm fine, let me show you."

"Malvina said you shouldn't exert yourself. That you need to be patient and gradually add in more exercise to get your strength back."

Her voice was breathy as he wound his hand under the heavy velvet of her skirt.

"Let's test my strength then."

He lifted her up with a slight wobble and covered the space to the desk in a few paces.

Ursula shrieked and flung her arms around his neck. "Elias! Be careful!"

"Come now, have a little trust. I didn't drop you on our wedding night."

Elias placed her back on the edge of the desk like she had been a few minutes before. This time her skirt was rucked up, and he knelt down between her long legs, his hand ringed around her ankle. He traced small circles across the fine wool of her stockings, and Ursula sucked in a breath as he pushed off both of her slippers.

"You see, since you've started working here, I've had this idea—or you could call it a fantasy—but I was too much of a coward to act on it. A week and half of that plump arse of yours pressed up against me every night without the ability to do anything about it has given me the confidence to try."

His hand skirted up the long line of her leg until he found the ribbon in her garter, undoing it with a gentle tug. His fingers skimmed along the soft flesh of her thigh, and he pulled the soft fabric down in a long, languid caress.

Ursula leaned back on her hands, her breathing shallow as she watched his every move. Elias went to the other leg and did the same.

She was perched on the edge of the desk, the balls of her feet lightly placed on the floor in front of him. Elias lifted her left leg and planted a chaste kiss on the inside of her ankle. Ursula gasped when his lips touched her skin. He growled in response, the sound reverberating through his chest as he ran his tongue up the delicate flesh and nibbled the back of her knee. Ursula's breathing became more staccato as he went.

Elias nibbled again at her thigh and stood. Delirious power surged through him as he saw her eyes glazed over and hazy with lust. He edged forward between her legs, a mirror to how he'd had her stand before him in the chair.

His hand followed the same path as before, but he kept going until he found the thin cotton of her underwear.

"Already so wet for me, Ursi. Have you thought of this, too?"

She gave him a tiny nod.

His fingers caressed the damp fabric. Ursula sucked in another shaky breath as he hooked his fingers in the hem and lifted her hips a fraction before tugging them down.

Elias began the same treatment all over again. His hands skimmed along her thigh, gooseflesh erupting in his wake until he palmed her damp curls. Ursula moaned when his finger finally entered her.

The restraint he'd held until now snapped, and Elias roughly thrust into her. He added a second finger and buried his face into her hair.

He wanted to be enveloped, *consumed* by her. To show her how maddening it had been to be next to her and not touch her. For all the weeks when he'd danced around her and done nothing.

Elias slowed his pace again, withdrawing his fingers as Ursula whimpered.

"Watch me. Watch me take you."

His voice was a shaky command as he undid his trousers and sunk into her. Ursula's gaze snapped to where their bodies met, her legs quivering as he drove deeper.

"Do you see what you do to me?"

She gave another tiny nod.

"Wrap your legs around me."

He pushed harder, holding onto the small of her back as his patience snapped. A zinging pulse ran down his spine, and Elias knew he was close to tipping over the edge.

"Ursi, where?"

He voiced the unspoken agreement that started on their wedding night. He'd instinctively known that she wanted to wait, to choose the size of their family. It would continue that way until she said otherwise.

"My mouth. Come in my mouth."

Elias had nearly spent himself there. It took all his willpower to not lose it again when Ursula got onto her knees.

She looked up at him, and while her amber eyes still had the hazy sheen of desire, they now sparkled with mischief as she took him in her hand and gave him a forceful stroke.

Her tongue glided along the underside of his cock, and Elias's eyes nearly rolled back in his head when she took him in her mouth. He watched as those plump lips moved along his shaft, joined by her hand when she sucked at the tip.

Elias ran his hand over her face and buried his head into her hair. The dark tresses snarled in his grasp, but he held onto her like a lifeline in a storm.

His climax pushed at him, crackling down his spine and through every nerve ending in his body. Pride shone in Ursula's eyes as he thrust into her mouth, the last vestiges of control falling away as he tumbled into his release, and she drank it down.

Elias sagged forward then, collapsing onto his knees in front of Ursula. They stayed there, silent and panting for a few long moments. He finally tidied himself up and fastened his trousers, then moved to smooth down Ursula's dress. When he had finished, he ran his fingers through her mussed hair.

She leaned into his touch as he cupped her face, his thumb tracing her lust-swollen lips.

"Ursi, I don't know how the stars aligned and sent you here, but I will never stop thanking our fathers and their schemes. No one has believed in me the way you have, and I want to spend the rest of my life to do the same for you."

Ursula kissed the pad of his thumb and ran a hand along his outstretched arm. "Elias, you silly goose, you already do."

"I hope so."

He pulled her onto his lap and kissed her fiercely. He really, really hoped she was right.

# 35

# Ursula

They sat in a companionable silence at the breakfast table. The pale light of early Spring streamed through the window, and Ursula could feel her spirits raise with the temperature.  Spring was in the air, and it was breathing new life into the world.

Mrs. Dyce had outdone herself with a thick potato omelette, sausage, and fresh fruit.  Ursula helped herself to a healthy portion, still as delighted by the rich foods as she had been on her first day.  She was just lifting a forkful to her lips when Rodger walked in stiffly, announcing mail had arrived for her.

Ursula's heart soared at the prospect of news from home. She ripped the letter open and froze.

"Ursi?" Elias eyed her cautiously across the table.

"It's here…or there…or he's there," Ursula babbled.  "The baby's been born."

She shot Elias a wide grin, tears spilling from her eyes as she flipped through the letter, her eyes racing over every line.

"Miranda says Mother is fine, but the labour was difficult. She's healing well, though. The baby is a healthy ten pounds, seven ounces, and has a shock of blonde hair. Blonde hair, can you believe it?" Ursula looked up at Elias again, feeling incandescent with joy. "He's the only one who has Father's colouring."

Her eyes raked over the letter again, darting frantically as she tried to take it all in.

"His name is Lucas. It's a good name, isn't it?"

Elias moved around the table and crouched beside her, an arm hung over the back of her chair. "It's a wonderful name."

Ursula felt weightless, like she was made of the spring light that streamed through the window. The shadow that sat at the back of her mind, a shadow she hadn't even realised was there, had gone, blasted away by the good news. She looped her arms around Elias's neck and pulled him close.

"We must go into town and get some gifts." Her words were muffled against his neck.

"Alright, where should we start?"

Ursula pulled back and looked into his shining blue eyes. She felt like he was reflecting everything back to her—her happiness, her love. She wanted nothing more than to melt into them.

He leaned up and brushed a quick peck on her lips. "Come on now, what shall we get the young Master Woodruff? I'm hopeless with these things."

Ursula felt her smile widen again. "I think we should get something for Mother first. We should go to the apothecary. I'm sure Malvina will have something to help her healing, and I'd like to tell Maisie."

She dipped her chin, and Elias caught it in his hand, bringing her eyes level with his. "And I'm sure she'd love to hear the news."

It had only been a few weeks since Maisie had left Cairden, and Ursula still missed her terribly. She had been such a beacon through those first few months in the north and again after the accident at the quarry. Time had slipped through her fingers since Elias's collapse. She had stayed close to home in the immediate aftermath, keeping a watchful eye on him as his strength returned. Elias had bounced back quickly, but she found more excuses than not to stay at home.

The weather had been pretty tortuous, too. Snow gave way to harsh sleet and rain that soaked you through in a second and left you chilled to the bone. Even her fur-lined cloak from Sinjorro Zavaran hadn't kept the chill out. Ursula had spent many a morbid hour in front of the fire dosed with Mrs. Clough's hot toddies, convinced she would never be warm again.

"Enough wool-gathering." Elias sprung up and Ursula craned her neck to watch him. "First one to be at the front door buys the other lunch."

He raced off, and Ursula scoffed before tearing after him, her heart so full it could burst.

The afternoon sun hung low in the sky, and Ursula held her hand up to shield her face. It was a brisk day with a clear blue sky.

The basket on her forearm shifted under the movement, and she fiddled with the wicker handle. It was overflowing with gifts already, and they hadn't even gone to the apothecary yet.

Elias held a teddy bear so giant he could barely see where he walked, but he peeked around the bear's beige, tufted fur and looked her up and down.

"Let me take that," Elias asked, holding out his hand.

"Please?"

Ursula tutted as the wicker handle pulled at her skin, relenting as it slipped lower again. "Only because you asked so nicely."

"Let's go sit by the fountain. It's too nice a day to be inside the whole time."

"Fine, but just a quick pit stop. I still have a lot to get."

Elias pumped his eyebrows, and Ursula gave her eyes an exaggerated roll. "What? It's the first time I've been old enough to spoil a sibling. Gwen came around when I was thirteen."

Elias stopped and kissed her on the tip of her nose. "Look at you, the proud big sister."

Ursula blushed and fluttered her eyelashes. It's true, she was proud. Proud of her mother, proud of the man who stood before her, and proud of herself for letting him love her way she always wanted.

They meandered across the square and sat at the edge of the fountain. The stone was warm underneath them, heated by the early spring rays, and the clear water tinkled like a melody just for them.

The afternoon rush had long passed, leaving a few afternoon shoppers lazily wandering through the square. Ursula inhaled; she could never take a breath like this in Currington. It was like she was breathing deep into her soul.

Elias shifted the giant bear on his lap and looped his arm over her shoulder. Ursula burrowed deep into his side. She could sit here for hours just being with him, the world flowing past them.

"Where's the apothecary from here?"

"It's a few streets up that way." He motioned to the right

with his head.

"I don't think I can move now," she said into his shoulder.

Elias dropped his arm and stood. Ursula made a petulant sound at his absence and looked up to find his hand outstretched to her. Her breath caught at the sight, his sleeve rolled up and forearm bare. How would she handle the summer if just the sight of his arms does this to her? Her pulse thundered as she thought of him sunkissed and glistening above her. Ursula clamped her legs together, trying desperately to not squirm in public.

Elias noticed her attention and raised a cocky eyebrow. "Everything alright there, wife?"

"Yes, yes, I'm fine." She bristled and reached for his hand.

Elias playfully tugged her to him, and Ursula fell into his embrace, squashed next to the bear. The basket batted at her hip, and she tried to grab it, but Elias swatted her hand away.

"C'mon, let's go see Maisie."

Ursula craned her neck to look for Maisie's golden-brown head through the foggy glass of the window.

"You won't be able to speak to her if you stand outside all day." Elias's words tickled at the shell of her ear, sending shivers down her spine.

"I know you're right," Ursula replied quietly. "But what if she's too busy to see me? Or I just get in the way while she's working? I don't want to be a pest."

"Maisie's not like that. You'll see." He hoisted the bear higher on his hip and shifted the basket on his arm before pushing the door open.

The air was moist and fragrant. Smelling like herbs and oils Ursula could never name. There were rows and rows of glass jars down one wall all labelled neatly on their shelves, and a series of tiny drawers took the whole width and height of the other.

There were only a few people other than them in the shop, but the atmosphere buzzed. The counter covered the whole back of the shop, and equipment puffed, bubbled, and twirled behind it. It was like a mini factory chugging away.

Malvina was dealing with a customer by the glass jars. A pair of spectacles precariously balanced on her nose as she gestured with two bottles in her hands.

Ursula looked around again, willing her legs not to bolt, when a tiny head popped up from behind the huge wooden counter.

"Mrs. Clearbould, is that you?" Maisie's exuberant voice filled the shop, and Ursula's skittish legs managed to carry her to the counter.

"I wanted to see how you were doing. I hope that's ok?"

Maisie beamed at her. "Of course, you silly goose. Now, anything I can help with? Or are you just in for a chin wag? Both are more than welcome." She looked past Ursula and waved at Elias, who was inspecting the wall of tiny drawers with the giant bear. He waved with the bear's huge paw. "Have you and Mr. Clearbould been at a carnival, or do you have news?"

Ursula beamed back at her. "News. My newest sibling has finally arrived, and I'd like to get something to send to my mother. We've been out all morning buying the baby bits, but I think she deserves a little something, too."

"Too right." Maisie nodded and pulled out a paper and pencil. "We have a great bath milk that is good for healing. Follow me, and I'll show you a few bits. I'm still learning, but Malvina's on hand if I get stuck."

Ursula followed, happy to hear about Maisie's new-found expertise.

They strolled through the streets of Allerbrock as the light faded and goosebumps danced along Ursula's skin. She buried deeper into Elias's embrace, enjoying his warmth and strength.

It felt as if they had circumvented most of the town by the time they wandered past the bookshop, the apothecary just a couple of streets away.

A large 'For Sale' sign hung in the window, and Ursula felt her stomach drop.

"Oh no. This can't be right!" she gasped and bolted through the door.

The bookshop had been the first place she felt at home in Allerbrock, and the thought of it closing and the community losing such a vital space tore her up inside. The shop was always bustling and was as much a meeting spot for locals as it was a business venture.

As usual, Kieran was at the sales desk, head in a book, a half-eaten apple dangling from the other hand.

Ursula raced up to the counter and slammed her hands down, eliciting a sceptical look from the clerk.

"Yes?" he asked, taking a laconic bite of his apple.

Ursula could read as many books as she liked, but she could never read Kieran. He was inscrutable as always.

"They're selling?" She waved around a bit too frantically and noticed the scattered shoppers eyeing her strangely. "Please, Kieran, you know how much I love it here. Can you tell me anything about why they are selling?"

He waggled his head and sighed, lowering his book and apple down as if it were a great imposition. Ursula would have assumed she had annoyed him if it wasn't for the fact he was like this every day.

"It's simple, Ursula. The Hubbards are old and want to move further south to live closer to their daughter. Kind of boring."

He shrugged and splayed his book open on the counter.

Ursula tapped on his shoulder insistently. "But…but…who will take over? Will it stay as a bookshop? Will you have a job?"

Kieran shrugged again, his face slack with boredom.

"Don't you care about any of this?" Ursula couldn't keep the pleading tone from her voice. She knew it was selfish, but this place meant so much to her. It was obvious it meant as much to the people in town, as well.

Kieran levelled his stare at her. "Ursula, obviously I care. It's my job, but I'm not going to cause a fuss, okay? The Hubbards have been good employers and now want a rest. That's more than fair. Do I know who's going to buy the place? No. Am I going to stick my oar in? Also no. I'm happy to bob along and see what happens. I live my life by the adage 'What's meant for you won't go by you', and I am happy to see where life leads. Worrying over things I can't control isn't going to help. I can't afford to buy it, but you seem to have enough money. Why don't you do it?"

Ursula was taken aback, firstly that Kieran had said so many words to her in one go, and also by his suggestion she should buy the shop. It was preposterous.

Well, maybe not completely preposterous—she was a merchant's daughter, after all. Plus, she had helped Elias with his work, which proves she had a head for numbers. And she had always loved books…

No. It was preposterous.

She shook her head to stop all the thoughts whizzing around. "Thanks, Kieran. You've actually been helpful."

He replied with a grunt and loud crunch of his apple, head firmly back in his book.

Elias was milling by the front of the shop looking at a tower of new releases. There was a memoir of a half-elf who circumnavigated the globe in a boat that caught his eye, he was just reaching for it when Ursula stormed up behind him.

"The Hubbards are moving down south! They want to be close to their daughter," she huffed.

Elias turned and the tower wobbled precariously. "Sounds reasonable. They've owned this shop for years and look as if they have a combined age of seven hundred and four."

Ursula playfully slapped him on the arm. "Enough, this is a serious matter. What happens if the shop closes?"

"Another one opens?" Elias shrugged and looped an arm around her.

She wrapped her hand around his waist, leaning her head on his shoulder. "Kieran said the strangest thing."

"That sounds about right. What did he say this time?"

"He thinks I should buy the shop." Ursula stopped walking for effect, but Elias just looked at her plainly and ushered her to continue on.

"Makes sense to me. You are obsessed with books."

Ursula gasped. "I'm not obsessed. I just like books, that's all."

"Uh-huh," Elias said sceptically, his voice full of mirth.

They ambled back up the slope to Cairden, but Ursula couldn't shake the feeling that this was meant to be.

# 36

# Epilogue

Ursula walked into the study, a wrapped present behind her back.

She went over to Elias at his desk, the usual pile of papers in front of him as she bent down to give him a quick kiss.

"Happy Anniversary, Husband!"

Elias looked at her, his sapphire eyes glinting in the light as his hand trailed up Ursula's calf. "No wool stockings today, Wife?"

"Of course not. It's too humid today. Silk is much better," Ursula replied with affected primness.

"A likely story. You know I'm a sucker for you in silk." Elias pulled her into his lap.

"This is for you," Ursula said, passing him the gift.

Elias ripped the package open, revealing a small rectangular box. He lifted the lid with glee.

"It's tickets to the theatre. There's a troupe due for Yule. Apparently you celebrate the first anniversary with a gift made of paper."

Ursula gave him a beaming smile, hoping she could convey all her happiness in that one tiny expression. She wanted to show him every day how much he meant to her. That they would do this year after year until they were old and grey, and she was too frail to sit on his lap. Elias gave her thigh an encouraging squeeze that said the same.

"Thank you." He pulled her close and gave her a heartfelt kiss that sizzled through her veins. "I have something for you, too."

Elias leaned forward, his hand clamped on her thigh anchoring her to him as he moved.

"Wait, there's something else," Ursula said tentatively. "There's going to be a new member of the family."

Elias stilled, looking deep into her eyes. "Does that mean? Are you…?"

"Oh no, not that!" Ursula chuckled heartily before jumping up and running for the door. She returned a few minutes later holding a small bundle of fluff.

"Here's your real gift. Say hello!" She brought the puppy over to Elias. "He's to keep you company."

The dog yawned lazily in her arms, his mottled fur at all angles. "You spoke so fondly of Colin that when Mrs. Dyce's daughter's dog had a litter a couple of months ago, I knew he had to be ours."

She deposited the pup in Elias's arms. His heart melted as he gazed down at the fuzzy bundle, snoring happily.

"Thank you, Ursi. I don't know what to say."

"How about what you will call him?" Ursula asked, sitting on the edge of the desk.

"I think it's only fitting to call him Paper."

Ursula let out a loud guffaw, momentarily waking the pup

who groggily opened an eye. "A dog called Paper. It certainly is unique."

She leant over to give the dog a reassuring pat.

"You still have your gift to open. It's in the top drawer. I'd get it for you but as you can see, my hands are full."

Ursula moved and opened the drawer, a small box inside. She opened it, finding a large iron key. She tried to keep her face serene and happy, even though she had no idea what it was for. Maybe it had some significance to him or was a northern custom she'd need to learn.

Elias gave a small chuckle. "No need to look so confused. It's just a key."

"I know that, but what's it a key for?"

"The old bookshop in town. It's yours now."

Ursula promptly dropped the key, and it tumbled a few times before landing in the middle of the room. Tears streamed down her face. She knew she must look a fright, but she couldn't stop the swell of emotion that raged within her.

Her husband had only got the best thing in her life—besides him, that is.

"Careful, you'll need that. It's the only one," Elias said ruefully.

"I don't think I'll ever be able to thank you enough," Ursula mumbled, tears still flowing. She staggered over to him, her heart so full, she thought it would burst.

Elias took her hand, kissing her palm. "Having you in my life is a dream come true. This is just my small way of returning the favour."

"But…but…how could you afford it?" she mumbled into his chest.

"I sold the quarry."

The words cut her tears short, cut her to the bone.

"Elias, how could you?!"

His face was a study of calm, although she could see the smile playing at the corner of his mouth. Ursula's eyes narrowed, suspicion bubbling through her.

"I sold the quarry to the town. Every person in Allerbrock now owns a stake in its future and can decide how it will be run. Even us."

Ursula felt the breath leave her lungs. Fresh tears pricked at her eyes as she wrapped her arms around his neck.

Elias ran his hands up and down her back, along her arms, and through her hair. She could have stayed like that for hours. She littered his face with small, delicate kisses.

"You wonderful, wonderful man."

He smiled at her, his oceanic eyes teary as he motioned towards the key, the dull metal glinting in the firelight.

"You better pick that up. Your family will be arriving soon, and we have a lot of news to tell them."

# Acknowledgments

They say write the book you want to read, so I did.

*Venturing North* came out of my own dive into the cozy fantasy world (yes, I used the US English spelling but I think it just looks better), and while I loved the stories, I found myself wanting more on-page romance. I love the fact that we could see characters forging a new life but I also wanted to see them kiss (and other stuff…).

This book was written alone on my bed (as I didn't have a desk), usually with my cat, Ed (to which it's dedicated).

Writing can be a lonely process but I'm an extroverted-introvert and I've loved pulling this story together. It wouldn't be here though without help from my brilliant editors Brit and Alyssa, my proofreader Gabby, and a great team of beta readers.  Thank you all, it means so much to my fragile neurodiverse heart that you all gave such thoughtful feedback that made *Venturing North* what it is.

It's also a love letter to Scotland, my home country.  I've lived all over and feel incredibly lucky to call this place home.

Being Scottish, I genuinely feel that people should own the land they work and where they live.  I was at a conference years ago where I learned about the community buyout of the Isle of Eigg (pronounced egg, for the uninitiated) and the idea stuck with me—hence the community buyout of the quarry at the end. I'd heard about land reform in the lead up to the

Independence Referendum of 2014 and it astounded me how much of Scotland is privately owned by absentee landowners, people without much interest or investment in Scotland or its people, beyond profit. The rules for community buyouts are still very stringent and I hope that we can change that, one spicy, silly book at a time—whilst putting pressure on politicians to change outdated laws.

My mum has to get a thank you as well, who has supported all my creative pursuits and backed any whim, fad, or trend I've followed. She's a good egg and a great mum.

I also have to say thanks to my husband, who probably won't see and couldn't care less about romance or fantasy books, but he supported and encouraged me all the way through. There's nothing like someone you love saying they are proud of you. It spurred me on when I was second, third and fourth guessing myself.

Finally, I'd like to say thank you, dear reader. You took a chance on an unknown indie author and I hoped you enjoyed my gentle, yet spicy, tale.

Please stay tuned for the next instalment of the Islands of the Northern Sea series. Theo's story is up next and it's proving to be even spicier (as if we'd expect anything less from that reprobate).

# About the Author

Alex McFarlane is Scottish born and bred. Originally from Edinburgh, they have lived all over Scotland and are back in their home town with their husband, cat, and dog in tow.

They have an MA in Art History and a Fine Art MFA, and draw a lot of inspiration from art, history and folklore.

Alex currently works in a library and enjoys reading fantasy, romance and contemporary literature, long ambling walks, visiting galleries, and lives off coffee and gin.

You can find her on Instagram/Tiktok @alex.mcfarlane.author and her Facebook page is @alex.mcfarlane.authorr (because someone else claimed the page without the double R. It may have been me, don't ask…).

Please post reviews for Venturing North wherever you like (no star minimum is required).

Get an extra spicy scene of Ursula and Elias as well as new releases, giveaways, and more, when you sign up to Alex's newsletter.

**You can connect with me on:**

- https://www.alexmcfarlaneauthor.com
- https://facebook.com/alex.mcfarlane.authorr
- https://www.instagram.com/alex.mcfarlane.author
- https://www.tiktok.com/@alex.mcfarlane.author

**Subscribe to my newsletter:**

- https://bit.ly/AlexMcFNewsletter